PRAISE FOR VIN

"Vincent Zandri explode
debut thriller of the year. 1.
paced, lyrical, and haunting. Don't miss it."
—HARLAN COBEN, AUTHOR OF CAUGHT

"A SATISFYING YARN."
—CHICAGO TRIBUNE

"COMPELLING...*The Innocent* pulls you in with rat-a-tat prose, kinetic pacing...characters are authentic, and the punchy dialogue rings true. Zandri's staccato prose moves *The Innocent* at a steady, suspenseful pace."
—FORT LAUDERDALE SUN-SENTINEL

"EXCITING...AN ENGROSSING THRILLER...the descriptions of life behind bars will stand your hair on end."
—ROCKY MOUNTAIN NEWS

"READERS WILL BE HELD CAPTIVE BY PROSE THAT POUNDS AS STEADILY AS AN ELEVATED PULSE...Vincent Zandri nails readers' attention."
—BOSTON HERALD

"A SMOKING GUN OF A DEBUT NOVEL. The rough-and-tumble pages turn quicker than men turn on each other."
—THE TIMES-UNION (ALBANY)

ALSO BY VINCENT ZANDRI

The Remains

Moonlight Falls

The Innocent (As Catch Can)

Permanence

Scream Catcher

Moonlight Rises

Moonlight Falls (UNCUT EDITION)

Pathological (A Digital Short)

Moonlight Mafia (A Digital Short)

True Stories (A Digital Short)

GODCHILD

Published by Thomas & Mercer
P.O. Box 400818
Las Vegas, NV 89140

ISBN-13: 9781612183435
ISBN-10: 1612183433

GODCHILD

VINCENT ZANDRI

THOMAS & MERCER

FOR LAURA ROTH ZANDRI

The Land Rover headlights drill through the early morning desert darkness, two fiery eyes burning on the silent horizon barely an hour before the sun rises over Monterrey.

Four a.m.

The appointed time.

She's been waiting for them, per instructions from her LA contact. The halogen signal promised just last night in Houston when finally, over caviar, Dom, and cocaine, she signed on to do the deal.

Her first and last (although that "last" bit will remain her little secret).

She is a writer by trade. But this morning, she is more like an actor, playing the role of the burrier. A border burrier (a bastardization of burro and courier), all packaged nice and neat in the guise of a beautiful woman. For the sake of the assignment, she has assumed the role of the in-between girl—the paid runner who takes the risk not just for the money, but for the sheer thrill.

That's burrier.

Not courier.

In the border world between Texas and Mexico, there's a distinct difference.

For the burrier, it's not about the need to run drugs. It's about the want.

Technically speaking, she doesn't need the money.

According to her phony bio, she doesn't have a family to feed, a brood of shoeless children living in a one-room shack with no hot water and no father to help carry the weight. What she's supposedly got instead is a two-bedroom town house in the Hollywood Hills, a loft apartment in Manhattan's Tribeca, a six-figure modeling contract with the Ford Agency, and a two-hundred-dollar-a-day coke habit.

But all this is not enough.

As a burrier, she can savor the elation of slipping into a skintight leather jumpsuit and motorcycle boots. The sheer power of firing up a Suzuki GSX1300 Hayabusa equipped with leather saddlebags and a CD/stereo combo with enough lethal amperage to scare off even the most rabid coyote.

The burriers are as beautiful as they are dangerous, and they are the only gringos the brothers will deal with these days.

Their philosophy: Why eat bread when you can have pure honey?

Her philosophy: What a story this is gonna make.

She may be acting out a role, but the one thing she can't fake is her beauty.

She is, as they say, drop-dead gorgeous standing out there in the middle of the desert with cropped auburn hair, blue eyes, and a black leather jumpsuit, the zipper running from breasts to navel. Like something out of a Bond film. And right now, as the headlights shine in the near distance, she can feel her heart beating, her throat closing, that little tingle shooting up her spine telling her, It's time, baby.

The desert is peaceful this morning.

Calm.

There is a sweet, dry, desert smell. And a slight hum that comes from the insects you never see in the dark of night. There is the bone cold and the occasional burst of wind to make it even colder, to send the fine granules of sand up into her face, make them stick to the red lipstick that covers her heart-shaped mouth.

When the doors on the Land Rover suddenly open, one at a time, and the silhouettes of two men appear—one tall and thin, the other short and stocky—both packing shotguns, she knows she's reached the proverbial point of no return.

No amount of acting can stop those bullets, should they start to fly.

She cannot deny the fear any more than she can deny the thrill of it all. She's the method writer, after all. She's not interested in facts so much as discovering what it actually feels like to experience something. What are the specific sights, sounds, tastes, and emotions that come together to create an experience? How do you translate these sensations and dimensions to the page so that the experience becomes more real for the reader than if the reader actually participated in it? That's method writing, and there isn't a soul on earth who can come close to her ability to convey a true life-and-death experience.

Now, with every step they take toward her, with every shell they cock into the metal chambers of their pump-action shotguns, she knows she is coming that much closer to death. The real thing. So she rubs her hip up against the saddlebag. Just to make certain that the money and her life are still viable options. Because if the money is not there, she knows she has no choice but to hand over her life. No questions asked, no excuses, no "Oh crap, I left it on the kitchen counter."

No begging, no pleading, no free sex.

She's done the research, so she knows what these brothers are capable of, even on a good day. How they strip you, strap you down naked on your back, all four limbs tied to stakes, baby oil poured over the skin, the hair on your head and sex completely shaved, eyelids taped back against your eyebrows so that when the desert sun also rises, the eyeballs fry while your skin bubbles and broils. What they find of you later—if they find you at all—stands as a coyote-chewed warning, a fleshless message not to fuck with the Contreras Brothers and their Mexicali turf.

But this morning, she has nothing to worry about as the two men in cowboy boots and Stetsons close the gap. She can feel the bulge that the cash makes in the saddlebag when her thigh contacts it. The sensation is oddly sexual. She swallows hard when the two men stop dead in their tracks, as though on cue (obviously they've been through the routine dozens of times before). One of the men—the shorter—takes four or five steps forward, meets her face to face, so close she can smell the tequila and cigarettes on his breath.

"Buenos días, señorita."

"It's still nighttime, case you hadn't noticed."

"Did you bring our money?"

"Did you bring our drugs?"

"Oooohhh, I like that. A beautiful woman who answers a simple question with a stupid question. Makes my job so much easier."

"Shall we get down to the job or shall we stand around and chat?"

"Well, what do you know. Beauty, brains, and—if you'll excuse the expression—balls."

He reaches out with his free hand, uses his dirty fingers to pull down her zipper. As much as his touch repulses her, she allows him to do it. Because it's all a part of the act, a small price to pay for the method writer.

And it proceeds like that. She standing there, he breathing on her, touching her, while his partner looks on in horny amazement. Until business must be tended to and the saddlebag is opened to reveal its *cargo of cash, and then the tailgate on the Land Rover is opened to reveal its payload. As the sun begins to show itself red-orange on the easternmost horizon, the whole deal goes down smoothly.*

That is, until another set of headlights appears. And another and yet another, the bright white lights clearly visible a split second before the trio hears the telltale wail of the sirens.

PART ONE

REMAINS HINT AT HORROR IN MEXICO!

MONTERREY, Mexico (AP) - US and Mexican authorities have resumed their search for bodies in the desert where at least six corpses have been unearthed. FBI informants claim as many as three hundred victims of a powerful drug cartel could be buried in the desert country between the city and the Texas border. Forensics experts, in cooperation with Mexican soldiers and police, have been systematically searching the vast area as well as two known desert ranches in Monterrey, once the undisputed territory of the Contreras drug cartel, at one time Mexico's most powerful and most violent drug-smuggling family.

CHAPTER ONE

I WAS SITTING INSIDE BILL'S BAR AND GRILL IN ALBANY, New York, listening to the hard wind that whistled through the cracks in the picture window embedded in the brick wall behind my back. The one held together with duct tape and striped neon piping that spelled out *Bud Light* and *Rolling Rock*. I had been kidding myself all afternoon, thinking it was possible to make myself invisible by hoarding a stool in the far, dark corner of the South End bar, all dressed up like a clown in my wedding-day blazer, charcoal pants, and virgin loafers with tassels.

It was March 21, according to the folded newspaper that sat ignored on the bar beside my right elbow.

REMAINS HINT AT HORROR IN MEXICO!

It was supposed to be one of the happiest days of my life.

But I never made the ceremony. That made it one of the saddest.

Instead, I'd been hiding out in the corner of this old bar, counting down the minutes until the happy-hour crowd left me alone and Bill the bartender dimmed the lights to make ready for some serious drinking, serious disappearing. If only vanishing were possible.

Horror in Mexico!

The world's business.

The blues in Albany!

My business.

After five slow hours inside Bill's I could tell you exactly who came and went like clockwork. An old man who called himself Kenny P. C. ("P for Pretty," he slurred, a toothy vampire smile on his ruddy face. "C for Cute.") and dressed himself in blue polyester slacks, a matching blue jacket, and a white rayon shirt. A man far older than his years, he sat five stools away from me toward the middle of the bar and drank bottom-shelf scotch. Until the head bob began and the space between the bar and his forehead became narrower and narrower. Until the bets were placed for which one final bob would send his skull bouncing off the hardwood. At which time he was escorted to the door, stage right, a taxi already warmed up and waiting for him just outside the picture window.

Then there was the woman in cheap Sears jeans and a white cotton T-shirt who'd come in sometime around one thirty. She had a pockmarked face and frizzy gray hair. She smoked Pall Mall 100s, one off the other, and carried on one hell of a conversation with herself in a *South All-benny* accent. On three separate occasions she found her way over to me, set her hand on my thigh, told me how sad and lonely I looked, and then offered her body. All three times I told her no. Finally I flipped her a twenty from my honeymoon bankroll, just to shut her up.

Maybe I liked being lonely, I told her.

And then there was the young Mohawk kid who sat four stools down from me, whose hands shook so bad he had to use them both to lift his whiskey glass off the bar, bring the rim to his thick lips.

I'd gotten to know them all during my disappearing act at Bill's. I had no way of knowing if my fiancée, Val Antonelli, or my best man (and lawyer), Tony Angelino, had attempted to contact me. No idea if they *wanted* to contact me. As I removed the pinned carnation from my breast pocket and set it down on the bar, I knew that by now I had to have been recognized. That I wasn't invisible. And if I had been recognized, then I was also sure that Val and Tony knew exactly where to find me.

I blamed the Albany cops.

Maybe I had no idea what their names were or what precinct they worked out of (though Albany wasn't that big). But as a former maximum-security warden, I'd gained enough experience over the years to be able to sniff out a cop at twenty paces. It was never the uniform that gave them away. No cop would dare enter this or any other bar for a drink dressed in his on-duty blacks.

The cops who came into Bill's were almost always young, almost always dressed in generous-cut Levi's jeans, immaculate running shoes, maybe a pastel-colored polo shirt or Notre Dame sweatshirt pulled over broad, iron-pumped shoulders. They wore gold Irish claddagh rings on their middle fingers, and their flattop hair always had that wet, just-out-of-the-gang-shower look.

And man, talk about the overwhelming aroma of Aqua Velva.

But if all this were not enough to convince me that the young dude ordering a pint of "Half and Half" was one of Albany's Irish finest, then I could be certain when he wrapped his arm around Kenny P. C.'s shoulder and addressed the drunk by his first name. Naturally Kenny would ask the cop if he could spare a couple of bucks. But then the cop would pull out the empty pockets of his jeans, allow them to hang there like little white wings. He'd hold his hands in the air and say, "Kenny, even Jesus Christ himself could touch only so many lepers."

You could always spot a cop at Bill's Bar and Grill, because everybody knew cops drank for free.

As a former lawman, I knew that the cops must have come and gone immediately after the eight-to-four shift or right after the four-to-midnight *action* shift. Just in time for last call. I'd seen quite a few of them during my afternoon inside the bar. Maybe I'd gone a little out of my mind by then, but I knew they spotted me just as easily as I spotted them. I also knew that it was only a matter of time until one of them placed a call to Tony's downtown law practice to let him know where the hell I was. Tony, in turn, would tell Val. On the other hand, why should she waste her time looking for me? Why even make the effort? I was the one who had left her standing at the altar all alone. I was the one who, for five long hours, had been pissing away our honeymoon money on beer, whiskey, and regrets.

❖

The wind whistled. Even with my blazer on, I could feel the cold March air on my back. I sipped beer from a long-neck bottle, fired up a smoke, and for the hundredth time that afternoon, hit the playback button in my brain.

It had just started snowing as I'd passed the stone pillars marking Albany Rural Cemetery's south-side entrance. Snowing hard in mid-March. I had pushed on past the old iron gates, feeling stiff and cold in my brand-new wedding-day blazer and loafers. Shuffling toward the plot that had been home to my first wife, Fran, for almost three years now.

As usual, I was running late.

In less than fifteen minutes, my best man would require my presence in the brick rectory behind Saint Mary's Cathedral on Eagle Street. According to tradition, Tony and I were expected to "sweat it out" in that back room among the spare chalices, bags of communion wafers, and the same Boone's Farm wine I used to sneak sips from back when I was still an altar boy. Sweat it out amid the smell of burning candles and incense, until my fiancée (and former Green Haven Prison secretary), Val Antonelli, began her long, slow march down the church aisle on her way to a second marriage.

Hers *and* mine.

In my right hand, collecting snowflakes, a weightless bundle of wildflowers wrapped in baby-blue tissue paper. Under my left arm—hidden by the blue blazer—a leather shoulder holster that cradled a two-and-a-half-pound Colt .45.

The low midday clouds showered the sloping landscape in wet snow. The white stuff came down fast and furiously as it fell against the crooked, leafless branches of the trees, against the bleached marble headstones and miniature churchlike mausoleums.

I stood over the five-by-ten plot with the granite marker at its head inscribed with Fran's birth and death dates.

Setting the bundle of wildflowers on the plot, I watched the petals begin to disappear in the falling snow. But what I saw was *a battered black four-door Buick sedan with tinted windows slamming directly into the passenger side of my Ford Bronco at fifty miles per hour; Fran's head and shoulders going through the windshield, the jagged edge of the glass taking her head clean off as though it were a razor blade; her body slumping back into the seat like nothing at all had happened. Like her life hadn't slipped away in the split second of time it took for that windshield to shatter. Then the screaming of the witnesses and the spattered blood and the sight of that black Buick tearing away. But not before the driver rolled down his window, just long enough for me to get a good look at his bald head, hoop earring, and the thin mustache that covered only half of his upper lip.*

The Bald Man...

I stood in the falling snow and recalled the two full years I'd spent in search of the Bald Man, only to come up empty. There were the endless hours spent sifting through mug shots, photographic kits, evidence folders, and case files. There were the posters printed with the Bald Man's likeness—the likeness I viewed for only a split second but committed to memory—that I stapled to telephone poles all across the state. There was the ten-thousand-dollar reward offered for any "verifiable information" leading to his whereabouts.

The entire two-year effort now resided in my brain, neatly categorized under FAILURE with a capital F. I knew that with my marriage to Val only a few minutes away, I had no choice but to give up the search for good; call it another unsolved mystery, just like the Albany cops did less than a year ago. All that was left was to move on with my life, remember Fran the way she had lived.

I stepped away from the plot.

The wildflowers were gone now. Completely covered over. I had barely ten minutes left to make it—you guessed it—to the church on time. Ten minutes to put the past behind me for good.

I might have made it too.

If it hadn't been for the battered black Buick sedan that drove in through the cemetery gates.

It was the car I remembered. The car that rammed into my Ford Bronco, sending Fran to her death.

The Buick.

My black Buick with the tinted windows, just sitting there idling, exhaust smoking out of the rusted tailpipe gray-black in the falling snow.

Here's what I should have done: pulled out my .45, blasted a couple of rounds over the roof of the car. Or maybe blown out a rear tire.

But here's what I did instead: not a goddamned thing.

I just stood there, as stuck to the ground as Fran's marker, while the driver of the Buick backed up, spun the front end around, and drove back out the same way he'd come in.

Some time went by before I was able to move.

I wasn't sure how much time.

Seconds maybe. Or minutes.

Time was relative. It was hard to read.

But at some point I forced myself up off my knees, made my way back to my 4Runner through the snow and ice to place a call to the APD, South Pearl Street Division, the precinct that had originally spearheaded Fran's hit-and-run. I sat inside the SUV, drinking sweet whiskey from the emergency fifth I kept in the glove box, fighting off the tremors, waiting for the cops to arrive, knowing I should have been calling Saint Mary's rectory to explain what had happened. Explain why I hadn't shown up yet for my own wedding.

But there was no explaining anything.

I just sat there, watching the snow fall, drinking from the bottle, feeling my body shake and my brain buzz. It was all I could do to swallow the whiskey without bringing it back up. And that was that.

By the time the cops pulled up, I was already ten minutes late for the ceremony. The two black-and-whites that parked outside the cemetery gates made me think of the black-and-white taffeta gowns Val had chosen for her bridesmaids to wear. I pictured the dark blazers and white button-downs my best man and ushers were wearing at that very moment. I imagined their blank expressions and their wide eyes staring into watch faces that didn't lie. From where I sat shivering inside the 4Runner with the heat blasting against my wet shirt, I saw the small beads of sweat that had begun to form on their foreheads when the guests who had filled the church pews started whispering to one another, "I'll be damned, Keeper's not coming."

It was the tinny drone of a cop radio that broke the spell as a tall, black-haired detective by the name of Ryan tapped on my windshield. Ryan claimed he was a new guy, having just been transferred from the New York State Office of General Services to South Pearl Street's Behavioral Sciences Unit. Together we walked to the spot where I'd seen the black Buick. Wearing a leather car jacket with wide epaulets and buttons, this thirty-something Detective Ryan checked my PI license along with my laminated permit for carrying a concealed weapon. He then questioned me calmly and methodically while we walked, sometimes asking and re-asking the same question two and three times to check for "accuracy and consistency of testimony." But then, sometimes cops forget that former wardens know as much about due process as they do.

It all went as smoothly as something like that can on a snowy day in March. That is, until we came to the spot near Fran's grave where I'd first seen the Buick. The problem, if you want to call it that, was that no sign of the Buick remained. The ruts that its tires had made when it peeled out were gone, wiped smooth by the still-falling snow. Or, in the words of Detective Ryan, "Just maybe, Mr. Marconi, the tire tracks, along with the Buick, were never there to begin with."

"The snow," I insisted. "It must have covered the tracks."

I slipped and skidded my way to Fran's plot. I dug my hand through the snow. I pulled up the bouquet of wildflowers, shook them off.

"I'm not imagining these," I said.

Ryan stood there, studying the white flakes collecting on the tops of his black lace-up shoes.

He let out a resigned breath. "You're that ex-warden," he said. "You lost your wife some years back. I've been over the file at Division."

"Hit and run," I said.

"And you're getting married again, is that it?"

I was missing the wedding as he spoke.

"You came back here out of guilt."

"What's your point?" I asked.

"Maybe you imagined the Buick."

I dropped the flowers.

"All I'm saying," he went on, "is that in times of emotional stress and turmoil, it's only natural to imagine things. Especially in a spooky place like this." He pinched closed his leather collar, cocked his head in the direction of the gates.

I took a couple of steps toward him. "Is this what a Behavioral Science cop is supposed to do?" I asked. "Convince me of what I didn't see?"

He walked up to me, brought his face to within inches of my own, sniffed me up and down with his nose. Like a police dog.

I knew he could smell the whiskey on my breath.

Because he could smell the whiskey on my breath, I knew exactly what he was thinking, although neither one of us said anything about it. In fact, the D word never came up. Not even in passing.

I cleared my throat. "I took a couple of shots," I said. "You know, to ease the jitters. After I saw the Buick." But I could tell by the furrows in his brow that he didn't believe me.

"Tell you what," he said finally, his gray breath mixing with the snow. "I'll have an officer take down your testimony. And if we see a black Buick matching the description, we'll pull it over, question the driver. How's that sound?"

"Don't go out of your way," I said.

"Call it a courtesy, Mr. Marconi," he said. "One lawman to another."

Back at the south-side gates, he called over another plain-clothes cop to take my statement.

As promised. One lawman to another.

The beefy cop dressed in uniform blacks asked if I got "a good look at the supposed black Buick in question…enough to create a composite image, that is."

He was trying so hard to hold back the laughs that he was making little raspberry noises through clenched lips.

When I finished with my description of the Buick, I made my way back to Ryan.

"Sorry I wasted your time," I said as he was about to get back inside the cruiser.

I was standing right beside him, the passenger-side door to the cruiser wide open, his left foot already inside, a wave of hot air blowing out of the dashboard heater onto my legs.

"You did the right thing," he said, taking hold of my forearm, giving it a sympathetic squeeze, as though the cops were still my fraternal cousins-in-arms. "Go get married," he said with a grin. He got in and closed the car door, smiling at me through the lightly fogged glass.

But it was way too late to get married. In more ways than one.

As I walked slowly back to my 4Runner, I couldn't help but look into the faces of each cop as I passed them, one by stinking one. I couldn't help but pick up on the way they whispered into one another's ears, thinking I had to be out of earshot when they referred to me as "one paranoid bastard."

That's what I remembered.

The rest was either repressed or just a dream, or both.

❖

I wasn't sure how long he'd been staring at me. Christ, I wasn't sure how long the entire crowd had been staring at me. But when I came out of my trance, Bill the bartender was standing across from me, his chubby face somehow tight, his receding hair slicked back, his customary white bar rag slung over his right shoulder.

"You OK?" he asked me.

My hands were wrapped tightly around the empty beer bottle to keep them from shaking. The bottom of the caramel-colored bottle made a *clickety-clack* sound against the solid wood bar.

"Maybe it's time to go home, Mr. Marconi," Bill said.

There, I thought. He said it. My name: Jack Harrison "Keeper" Marconi. He knew who I was. Just like everyone else probably knew who I was—Keeper Marconi, former maximum security prison warden turned unemployed private investigator.

"Tell you what," Bill went on. "I'll call you a cab."

I'm pretty sure it was then, when Bill went for the phone, that I pulled out my Colt. Come to think of it, that's exactly when I got a good look at my sad face in the mirror behind the bar, pulled the piece out, and emptied the entire eight-round clip, blowing away Jim Beam and Jack Daniels and even managing to nail some Wild Turkey in the process. It was a damned shame, too, having to waste good booze like that. But I suppose, in the end, it would have been a worse shame to have wasted me.

CHAPTER TWO

THE COPS HAD TO HAVE BEEN ON THEIR WAY BEFORE I decided to blow away my reflection in the mirror. Not those off-duty cops scamming free beer. But on-the-job cops in black uniforms who stood out in the white light of the aluminum-and-glass entryway, black 9mm automatics drawn and poised—combat position.

But then, the cops came as no surprise.

It was the sudden appearance of Tony Angelino that came as the real shocker. He stood square at the head of the pack, dressed in a camel-hair overcoat and a blue blazer, just like mine. His dark gray slacks had been cut and tailored for his medium but stocky build. His white wedding carnation was still pinned to his lapel, and the wide-brimmed fedora on his head matched his threads.

To a T.

He wasn't smiling.

Neither was I.

"How about a drink," I said.

He just stood there, staring at me with those deep-set brown eyes of his, the rhythmic flash of red, blue, and white cruiser lights streaking across the wall.

I stood up then, on the rungs of my stool, towered over the entire bar, the faces of all those regulars looking up at me, their hands gripped around their drinks even now.

"Bill!" I shouted. "Whiskey!"

But Bill never moved a muscle. He was still on the floor, covered in spilled booze and shards of glass.

Tony came closer. Slowly.

He raised his fists to chest height. The fists were covered in brown leather driving gloves. He rubbed them together, like a boxer waiting for the bell to sound.

"No drink for me," he said, eyes on me, going through me.

I sat back down on the stool. "Was it something I said?"

But I guess Tony didn't have the time for stupid questions. He simply raised his right fist high and knocked me cold.

CHAPTER THREE

I FULLY EXPECTED TO WAKE UP INSIDE THE COUNTY lockup. But when I opened my eyes there was no concrete plank ceiling to close me in, no bright overhead lamps to sting my retinas. There was no concrete floor, no iron bars, no Plexiglas shield. Instead, I saw a white vaulted ceiling and a long wall of glossy black bookshelves filled with colorful volumes.

Without having to look too much further, I knew I'd come to on the leather couch in the living room of Tony's downtown condo.

Facing me directly: a long, winding staircase that accessed the second and third floors. Embedded in the bottom of the stairwell: a two-way fireplace. I didn't have to turn over to know that behind me, a wall of windows looked out over Eagle Street and the governor's mansion, which almost never housed the governor and his family (who preferred to reside "where the action is" in Manhattan). After all, I'd been inside this room a hundred times over the years. Maybe a thousand.

For now the windows were covered in dark, floor-to-ceiling drapes. And had I not closed my eyes again, I might have screamed out in pain from the splitting hangover. But I suppose there's something to be said for self-control. Because when I opened my eyes once more, a very stiff-looking Tony was standing in the center of the white-and-black-checkered marble floor.

I knew without asking that he had been responsible for keeping the heat off, keeping me out of lockup. Now he stood there with arms crossed at his chest, staring at me with distant, glassy eyes, as though I'd never woken up on the couch at all but had died in my sleep.

"Morning," I groaned, the back of my throat feeling like it had been scraped with a razor.

"Exactly," Tony said.

He had dressed down since the night before, when he'd knocked me cold. Now he wore only the dark gray slacks, along with the white oxford, sleeves rolled up neatly, all the way to the elbows.

Without another word, he turned and stepped into the kitchen.

I forced myself up and lit a smoke.

When Tony returned, he was carrying his leather briefcase. He laid the case flat on the lid of the grand piano, thumbed back the spring-released latches, pushed open the lid. He pulled out a number-ten envelope, tossed it onto my lap. When I looked down, I could see that my name had been written on it in Tony's unmistakable, loopy handwriting.

"Don't open that yet," he said while stepping behind the couch, pulling hard on the drawstring that opened the drapes and let the blinding sun shine in.

I knew the envelope must have had something to do with the wedding.

Maybe that's why the panic alarm sounded, the little voice inside my brain that told me to get up and head straight for the door. No bothering with good-byes or *It's been swell, Tone*. Just get up and get the hell out.

But when I stood up, I felt a hand grab at my collar. The hand yanked me back down onto the couch. That's when Tony made a beeline for his briefcase. He reached inside, pulled out a Colt .45.

I patted the space under my left arm where my own Colt should have been.

The holster was empty.

"That's my piece," I said.

"You can have it back," he said, "after you listen to what I have to say."

"You're supposed to be my best friend," I said. "Or did you forget?"

"Who are you to talk about friends," Tony said, "when you don't give a rat's ass about standing them up?"

Tony set my gun down inside his briefcase.

He stood straight and stiff, right foot planted on a square of black tile, left foot on a square of white. His heavy forearms were crossed at his chest. He was just five-foot-eight, but from where I was sitting he looked big and powerful.

"I've got a job for you," he said.

"I'm not working right now," I said.

"You can't afford not to."

"Who says?"

"Your bank account says."

He went back to his briefcase, pulled out an envelope with a Key Bank logo printed on it. The kind of envelope a bank statement usually comes in. My bank statement.

"You've got a couple of C-notes to your name. That's it. How the hell did you expect to pay for a wedding?"

"Val was footing the bill," I said.

He laid the statement back inside the briefcase. "Val's gone now."

That hard sinking feeling in the pit of my stomach. "I already know that," I said. "I should have known."

"One of my clients has an emergency," Tony explained a minute later, after handing me a mug of coffee. "Man by the name of Richard Barnes."

I recognized the name and said so to Tony. But that didn't stop him from telling me a whole lot of what I already knew. Barnes was a rich guy, a producer who ran public-relations campaigns. Mostly for politicians, if I remembered correctly. And the only reason I remembered correctly is that I recalled how his Reel Productions worked on the governor's campaign during the last election. During a time when any employee of New York State worries about job security. Or the lack of it. Which I used to do. Until I lost my job: suddenly elections meant nothing to me.

I took a drag off the cigarette, drank some black coffee.

I asked Tony to give me the short of it. So I could get back to my motel, get a shower and a shave. Maybe a nap before I headed south to Stormville. From there, who knew where.

Tony looked directly down at the tops of his tassel loafers. Loafers identical to my own. "Richard's wife, Renata, was busted by Mexican police for attempting to smuggle cocaine out of the country," he explained. "From a border town called Monterrey into Brownsville, Texas."

I stubbed out my cigarette, sipped more coffee.

"I thought Barnes's wife was a writer," I said. Tony went into the kitchen and came back out with his own cup.

"That's part of the point," he said, blowing into his cup with pursed lips.

I made a time-out T with my hands, shook my head from left to right and back again. "Maybe I'm missing something here, but anyone with half a brain knows the penalties for running dope across the border."

Tony drank some coffee and set the cup down on the grand piano beside the briefcase. "She wasn't interested in selling drugs so much as she had an interest in experiencing the *process* of selling drugs." A bewildered wave of his hands. "At least that's Richard's story."

"She took a chance like that for a book?" I asked.

"For an article, actually. But that's not important."

"What is important?"

"There are two kinds of drug runners presently operating in Mexico," Tony explained. "There are the so-called burriers, a term derived from burro, or mule, combined with courier. The burriers are usually rich women who like to move cocaine not for the money, but for the sheer thrill of it."

And the second kind?

"The second group," he said, "is made up of poverty-stricken women who have no choice but to move small amounts of cocaine paste."

I drank some coffee. It was getting cold.

"If the burriers are rich already," I asked, "then why risk taking that kind of chance? They need the rush that badly?"

"I suspect Renata was on her way to answering that question, *paisan*, before she was nabbed at the border."

It all came back to me in tidal waves: Renata Barnes. A petite woman with short auburn hair and wild blue eyes. I'd seen her on the *Today* show a while back when her best seller *Godchild* had just stormed the country, thanks to Oprah. I recalled how she was forced to respond to allegations about the suspicious drowning death of her own kid. How it mimicked in absolute detail the fictitious drowning death of the child in the novel—a drowning death that was the result of murder. In my mind, I saw Renata once more, storming off the set of *Today* in tears.

When Tony went upstairs I got up from the couch, stretched. I felt silly and somehow dirty, still dressed in my wrinkled wedding blazer and slacks. I wanted a shower and maybe a drink. Both would have to wait.

I stood by the window wall. Outside, a clear blue sky. A layer of fresh snow covered the front lawn of the governor's mansion. The snow contrasted sharply with the black parking lot directly beside it. It hurt to look at the snow when it reflected the sun. I ran my hand over the small bruise on my chin. It must have formed when Tony walloped me. I looked down on the guard shack at the mansion gates and the tall, wrought-iron fence that ran the perimeter of the property. Despite what Tony had told me about Renata, he never once had pressed the matter of my walking out on him and Val. Not really.

While I fingered the business-size envelope folded up inside my jacket pocket, I half wanted to blurt out what had happened. How the black Buick had just shown up. Then maybe beg forgiveness, as if Tony were in the business of forgiving. But I knew that he was smarter than that. In his own way, I knew he'd get to what went wrong with my second wedding in due time. For now, the thing to do was concentrate on the business at hand, absorb all he had to tell me about Renata, regardless if in the end I decided not to take on the job.

When Tony came back down, he was dressed in a clean blue suit. He was fixing the sleeves of his jacket by tugging on the cuffs with the tips of his fingers.

"So what is it you want from me?" I said.

"Renata was busted three days ago."

"In the desert." A question.

"Just outside Monterrey," he said. "Far as we know, she's locked in a holding cell in the basement of the town's maximum-security prison, where she's awaiting trial."

"You're sure of this." Another question.

"I have a communication from the Mexican attorney general. Man by the name of Jorge Madrazo."

"Anyone tried to contact her?"

"She was allowed one phone call. She used it to call Richard."

"If she's indicted?"

"Full indictment will result in a very lengthy prison term. A lengthy prison term could very well be a death sentence."

I looked out the window once more. A limo was pulling out of the gate beside the guard shack. Probably the governor himself, hightailing it to New York City and civilization.

I turned back to Tony.

"Barnes is a powerful guy," I said. "Why doesn't he strike a deal with the attorney general, negotiate her out? At least try and have her extradited?"

"Richard's business has already suffered plenty over the negative press that Renata received when she published *Godchild.*" He was putting on his camel-hair overcoat. "The DA was prepared to indict her for second-degree murder in the death of her own baby boy, Charlie. Only he couldn't find enough credible evidence to substantiate an accusation of murder by forcible drowning."

"Then get the magazine to confirm her side of the story. Have them prove she was on assignment in the desert."

"What magazine? There is no magazine. She was going to sell the piece on spec." Now he was putting on a blue fedora, pulling the wide brim down over his forehead, cocking it just slightly over his right eye. "Besides, sounds like a weak attempt at a false alibi." Outside the window, yet another limo pulling up, the electronic gates swinging open. "Barnes fears that if it gets out about Renata being busted on Mexican soil, he'll have to go through the same kind of public shit storm all over again."

"If Renata is such a great author," I said, "why risk writing an article about smuggling drugs? Why not hang out by the beach, pump out a novel once a year or so?"

"Renata is a hands-on writer. Apparently she needs to be in the middle of a battle if she's going to write about war or in the middle of a homicide if she's going to write about murder or in the center of a drug-trafficking operation if she's going to do something on drugs and the women who smuggle them. She's not content to write a piece based upon outside observations, third-hand accounts, and the Internet. What she wants is the real experience."

"Thus all that commotion over *Godchild*?"

"She's what they call a method writer, Keeper. Meaning in order to accurately translate the experience on paper, she must in some capacity participate in the experience."

"Thank God she isn't writing about suicide."

"Save those remarks for me, *paisan*," Tony said. "Your future client will not find them the least bit amusing."

For what seemed a while, I watched the sun shine against the marble floor.

Then, "What Barnes wants from me is to find a way to get her out. Is that it?"

"What he wants is for you to go down there and use any means necessary to break her out. And he's prepared to pay extremely well for it. Two hundred thousand cash, plus expenses, no questions asked, absolutely no press. Plenty of money to repay me for the repairs at Bill's and for keeping you out of the joint and for protecting your license."

I exhaled. "I saw the Buick," I said. "In the cemetery."

"I know about what you *think* you saw," Tony said.

"It happened," I said. "I was there."

He nodded, but like the cops before him, I knew he didn't believe me.

"Did you see a driver?" he asked.

"The windows are tinted."

"And there was a blizzard," he said.

I turned back to the window. The two guards who manned the shack were standing outside in the cold, smoking cigarettes and laughing. I was thinking about risk. How I didn't stand a chance of getting past the visitor's gates of a Mexican prison without getting shot to pieces. A plan like Tony's would require connections inside and out, not to mention maps, layouts, guns, ground and air transport, and a safe house. Just for starters. I was certain Tony had to have considered all this and more even before asking me to take the job.

I turned back to him. "This rescue in Mexico," I said. "It's a crazy idea."

He took a breath, secured the closers on his briefcase, and picked his keys up off the grand piano. "I know it's dangerous. But besides the payday, it could be just the thing you need to put Fran's death behind you. For good."

Outside the window, across Eagle Street, the two guards stamped out their spent butts.

"At least talk to Barnes," Tony suggested. "Then make your own decision."

"And Val," I said, facing him again. "Can you arrange for me to see her?"

Tony suddenly lost the color in his face, like the blood had simply drained out of it. And it had. "There's something else I have to go over with you," he said, his voice little more than a whisper.

I pulled the number-ten envelope out of my pocket. "It has something to do with what's inside here, doesn't it?"

He pointed toward the door, car keys dangling from his fingertips.

"Let's go for a ride," he said.

CHAPTER FOUR

SHE KNOWS SHE'S ON AN ELEVATOR. BECAUSE SHE CAN feel herself falling. Slowly. The hot, airless box shuddering. Invisible wheels and gears grinding, cables stretching, straining. Like at any moment the cable is going to snap and send the car plummeting to the concrete bottom.

She is blind.

The black hood they pulled over her head in the desert prevents her from seeing anything. Her present world is black. The soldiers have been leading her around, one on each arm. They act as her eyes. She can feel the stifling heat of the elevator car, can feel her wet breath soaking the cloth where her lips press against the fabric. She tries to keep her cool, tries to keep her head. Because if she gets out of this mess alive, she might just write about it. What a story it could make. A firsthand account. Busted in the Mexican desert and alive to write about it.

When the elevator stops suddenly, she feels her knees buckle. She feels the compression of her stomach wall. She is forced to swallow. The world inside her hood is still black, still stiflingly hot.

When the metal doors slide open, she feels the rush of cool, damp air. There is the steady buzz of mechanical equipment coming from somewhere off in the distance. She knows she must be at the bottom. The basement. But then, the machinery cannot drown out the distant voices. Hundreds of them. Shouting, laughing, crying.

The soldiers yank on her arms, pull her out of the compartment into a concrete corridor she has no way of seeing. They lead her closer to the voices. The closer she comes, the louder the voices get.

And while she walks blindly, the morning's events come back to her. From the very moment the mission went all to hell.

❖

The halogen spotlights burned brightly from the roofs of the big trucks' cabs; sirens wailed; a soldier who stood foursquare on the exterior flatbed screamed, "Alto, alto, alto," through a bullhorn over and over again while the military trucks proceeded to form a tight circle around the Land Rover and the motorcycle.

The dealers had turned their backs on her to get a good look at the dozens of soldiers who now blocked any path of possible escape. But the tall dealer was not intimidated in the least, as he positioned his shotgun at his hip and began blasting a hole in the line. That is, until a burst of automatic fire tore him in two at the waist.

The second, shorter dealer was not so gutsy. He dropped his weapon to the ground, raised his hands in surrender. She raised her hands too, although she was not carrying a weapon.

A moment later, a soldier broke away from the line and approached the two (she was not at all certain if they were soldiers or police, because they were dressed in green fatigues and combat boots. They carried automatic weapons slung over their shoulders. But then, the word POLICÍA had been stenciled onto the white side panels of the four-wheel-drive trucks in big, bold, black letters).

What happened next happened fast. The soldiers poured all over the Land Rover and motorcycle like ants on sugar. They aimed their rifles at her and the short man, forced them to lay down flat on their stomachs, hands locked behind their heads. It was while she was on the ground, all those black shiny jackboots shooting past her line of sight, that she first noticed the short man's sobs. He whispered to her through the tears, "They will kill us all. You and me. We are all dead."

She lay there on the ground, the cool sand touching her lips. What happened to the tough guy, she thought. Where's the hard son of a bitch who ran his filthy fingers down my chest?

It would please her to see him die. Even if she had to die along with him.

That was the last thing she remembered thinking before she was picked up off the ground, carted over to one of the flatbed trucks, and thrown down on her back—on a mattress, of all things, as if they had been planning this all along. Two soldiers aimed their M-16s at her while another man ordered her to unzip her jumpsuit. "Do it now," he said in English. On her back, she swallowed something hard, began to unzip the jumpsuit, slowly. All the time she was watching the eyes of her captors, watching their Adam's apples bob up and down with every inch of bare skin she revealed. But then, just as she was about to remove the jumpsuit, another man appeared from out of the twilight.

He was not a soldier. At least he was not dressed like one. He was wearing a suit. A black suit in the desert, with alligator shoes. He was a dark-haired, mustached man with a tiny diamond in his left earlobe. He carried a black pistol. A six-shot .45 maybe, or a 9mm. Whatever it was, he pressed the barrel of the pistol up against the temple of the soldier to her immediate left.

"That's enough," the suit said in broken English. "We're taking them to the pit."

Several bumpy miles later, she found herself standing on the very edge of a wide-open pit. A mass grave really, dug out of the desert.

Maybe twenty feet wide by thirty feet long. There must have been a hundred bodies in it, stacked like cord wood. Bloated bodies covered with some kind of white, sulfurous powder. The smell was revolting. Rotting meat and skin.

She stood there, shivering in the early morning coolness, but it was not the air that made her tremble. She was reminded of the old films she once saw of the Holocaust. Black-uniformed Nazis surrounding entire groups of Jews who had been stripped naked to the waist. Women, children, and men shot pointblank in the back of the head, their bodies slumping lifelessly, one by one, into the grave.

And then it happened. Two soldiers dragged the short dealer, kicking, screaming, and clawing the entire way, to the very edge of the pit. He didn't want to die. Not now. Not like this. Then a third soldier went up to him, pressed the barrel of an M-16 against the back of his skull and triggered a round that sent his forehead into the grave just a couple of seconds before the rest of his body followed.

She stood at the edge of the pit, watching the short man's body rolling end over end, like a rag doll falling down the stairs, until it joined the others. So this is what it's like to die, she thought. This is what it's like to just disappear off the face of the devil's earth.

She waited for her turn. But then she discovered that they had something else in mind for her. The suit approached her once again. He was carrying something in his right hand. A piece of black cloth. When he opened up the black cloth, she could see that it was really a hood. When he pulled the hood over her head, everything went black. He dragged her across the sandy floor until he told her to stop. She heard the sound of a truck door opening. "Watch your step," the man said as he helped her up into the seat.

"Just what the hell do you think you're doing?" came an accented voice from out of the near distance.

"She rides with me," said the suit as he got into the driver's seat.

"And why is that?"

"Because you and your men are pigs," he said, slamming the truck door closed.

❖

Now, as the two soldiers tug on her arms, signaling for her to stop, she is startled by a sudden electronic buzz and an equally loud clatter of metal slamming against metal. Like gates being electronically opened.

She feels a hand shove against her back, pushing her inside. Then abruptly the hood is pulled off. Her eyes burn and she is forced to cover them with her palms. She goes to her knees on the concrete floor as the soldiers leave and the prison gate slams closed.

CHAPTER FIVE

THE FIRST TIME I SAW TONY ANGELINO THE *LAWYER* IN action, he was being dragged to county jail for contempt of court. I'd been going on my seventh hour perched up in the marble balcony of the State Supreme Court in Albany when the presiding judge had referred to Angelino's murdered client, Corrections Officer Donna Payton, as a promiscuous femme fatale: "A woman who had no business being a prison guard regardless of New York's acceptance of what common sense tells us should be a male-dominated field."

Whatever the hell that meant.

But the assessment had caused Tony to shoot up from his chair, raise his left hand, point it directly at the shackled prisoner seated at the defendant's table. "Your Honor, this piece of scum deserves the death penalty," he shouted. "And since we can't get him that, he deserves castration."

That's when Tony pulled a stiletto out of his jacket pocket and triggered open the six-inch blade, causing the black inmate to duck down under the long wooden table, screaming for someone to get that "madman" away from him.

The bald-headed Judge Howe called out for the police just as Tony buried the knife a good two inches into the table. Tony then called the judge a "no-good, head-up-your-ass, woman-hating son of a bitch," prompting the entire courtroom, including the twelve-member jury (two-thirds of them women), to explode in applause.

In my humble estimation, it took only twenty seconds flat for the armed security to pounce on Angelino, cuff him, and drag him out of court to a waiting mob van for an all-expenses-paid visit to the Albany County lockup.

It had been one hell of an introduction.

But I'm getting ahead of myself.

Actually, it all goes back to one Friday night in September 1984 when I was still the acting deputy superintendent for security at Coxsackie Correctional Facility in Greene County, during which time one of my corrections officers—a very attractive young woman by the name of Donna Payton—was raped and killed while working the four-to-midnight action shift. Around six that evening, not long after chow, a disturbance had been reported in the vicinity of the prison chapel. Against the better judgment of her shift commander, Donna volunteered to check it out.

But what should have been a routine check turned into something else entirely. Lenny Jones, the Schenectady-born-and-raised serial killer whom I'd placed in charge of chapel maintenance at the direct request of the prison padre (thinking perhaps that he and Jesus could somehow rehabilitate the cold-blooded killer), lay in wait for Payton.

When she entered the chapel, nightstick in hand, Lenny closed the wood door behind her and barricaded it with a church pew. He cornered her and beat and raped her with her own baton. Because the religious worship areas were located on the opposite end of the prison, her screams and cries for help could not be heard. Not that old Lenny ever attempted to muffle them.

Screams and cries made up just a part of his MO, made up just a small portion of what got him off on the killing experience. That and literally biting off her nipples while she lay on the altar beneath a wooden statue of the crucified Christ, bleeding hopelessly, inside and out.

So it was during that murder one trial that I was finally able to get a glimpse of what would one day come to be known as, and I quote, the "Tony Angelino Experience."

All morning and most of the afternoon, I watched Tony in action from up in the marble balcony of the State Supreme Court. I watched him meticulously lay out the facts of the Lenny Jones/Donna Payton case for the jury, not just with the spoken word but with the use of storyboards tacked to four separate bulletin boards. To add some real emotional weight to the case, he then proceeded to pass around graphic photos of the dead corrections officer, causing one jury member (a twenty-something white man) to become physically sick. And at another point in the trial, when his oration in defense of Payton's heroics (heroics that "defied all boundaries of gender") caused another jury member (an elderly black woman dressed entirely in white) to burst into tears, I became convinced that Tony had the talent to fool Jesus Christ himself.

What he did not have, I would later discover, was the talent to change the mind of a bigoted and biased old judge who took perverse pleasure in handing out thirty-day jail sentences for contempt of court to lawyers who would never see things his way. Regardless of who was in the right, who had been raped, who had been murdered by a convict already serving out a life sentence for murder one.

As for the upshot of the trial?

Tony did do his thirty days in the county lockup as decreed, while the jury handed Jones yet another life sentence in Coxsackie Prison's general populace. The new sentence didn't deter him from killing two more young inmates, both transvestites hooked on smuggled hormones and synthetic heroin.

But as you might have already guessed, no number of bigoted old judges or bleeding-heart prison padres or repealed death penalty laws or even Jesus Christ himself could save Jones from dying—dare I say it—by the sword. For on the late afternoon of December 24, 1989, almost five years to the day after the brutal murder of Donna Payton, Lenny found himself cornered inside that same prison chapel by a couple of inmates who harbored no grudge against him in particular.

In the end, the strangulation and mutilation of Lenny Jones had been nothing personal. Call it another day's work for the two killers, both of whom were already serving life sentences. In other words, they had nothing to lose on an outside they'd never see again. But then, they had everything to gain inside a concrete and razor-wire world that placed a certain value on men who had the balls to take out an infamous serial killer.

But here's the real sweet spot of the story:

It couldn't have been more than an hour after Lenny Jones's murder that Fran and I were attending a party at Tony's condo. Naturally I assumed the purpose of the party was to celebrate the final Christmas of the 1980s, but later on I learned through a very trustworthy source that the party had been intended to celebrate the "very sudden and very unfortunate death" of Jones.

In fact, at the party Tony passed out little Mass cards with a portrait of the Virgin Mary on the front and the Hail Mary printed on the back along with the name Leonard L. Jones and his—get this—birth and death dates. The cards were beautiful, with fine gold lace embroidered around the edges and embossed printing.

A time-consuming and expensive job, at least according to Fran. A job that would take a week or more to produce.

So when Fran asked about how in the world Tony would know that Mr. Jones was going to die that very afternoon, my confidential source simply raised his hands in the air, stuck out his bottom lip, and went back to the bar to freshen his drink. And when Fran turned to me, looked me in the eye, and said, "Oh, my sweet Jesus, he had him killed," I quickly pulled the drink out of her hand and dragged her onto the dance floor under a piece of mistletoe that hung on a string from the cathedral ceiling. I kissed her until embarrassment alone caused her to forget—at least for the time being—about the death of Lenny Jones and the legal counsel who had arranged it.

Now, ten years later, you could say that Tony had calmed down a lot. But as a lawyer, he was still arranging deaths. In this case, the death of Val and me.

We were sitting inside his Porsche Carrera, parked at the Port of Albany. To our right, the rusted hull of a massive cargo ship was being loaded with wooden pallets that contained four fifty-gallon drums apiece. The stenciling on the black drums spelled out MOLASSES in bold white letters.

Not ten feet from the car, a telephone pole was embedded in the macadam-covered dock. The pole was leaning drastically to the right, as though all it would take was a stiff gust of wind to send it into the river. Stapled to the pole was an artist's rendering of the Bald Man and the ten-thousand-dollar reward leading to any verifiable information as to his whereabouts. It was still there after two years, a faded reminder of my failure.

Tony asked for the envelope he had given me earlier.

From the passenger seat I watched the powerful movements of the enormous booms and cranes that lifted the pallets off the dock. The booms swung like giant arms, hauling the cargo up to the ship's deck, then loading it down inside a hull I had no way of seeing from where I was sitting.

"The envelope, please," he said.

Without looking at him, I reached inside my blazer, slid the envelope out from the interior pocket. Not ten feet from us, the Hudson ran fast and wide and very dark. Seagulls flew circular patterns around the cargo ship. You could feel the Carrera bucking in the wind. The gusts caused the pallets of molasses to sway like pendulums as they rose up off the docks.

Tony snatched the envelope out of my hands. "I'll do it for you," he said.

He tipped back the brim of his navy-blue fedora and slipped his thumb inside the flap, ran it down the length of the envelope, tearing it neatly open.

"I'll get straight to the point," he said, holding the contents of the envelope in his hand. "Last night Val obtained a court order preventing you from having any contact with her whatsoever. With her or her son, Ben. This is your copy of the order."

"Are you issuing me an affidavit, Counselor?" I said, staring at a family of black ducks floating on the surface of the water, bobbing up and down in the wake.

"Yes," he said, softly.

I took the document in my hand, unfolded it, stared down at it. The very top of the paper had been dated for the day before and stamped with the number 813.12 in the left-hand corner. In the top center appeared the words *Family Restraining Order and Injunction*. A few spaces below that could be found *Definitions*.

I read the first paragraph.

In this section of the document, domestic mistreatment means any of the following engaged by an adult family member or adult household member against another adult family member or adult household member against his or her former spouse or, as in the case of cohabitation, common-law spouse, or by an adult against an adult with whom the person has a child in common, biological or guardian. Intentional and/or possible infliction of physical pain, physical injury or illness…

I was tired of reading. The words meant nothing to me anyway. I folded the document up, stuffed it back inside the envelope, and back inside my jacket pocket.

"They just don't pass out restraining orders at will."

"You're no stranger to the process," Tony said. "Restraining actions can be easily filed even without the help of an attorney. County clerks have the forms on hand. From there you hand in the completed form along with a certified check for one hundred eighty bucks. Within a few hours, you're in business."

I focused on the Bald Man's face, flopping in the breeze coming off the river—the smooth egg head, the wide eyes, the thin mustache, the hoop earring in his left earlobe.

"How'd she get the state to act on it so quick?"

"Val has as many contacts in the legal field as anyone else who's spent their entire adult life in law enforcement," Tony explained. "After she got wind of your performance last night at Bill's Grill, she thought it prudent to pull a few strings. In the protective interest of her and her son. As you know, her first husband was abusive—"

"I know what the hell he was," I said.

Tony looked directly out the concave windshield of the Porsche toward the river. He inhaled gently and then released the breath. "I know you're not dangerous," he said. "I'm sure, deep down, Val knows you're not dangerous. It still does not change the fact that you walked out on her or that you shot up a local bar with your own personal hand cannon."

"The Buick, Tony," I said. "The fucking Buick showed up again." I looked down at my lap. "I want to go back to the cemetery, Tone. Take another look."

"You do that, *paisan*, and you will never forgive yourself."

"What if I find something?"

"What if you don't?"

He was right. The thought of not finding something frightened me way more than finding something that would finally lead me to the Bald Man. I looked one last time at the artist's rendering. I actually made eye contact with the poster. One day I would find him. Sooner or later. I wanted it to be sooner.

"Oh, for Christ's sake, Keeper," he said. "You can't carry Fran's cross forever."

I turned to him. "Go to hell," I said.

"But here's the reality of it," Tony said. "If you try anything, anything at all, if you even breathe in Val's direction, she'll call the police and they'll bust you, and by then there'll be nothing more I can do for you."

"Cut the bullshit, Tony," I said. "What's this court order stuff really all about?"

He turned slowly, back to facing the river. He pulled the brim of his fedora down low on his forehead. "Revenge," he said. "Simple revenge. For walking out."

"Just like that," I said. "No second chance?"

Tony raised his hands in the air, dropped them in his lap.

"You left her standing at the altar," he said. "Now tell me, how would *you* feel?"

The river.

Black and deep.

I felt like jumping in.

Drowning. For a little while at least. If it were possible.

"No comment," I said finally.

"No further questions, Your Honor," he said.

CHAPTER SIX

"I'VE DONE SOME RATHER EXTENSIVE—AND *EXPEN-sive*—research in the days since Ms. Barnes was arrested in Monterrey," announced Don O'Brien, the tall, balding, nattily dressed young lawyer belonging to Richard Barnes and his Reel Productions. "And, in turn, I've learned quite a bit. The main point being that Mexico is a country consisting of two worlds. *One* of extreme wealth and resource. Another of poverty and not-so-silent desperation."

We were sitting in Tony's rectangular-shaped office. Like Tony himself, the penthouse office was sleek, with polished hardwood floors and mahogany-paneled walls accented with custom-framed prints, including an original Picasso torso sketch.

On the glass coffee table in the far corner of the room sat the remnants of our lunch—mostly just the white deli paper in which our roast beef sandwiches had been wrapped. Tony sat at his desk, jacket off, the sleeves of his white oxford rolled up to his elbows, the thumbs of each hand positioned under gray-and-black-striped suspenders.

Barnes sat in the wooden chair beside me.

If I had to guess, I'd say he was about forty, with well-groomed salt-and-pepper hair and a narrow face. He wore a charcoal-gray single-breasted suit, similar to the one his lawyer wore, and rimless eyeglasses that made him appear the filthy rich public-relations man he had become in recent years since latching onto political candidates and their causes, including our present Republican governor. As for me, I had changed into my power-lunch best: Levi's jeans, Tony Lama cowboy boots, and a black leather jacket.

O'Brien paced the floor. "What we're clearly looking at in Mexico, gentlemen," he said, hands folded behind his back, eyes gazing out the window like a professor who's been over the same material a thousand times before, "is a land of haves and have-nots."

"Brilliant," Richard Barnes interrupted from his chair. "But can we please dispense with academic jargon and get to the heart of this matter, Donald, while my wife still has a shot at staying alive?"

O'Brien looked like he'd just been kicked in the shin. Both shins. "Please. Richard," he said, "I feel it's of the utmost importance to establish a little historical background."

Barnes shook his head. "Just make it quick, please."

I looked at Tony. He was leaning back in his swivel chair, elbows planted on the armrests, fingers locked together and pressed up against his mouth as he choked back a laugh.

O'Brien coughed. "Now where was I?"

"To have and have not," Tony volunteered, speaking through his fingers.

"Oh, yes," O'Brien said. And then he began pacing again. He told us that during the sixteenth century, Mexico was considered El Dorado by the Spanish-speaking hunters blinded by greed over its vast gold treasures. "That precious gold," he went on saying, "has now been replaced by cocaine, heroin, marijuana, and cheap labor."

While O'Brien went on with his lecture, I sat far back in my chair and noticed that on the floor beside Barnes's feet was O'Brien's briefcase. The case was wide open. Set on a stack of papers was a small paperback book. From my chair, I could see that the book was titled, *In Focus Mexico: Guide to Politics and Culture*. The cover photo depicted two Mexican natives dressed in festival garb—wide-brimmed hats, bright red vests with swirling patterns of yellow and purple over plain white linen pullover shirts. The natives appeared to be members of a larger team carrying a heavy wooden platform that supported a tall statue of Jesus Christ. Draped around the statue was an array of gold vases filled with colorful flowers.

I'd been sitting in one spot for too long.

I decided to cross my legs.

In the process, my foot hit the open lid of the briefcase, tipping it back and spilling out the contents, including the papers and travel guide.

"I'm sorry," I said, bending over to collect the papers and the book. "Let me get that for you."

"That's not necessary, Mr. Marconi."

I sat up, handed him the papers, but slipped the travel guide into the side pocket of my leather jacket. While an annoyed Barnes once again focused on O'Brien, I slipped the book back out and scanned the first few pages until I came to a chapter that had been marked with a yellow Post-it note. Some of the type on the pages had been highlighted in transparent yellow marker.

"You see, Mr. Angelino, Mr. Marconi," O'Brien went on, now standing at the window, hands casually in pockets, "my extensive knowledge of Mexico tells me that this is a land of un—"

"—predictable extremes," I said, reading directly from the guide. I lifted the book up high so everyone, including Barnes, could make it out.

"What's the point, Keeper?" Tony asked.

I slapped the paperback down on my lap.

"Let's face it," I said. "This man doesn't know squat about Mexico. Nor does he know squat about how to get Barnes's wife out. Meanwhile, it's my ass that goes on the line if I decide to take the job."

O'Brien affected a hand-caught-in-the-till kind of smile. I turned to look at Barnes. He had a tight, that's-my-till-you're-stealing-from expression on his face.

"You're right, Mr. Marconi," Barnes said in a calm, dry voice, eyes never veering from O'Brien. "We don't know 'squat,' as you put it, about Mexico and its recent wave of drug-related atrocities, other than what's reported in the papers. So there's no use pretending we do." He turned to me. "But we do know this about Monterrey Prison." He reached inside his suit jacket and pulled out two neatly folded sheets of 8½-by-ll-inch paper, which he then smoothed out on his lap.

Tony sat up in his chair.

Barnes handed the article to Tony, who perused it quickly but then handed it to me directly across his desk.

I glanced at the headline on the first page: IN MEXICAN PRISONS, HOPE IS QUICKLY ABANDONED!

"All we had to do," Barnes said, "was Google the subject of 'Mexican jails' and voilà." He made quotation marks with his fingers when he said, "voilà."

"I did a little more research than that," O'Brien insisted.

"You know, you're absolutely right, Donald," Barnes said, lifting the paperback off my lap. "You also took a little trip to the bookstore. Now there's an excursion I'm going to insist you bill me double for."

O'Brien's lower jaw seemed as though it were hanging off his belt buckle. "I did spend a night in the library, Richard. My wife had to miss her bridge—"

"Oh, shut up," Barnes said.

CHAPTER SEVEN

TONY SUGGESTED THAT WE ALL CALM DOWN AND take what he referred to, among men, as a "piss break." Barnes retrieved a cell phone from his briefcase. He said he needed a few minutes to check up on some of his clients anyway. That left me alone to read the Internet article, which, I noticed, had been penned originally for the *New York Post.*

A man making his way past the iron bars and concrete walls in the half light and foul stench of Monterrey Prison emerges upon a nightmare of humanity: dozens of tranquilized men and women packed together like sardines in six separate holding cells.

I stopped there and read the paragraph again.

First off, I was trying to comprehend co-gender incarceration. Then I was trying to imagine dozens of inmates packed into a few narrow holding cells where finding enough space to sit down would be a major problem. Even for a man who had spent most of his life in some of the most crowded prisons in New York, I couldn't fathom how a prisoner would be expected to eat, sleep, and clean up in that kind of environment, let alone survive from one day to the next.

Maybe that was the point.

I read on.

If the prisoners behaved themselves, they might have the "opportunity" to move into a four-person cell after only a couple of months. A cell block guard who had agreed to be interviewed stated that he'd been forced to maintain five inmates to a ten-foot cell while a total of 344 men and women in his block had no choice but to share three toilets.

Señor and *señorita,* welcome to your worst nightmare.

The more I read, the more I realized it wasn't the lack of personal space or proper sanitation that posed the greatest threat to Renata. According to one Amnesty International official named in the report, from January 1993 to April 1998, more than a thousand inmates had suffered violent deaths inside Monterrey Prison, not only at the hands of other inmates but also at the hands of the guards. It was even suspected that the prison warden himself (a suspected member of the Contreras Brothers crime family) partook in executing the death penalty from time to time. The stats, if they were accurate, astounded even me. Last year alone, Monterrey experienced 232 homicides, over a hundred attempted intentional body-damage incidents, eighty or so rapes, fifty-two inmate-to-inmate robberies, and over eighty drug-related, nonviolent crimes.

Because the prison's total population stood at around four thousand, it didn't take a genius to figure out that Renata had about one chance in four of making it out alive. Maybe less, considering the rancid conditions. That is, unless someone or something acted fast.

That's where I came in.

Or didn't.

❖

Tony was the first to return.

He took his usual place behind the desk.

Then came Barnes, O'Brien on his tail.

Barnes folded his cellular. Instead of packing it back in his briefcase, he stuffed it inside the interior pocket of his suit jacket.

I set myself on the edge of Tony's desk, crossed my arms. Very official-looking.

"I know why you want to hire me, Mr. Barnes," I said. "And I think I know what the job entails. But maybe you can shed some light on how exactly you'd expect me to pull it off."

Without hesitating, O'Brien stepped forward. But then he stopped dead in his tracks when Barnes shot up.

"Please, Donald," he said. "Just stay out of the way for now."

There was a weighty silence in which I wasn't quite sure if O'Brien was going to cry or throw up or both. Both, if I had to place a bet. But he just backed into the far corner where the glass and mahogany walls met and lowered his head like a scolded kid.

"I'm not going to pretend you can go this one alone, Mr. Marconi," Barnes said, looking me in the eye. "I'll be providing you with a contact."

"What contact, Mr. Barnes?"

"Richard," he said. "Please call me Richard."

"Who would act as my contact, Mr. Barnes?"

He swallowed. "I have a man in mind who would be happy to take the job on."

"Mexican man?"

"Of American and Mexican descent, actually. An antiquities trader who, on occasion, hires out as a guide."

"How'd you find him?"

O'Brien tore himself away from the wall. "It's none of your business how we run our operations, Mr. Marconi."

I caught O'Brien's eyes with my own, locked onto them. I was just about ready to tell him to shut up when Barnes made it

GODCHILD

perfectly clear that his "services would no longer be required for the remainder of the proceedings."

O'Brien's face turned Harvard red. "But who will you use as a witness, Richard? You just can't solicit the services of a private investigator you know nothing about, even if he claims to be an expert on prisons."

"That's enough, Donald," Barnes snapped. "Now please leave the room before I ask you to return my retainer."

Another silence. You could almost hear the pigeons perching outside Tony's window. If there were a ledge for pigeons to perch on in the first place. O'Brien pursed his lips, bent over, and packed up his briefcase. "Well then," he said in a strained voice, "since I am no longer wanted, I'll take my leave."

As he was going for the door, I shouted out for him to stop.

I grabbed the travel guide off Tony's desk, flung it to him from across the room. O'Brien bobbled the book with his free hand but somehow managed to hang on. Not bad, I thought. For a dweeb.

He let out a breath and stared at the book's cover until a broad smile appeared on his face. He raised his head and, at the same time, positioned the book in his right hand like a Frisbee.

He tossed it back to me.

I caught it one-handed.

"Actually, Mr. Marconi," he said, "I believe it's you who's going to be needing it more than I."

And then he walked out.

After apologizing on behalf of his counselor, Barnes loosened the knot on his tie. His way of getting down and dirty, I supposed.

I asked him how he expected me to recognize this contact.

"He'll recognize you," Barnes said.

"What about weapons and a safe house?"

"You won't have to worry about a thing. They'll already be there waiting for you. Nor will you have to worry about customs giving you a problem."

Tony sat up straight. "If I may," he said.

"Please, Anthony," Barnes said.

He explained to me that Richard already had several business ventures in Mexico and parts of Central America. "Some people owe him favors here and there," he went on. "So you won't have problems getting in and out, if you know what I mean."

I knew what he meant. But the whole operation sounded a little too good to be believable. Just cruise into Mexico, break into a major Mexican prison, steal the damsel in distress, escape to the border, fly off into the sunset, run the credits and the closing music. Just one big easy. If Tony weren't my friend, I'd swear he and Barnes were feeding me directly to the dogs. Or, in this case, coyotes.

"What about your wife, Mr. Barnes?" I said. "I don't know anything about her other than what I've read in the papers or seen on TV."

Barnes reached down to the floor, picked up his briefcase, set it on the edge of the desk. He took out a manila folder. "In here you'll find all you need to know about Renata. Photos, bios, and a copy of her novel."

He set the package on his desk.

"*Godchild*," I volunteered.

"Yes," a suddenly morose Barnes said, as if the very mention of the novel caused the plug to be pulled on his heart. "*Godchild*."

He closed up his briefcase. "Well, if there's nothing else…" He let it dangle.

He forced a smile and held out his right hand. I took it, shook it loosely.

"I trust the money would be to your satisfaction."

"So long as it's OK with Tony," I said.

I took my hand back. It felt cold and wet.

"You won't speak with me again," Barnes said. "You can give your answer to Mr. Angelino. He in turn will relay your decision to me."

He took his case and left, leaving me alone with Tony.

I turned to him after a time.

"Well," he said, holding out his hands. "Yes or no?"

"I don't know," I said.

"When *will* you know?" he said.

"Can you give me until tomorrow morning?" I asked.

He nodded. "OK, sleep on it. But I can't wait much longer than that. Renata doesn't have that kind of time."

I glanced at the Internet article on his desk. He was right.

"I'll let you know first thing," I said. "Now how's about a ride back to my motel?"

CHAPTER EIGHT

THE WINDOWLESS CELL MEASURES ABOUT FIVE FEET BY five feet. Almost a perfect square, with a tile floor and drain in the center.

A steel-framed bunk that supports a thin mattress is pushed up against the concrete wall to her right. When she looks out the vertical iron bars that make up the door to the cell, she can see a gray concrete wall.

The cell is lit by only one exposed overhead lightbulb.

All around her come the moans and groans of the inmates. Sleeping the restless sleep of the drugged.

She zips up the front of her jumpsuit, as if this makes her more secure, and moves toward the front of the cell.

"Hello," she whispers out across the iron bars. "Is anyone out there who can hear me?" A deep, stale breath. In and out. "Hello… anybody?"

After a short time, she hears a man's voice. "Hello," comes the whisper.

She feels herself smiling, the muscles in her face tightening up, a shot of warmth and security shooting up her spine. "My name is Renata," she says. "Where am I?"

"Beautiful Monterrey Prison," he says in a heavy, throaty voice like the voice of an old man, although Renata has no way of knowing for sure.

She wishes she had her reporter's notebook, a pad of paper, a scrap, anything to write on. And something to write with. But she has nothing. *They stripped her of everything when they dragged her in with that blindfold on.*

"Where in the prison?" she asks.

"Basement isolation," the man says. "Consider yourself lucky. Upstairs you have to share a box with ten or twelve people. Don't take this the wrong way, but a woman like you…well, you wouldn't last long."

She wants to tell him that he has no idea who he's dealing with. But she lets it go.

"What's your name?" she asks.

"Roberto."

"Why are you here, Roberto?"

"They say I murdered my wife's lover."

"Is it true?" she asks. *If only she had a pen and paper.*

"This man I speak of, he used to come across the border from Texas on Thursday afternoons. When I was at work."

"Is that a yes or is that a no?"

"It was wrong for him to come across the border and do what he did to my wife."

"I'll take that as a yes."

"What are you in for, Renata?" he asks. "If you don't mind?"

"I write books," she said.

He laughs.

"What's so funny?"

"Good material here," he says.

She smiles, although he cannot see her smiling.

Just then there is the sound of a lock being unlocked. A metal door swings open and hard leather soles shuffle on concrete. There is the sound of chains and keys rattling and shaking.

They are coming for her. She has no way of knowing for certain, but then she can feel it like a lump in her chest.

"Miss," the invisible man says, his voice now urgent. "Here they come. Do not talk. Just do what they tell you."

She feels her heart racing as she slides back against the far wall, knees tucked up against her chest. She sees them then. Three men. Two soldiers. Perhaps the same two who brought her in here from the desert. Standing in between the men is the mustached man also from the desert. He is still dressed in his black suit. The soldier to his left is holding a plastic tray containing a plate of food and water. The soldier to his right holds an identical tray that supports something else entirely. A syringe and a vial containing a clear liquid.

The mustached man calls out for the guard to open the door. "Numero dos!" *he shouts.*

An electronic buzzer sounds and the gate slides open.

The mustached man steps in. The soldiers follow.

"Are you hungry, Ms. Barnes?"

She stares at him, stone-faced.

"I must apologize for the way you've been treated."

"Don't bother," she says, feeling her teeth begin to chatter.

He crouches, meets her eye to eye, his face so close to hers she can smell his Bay Rum aftershave.

"If it is any consolation," he says, "I spared your life out there in the desert. Running drugs, as you know, is a serious crime in this part of the world."

"Is it?" she asks, as if she doesn't know.

"I'd like to go on sparing your life," he says, "so long as you cooperate with me."

She breathes in and out. Twice. "What is it you'd like me to do?"

He reaches out with his right hand, gently fingers the zipper on her leather jumpsuit.

"Answer some simple questions."

She slaps his hand away. "Touch me again," she says, "and I'll find a way to kill you."

He stands.

His face is serious, with heavy, black-and-blue bags under each eye, creases in the tan skin that covers his cheeks and forehead.

"Take away the food," he says to the soldier on his left, who immediately walks out with the tray. Then to the second soldier, on his right: "Shoot her up. It'll help clear her mind."

The soldier to his right takes the syringe and vial in one hand and, with the other, sets the tray down on the floor.

"Don't you touch me with that thing," she screams, quickly shuffling back into the corner.

The mustached man approaches her, grabs her by the feet. "Your resistance is nothing to us," he says. "As is your life."

The soldier is sticking the needle into the vial, pulling back on the plunger, sucking the liquid up.

"Get away from me!" she screams, trying to kick. But he's got her tight by the legs.

"Just stick it through her clothing," he orders the soldier.

The soldier holds the syringe up at chest height. He depresses it just enough to allow a bit of the clear liquid to spray out. He comes for her.

"No, goddammit, no!" she screams again.

"Just do what they tell you to do!" shouts an invisible Roberto.

CHAPTER NINE

YOU WANT TO KNOW WHAT SLEEP WAS LIKE FOR ME? Let's just say I hadn't slept well in years. Not for lack of trying. Drink, pills, television, staring at the ceiling—nothing helped. Nothing could stop the memories that sped through the screen of my imagination like a videotape gone wacky.

This had always been the trick:

Attempting to sleep with my eyes wide open. If such a thing were possible, with my Colt laid flat on my bare chest and the radiant heat making boiling and pinging sounds that reverberated against the paper-thin walls of the motel. I fixed my eyes on a popcorn ceiling that exploded in red neon with every flash of the Coco's Motor Inn sign. Soon enough the events were on their way back to haunt me in their perfectly calculated nap-time brilliance.

Me, at the wheel of the Ford Bronco, inching my way into a four-way intersection. Fran, seated on the passenger side. She screams. I hit the brake in the middle of the intersection, as if my life depends upon it. And it does. Only a split second later, the Buick runs the red light, rams us, dead-on. Suicide seat. Fran slams forward, her head through the windshield, the sharp edge of the glass taking her head clean off at the base, her body falling back into the bucket seat as though nothing at all had happened. As though it was all a mistake. This is what immediately registers: the battered black Buick backing up fast, the tires burning rubber against the asphalt. Then the car quickly shifts into forward, swerving around the wrecked Bronco, shooting on past, but not before I get a good look at the driver. A bald man with a hoop earring and black John Lennon sunglasses. He looks at me before he takes off.

Forever.

But then he is back. Just like that. Driving through the gates of the Albany Rural Cemetery.

The battered black Buick come back to life.

Or maybe that too is just another dream.

I woke up like I always did: in a pool of sweat, the .45 having slid off my chest onto the bed. Outside the motel room came the stop-and-go sounds of the jets taking off and landing at the Albany International Airport and the perpetual murmur of commuter traffic growing heavier and heavier. Men and women rushing home to their private suburban hells.

I lay there on my back staring at the flashing red neon letters. Suddenly my thoughts shifted to Val. I saw her almond-shaped brown eyes and her chiseled cheekbones and her smooth, shoulder-length, sandy-brown hair. I remembered her warm smile and her low, smooth voice. I wanted to call her. But then I rolled over onto my side and saw the folded restraining order on the bedside table and I knew it would be wrong to even try. I had to consider the consequences. Consider the fact that not only would I be breaking the law but that I would be breaking her heart, and mine, in more ways than one. I knew the best thing was to let it all go. For her, for me. Forget there had ever been a wedding, or an engagement, or even a proposal.

Forget there had ever been any such thing as Keeper and Val. As the sun set on Albany, I folded back the metal clasp on the manila envelope that Barnes had handed me that afternoon at Tony's office. I flipped it upside down and spilled the contents onto the bed.

There was a paperback copy of Renata's novel, *Godchild*, along with what looked to be a press kit that had been prepared by her New York publisher. There were also three or four newspaper clippings that Richard must have added to the mix. The press kit was held together with a heavy black clip. It consisted of a press release announcing publication of the novel, a short Q-and-A piece, and a brief article about the book. There were also three eight-by-ten color glossies. It was these images of Renata that caught my full attention.

Her hair was vivid auburn and cropped short, with little strands hanging over her forehead. Her eyes were deep blue and her nose was small but as pronounced as her lips, which, when they came together, made the shape of a heart.

I can't say how long I actually sat there and stared at Renata's image. Let's just say I looked at it until, at very least, I might be able to spot her on a busy street corner.

Or should I say a cell block in Monterrey, Mexico?

I laid the three photos out side by side and picked up the first of the written pieces. There was a fairly detailed bio that told me she had been born upstate in Cairo, New York, a small town just outside Catskill. There, she had been raised in the public school system. She'd gone on to Vassar to major in journalism before blowing another two years on a master of fine arts degree in writing at Vermont College. From there she did a stint as a reporter at the *Times-Union* in Albany and then on to a freelance career with *Time* and *New York Newsday* and some other papers.

It was during this time that Renata began to publish some of her early fiction in a whole bunch of journals I'd never heard of before, nor ever would again. Soon came the marriage to Richard and a short-lived career in public relations and script writing for

Barnes's own Reel Productions. Then, curiously enough, she went back on the road as a freelancer, this time to some pretty far-off locales like Florence, Moscow, Beijing, and even Benin, West Africa.

She covered the Gulf War for *Mademoiselle*, reporting on women in the front lines, which resulted in her nomination for the "prestigious" Polk Award for "accuracy and clarity in reporting while willingly placing her life at risk." She'd later suffer a case of the bends while writing about vampire bats in the underground caves of Sri Lanka for *National Geographic*, come close to arrest in Kosovo during the Balkan wars, and nearly have her brains blown out by an irate mobster while preparing a feature on the emerging black market in Russia.

She stayed at home long enough to bear and, for a time, raise her little boy Charlie, until the child's untimely death in 1995. After which she took off again, this time for the south of France where she wrote *Godchild*, her only novel to date.

I took a few more seconds to look through the rest of the publicity material, all of it either regarding *Godchild* or the actual writing of the story; all of it stressing that it was fiction as opposed to memoir. Deciding to cut to the chase, I picked up the novel itself and glanced at the jacket copy.

Godchild *is a psychological tour de force that exposes the madness behind a mother's recounting of her child's drowning...*

I stopped right there.

Not exactly light reading. No wonder Barnes looked as though he was about to cry when he handed me the copy. I knew that if the emotions he had for his son bore even a fleeting resemblance to the ones I still carried for Fran, then there would be no getting over his kid's death. It just wasn't possible. And then his wife has to go and write *Godchild*, a constant three-hundred-page reminder of the sadness.

I picked up the newspaper clipping. It came from the spring of 1995.

BARNES CHILD DROWNED IN BATHTUB

I read the article. In the end, it offered little more information than the headline itself had. Only that the kid had been discovered by his mother after she had left the room for *two minutes, no more.* And in that time—that space of one hundred and twenty seconds—Charlie must have hit his head on the ceramic tub and drowned.

As of that writing, Renata had not been charged with negligence or murder. Another short piece was published two days later with the headline, AUTHOR BARNES DENIES KILLING CHILD. Under that clip was another, and it was this one that nearly made my heart stop.

It was a news item published May 5, 1995, the day of Charlie Barnes's funeral, almost a year to the day before Fran would be murdered. But it was not the article that got to me, or the description of the service and the moving eulogy given by Bishop Hubbard himself. It was the UPI photo that went with it. The one conspicuously placed under the headline, BARNES CHILD BURIED, PARENTS IN MOURNING.

It was a black-and-white photo I had probably seen before in passing—maybe back in 1995 while I was still warden at Green Haven Prison. A photo that showed a man who would mean absolutely nothing to me until a year later when he would mean everything. Just a simple, grainy black-and-white shot of a defeated Richard tightly clutching Renata's arm—more for his own support than hers—as they descended the stairs outside Saint Mary's Cathedral dressed in black. But it wasn't the Barneses who caught my eye. What concerned me was the man who stood only a couple of feet back in the crowd as the mourners moved toward what must have been a long line of waiting limousines. A burly man with an earring in his left earlobe and a thin mustache that barely covered his lip and a shiny, shaved head.

The Bald Man.

Up close and personal.

CHAPTER TEN

I DIALED TONY.

He answered after the third ring. Music in the background, some voices spilling across the earpiece. Men and women. "What's up?"

I said, "I'll take the job."

He breathed. "I thought you wanted to sleep on it."

"I can explain tomorrow."

"I'll get started," he said.

I hung up.

CHAPTER ELEVEN

IN THE DREAM, SHE HOLDS THE NEWBORN CHARLIE IN her arms. She is crouching, cradling the baby on her shoulder while she runs the bath, holding her free hand under the warm—getting warmer—water. She feels the good feel of Charlie's warm face cuddled into that sensitive space between her shoulder and neck, feels his warm breath. She can't remember ever being so happy. So happy she hasn't even thought about writing. Her computer just sits there on the desk in the bedroom, idle. And she doesn't care.

'What a trip. 'Having a little baby. 'What a fantastic trip.

And as she sets the baby into the water, she feels the bathwater soaking her cotton shirtsleeves, feels it soaking her entire shirt, as the baby slips under the water, headfirst...

She awakes in a pool of wet

Startled.

The mustached man is back in her cell. He's alone this time and he's just tossed an entire bucket of water on her.

"I hope you're ready to talk," he says.

CHAPTER TWELVE

AT HALF-PAST SEVEN IN THE MORNING, I WAS SITTING at the counter of the downtown Dunkin' Donuts. While the early bird suits rushed past the picture windows, briefcases in hand, on their way to their office cubbies, I was attempting to sort out my intentions regarding the Barnes job over black coffee and two blueberry cake doughnuts. The Dunkin' Donuts was set between a Burger King and Bruegger's Bagels and was only a short walk from Tony's Pearl Street office. The place was new, and it occupied what had been a Buster Brown Shoes back when I was a kid. Back before all the downtown shops were forced to vacate the empty city streets and move out to the mall, where they died an even slower death. Before people could eat doughnuts at plastic-covered tables and look out windows that once displayed the newest in children's footwear.

The night had been a long one.

What little sleep I got had been interrupted by long interludes of lying on my back, staring up at the red neon letters that reflected backward against the ceiling, thinking the same thoughts I was thinking now. Thoughts about the Bald Man, thoughts about Barnes and Renata. Thoughts about connecting the three together. If the man in the photo was actually the Bald Man, what had he been doing at Charlie Barnes's funeral? Were the Barneses and the Bald Man friends? Were they family? Was I out of my mind for even making the connection? Or was I just plain reaching for something that didn't exist?

Without a name or identification of some sort, I had no idea who the man in the photo was. What I did know was that he looked an awful lot like the man I saw driving the black Buick. But in a real way, it was reason enough to take on the job of going after Renata Barnes.

I sipped some coffee, took a bite of doughnut, and pulled the newspaper clipping out of my pocket. I spread it out on the pink Formica counter, stared down at it, past the clearer images of Richard and Renata, two rows of mourners back, to a somewhat blurrier image. The bald head, the mustache, the earring, the round John Lennon sunglasses. How many times was I going to go over the description in my head? Countless times. But the fact remained that this piece of newspaper was probably the largest clue I'd been able to come up with in two years of searching. And I had just happened to stumble upon it.

The girl working the counter came up to me. She held a fresh pot of coffee in her right hand. She asked if I wanted more. I did. She poured some coffee into my cup and smiled. She was a young girl with blonde hair pulled up behind her head in an untidy bun. A kid really. Maybe eighteen or nineteen. Dressed in a tight pink-and-white dress that matched the vinyl wall finish, with a Dunkin' Donuts logo on her breast and powdered sugar on the little apron that covered her lap. She wore Nike Airs on her feet, with white socks around her ankles.

I asked her if I could smoke.

She reached behind the counter, found a small tin ashtray, set it beside my plate of doughnuts. "Be my guest, sugar," she said. The "sugar" part made me blush.

I folded up the article, slipped it back into my pants pocket.

I lit one up, let out the initial hit of smoke, followed up with a sip of the too-hot coffee.

There was more to think about and it was no use ignoring it. A whole second side to the equation that I had to consider. I had to calm down, consider the fact that I could very well be overreacting. That the man in the photo could be someone else entirely. After all, I'd only had a fleeting glimpse of the Bald Man. As much as I think I committed his looks to memory, I could have been all wrong about his identity.

The fact of the matter was this: Barnes's job was dangerous. It would be suicide to go into it with anything on my mind other than the job at hand. Which was to get his wife out of that Mexican hellhole.

The end.

Professionally speaking, it *should* not have made an ounce of difference to me just what skeletons the Barneses may have had stuffed away inside their walk-in closets. It should not have made any difference if their marriage was a good one or a bad one, or if Richard was a slimy producer of slash-and-burn political propaganda or if Renata had killed their child and somehow fictionalized it in *Godchild*. More importantly, it should not have made a difference if the bald man in the newspaper photo was my Bald Man.

I no longer worked on the side of the law.

I worked for myself.

In the end, what difference did any of these things make so long as Barnes's two hundred under-the-table Gs were good? I hadn't been a PI for long, but I knew that the number one rule for any detective was to stick to the job at hand. Don't ask questions that'll get your ass in a sling. Don't get personally involved, don't go off half-cocked on a personal vendetta.

End of story.

As far as my relationship with Barnes was concerned, it could easily be summed up like this: I give you the girl, you give me the money. Thank you very much, have a nice, rich life.

I smoked and sipped more coffee. It was cooling off now. Enough so that it didn't burn my tongue. In the meantime, the counter girl drifted her way back. She carried a pot of coffee in her right hand. Steam rose up from the opening in the top of the pot. She asked me first if she could freshen up my cup. I liked that. I told her no, that I had to get going. I did, however, order a large cup of black to go. With her left hand, she reached into her apron and set a small slip of paper on the counter. My tab. A whole one dollar and ninety cents. I stamped out my butt, popped the rest of my second doughnut into my mouth, slipped off the stool, and fished for my bankroll in my left-hand pocket. I peeled off a five and slipped the bill under the empty white plate.

On my way out, while I was zipping up my leather, I spotted her across the glass case, where she was in the process of filling a pink box with some muffins.

"Thanks," I said.

"Don't forget your coffee," she reminded me.

I stopped and made my way back to the glass case. She handed the cup to me.

"Forget your head…wouldn't you, sugar?"

"Exactly," I said, turning for the door.

Sugar. How sweet it is.

CHAPTER THIRTEEN

"I NEVER SAID I DIDN'T BELIEVE YOU, *PAISAN*. IT'S JUST that I agree with Detective Ryan when he attests that you've been under a lot of strain." Tony, talking from behind his mahogany desk. "It's easy to let your imagination run wild."

I had just shown him the newspaper clipping of Charlie Barnes's funeral, just pointed out the image of the Bald Man. Or *a* bald man anyway. Now Tony was removing the plastic lid from the Styrofoam cup of Dunkin' Donuts coffee I brought for him. At the same time, he was trying to talk me out of believing that the man in the photo could be anything other than a man with no hair and that the battered black Buick I'd seen driving in and out of the Albany Rural Cemetery on Saturday was anything other than a figment of my over-stressed imagination.

But then something different happened.

Something I never expected.

Tony let out a breath while the color of his complexion went from tan to red to white. Not an easy task for a *paisan*.

He sat up straight in his swivel chair, planted his elbows firmly on the desk, and stared down at his fingers, locked together at the knuckles. "OK, let's cut the bullshit," he said, his voice just one great big resigned sigh. "I've known about the Buick for a while now. A few weeks, in fact. So has Ryan."

I set the article down on the desk.

There was the inevitable adrenaline head rush. The slight dizziness. The anger that started at the tip of your brain stem and didn't stop until it fried your brain.

"And you never fucking…" An outburst. I breathed. "And you never told me." Controlled now. Whispering. Swallowing the anger.

"I didn't want to alarm you."

"You didn't want to alarm me." I kept whispering.

He nodded. "I was afraid you'd do something stupid."

"So Ryan tries to convince me I'm imagining things. And you do the same."

He nodded. "It was for your own good," he said by way of explanation. "But then, you can only go on pretending for so long. Then it gets serious."

"More serious than this?" I asked. "For Christ's sake. I missed my own goddamned wedding."

We sat there silent for a few seconds while Tony sipped the coffee.

My head was spinning, trying to keep up with itself.

"I don't get it," I said. "On one hand, you're willing to send me to Mexico on this suicide mission, and on the other you don't let me in on the Buick until now."

Tony stared at the steam rising up out of the coffee cup. He rolled up the sleeves on his pressed white shirt, neatly, to the elbows, as if to give him something to concentrate on other than me. My problems with the past and present.

"OK," he said. "Just suppose the Buick is *your* Buick. Just suppose the man in the photo is *your* Bald Man, and just suppose Barnes is somehow connected to him."

"Just suppose," I said, "that the Bald Man has shown up with the intent to finish the job he started. To see me dead."

More thinking on Tony's part. And then: "Let me ask you a simple question: Who, in your opinion, would like to see you dead, Keeper?"

The answer, of course, was so obvious that it took me a few seconds to come up with it. "I was a warden, for Christ's sake. Who the hell doesn't want to see me dead?"

"Exactly," he said. "Without going over the lists of inmates who've been paroled during the past three years or inmates who presently have major connections with the outside, it'll be impossible to come up with any one name or any one scenario."

"So what are you saying?"

"What I'm saying is you came down hard on the drug trade at Green Haven, especially in '94 and '95, getting in more than a few people's way, if you get my drift."

"And?"

"And anyone in the can or out could have found out about your past, about the black Buick. These guys have access to newspapers and the Internet. Somebody could have found out all about your past and has simply initiated a game of emotional blackmail. And you're just playing right into his hands."

"What about Wash Pelton?" Pelton had been a former friend *and* enemy. A paunchy, gray-haired political appointee whom I personally sent up to Dannemora for life. A former commissioner of Corrections whom I busted after a particularly dangerous game of catch-as-catch-can, when he tried to pin both a murder rap and a major drug ring inside Green Haven Prison on yours truly.

"Pelton's stomach cancer took him six months ago," Tony pointed out while taking a sip of his coffee. "If he's suddenly interested in tidying things up, he's got to do it from the grave."

"Then how the hell do you explain the bald man in this clip?" I held up the article once more.

"Coincidence," he said. "Or bad timing."

"Or a perfectly logical series of events," I said.

Tony drinking coffee.

Me looking out over his shoulder, through the floor-to-ceiling tinted glass, at the Hudson River on a bright, clear March morning.

"Look," he said, breaking the silence. "I admit, there is one thing we should consider."

I caught his brown eyes with my own, nodded.

"The black Buick could be intended as some kind of warning. A message from any number of drug bosses or their soldiers you once incarcerated. It doesn't necessarily have to be someone like Pelton or even one of his living apostles." He took a quick breath. "But there is one thing that's gnawing at me." He picked up a number 2 Ticonderoga pencil from his desk, tapped the eraser against the furrowed skin of his brow. "If somebody does want to go after you—I mean if somebody is making a serious play—why not just get it over with?" He wrapped the index finger on his right hand around the pencil, held it over his desk, like an imitation pistol. "Bang, one shot to the head and you're done. Quick, easy, effective. Least that's the way I'd do it."

"Comforting," I said.

"I mean, why go to all the trouble of sending out a car that matches a description of the one that killed Fran? Or, on the other hand, if it is the real car, why take a chance putting it back on the road?"

"Maybe just a warning, like you said."

"Or maybe a way to torture you while they bide their time, wait for the right moment."

"There is something you're leaving out," I said.

He set the pencil back down and picked up his coffee. "What would that be?"

"Why now?" I said, setting the article on his desk. "Why after two years of nothing do the Buick and this bald son of a bitch decide to show up at precisely the same time Barnes and his dilemma show up?"

"You saw the car on Saturday, one full day before Barnes inquired about hiring you. If you're trying to connect this thing with my client, the timeline doesn't jive, *capisce*?"

He was right. But that didn't mean I had to believe in his logic.

"Besides," Tony went on, "doesn't make sense for a guy to hire you with a cash down payment only to knock your ass off in the end."

"Or maybe it does."

"Damn it, Keeper. If you think you can accept this job just because it'll lead you to this bald guy, think again. It's extremely dangerous. You're going to have to concentrate on one thing, one thing only: getting Renata Barnes out, getting her home, getting two hundred Gs to start over with. After that you can do all the searching you want. Until then, stick to the job and nothing but the job, *capisce*?"

"You're leaving me nothing to hang my hat on, Tone," I said. "And a whole lot of nothing makes me real nervous."

"I hear your concern, *paisan*," Tony said, picking up the telephone receiver, bringing it to his ear. "And I feel for you. But I'll say it one more time: in the end, it's probably just someone fucking with your head. And that's all."

"And if it's not just child's play?"

"I've already got that one figured out." He punched a button on the phone unit. "A little preventive maintenance," he said, bringing the phone to his ear, hand cupped over the mouthpiece.

"Can't wait to hear all about it," I said.

"Get me Albany Medical Center," Tony said into the phone. "The morgue."

CHAPTER FOURTEEN

*SHE COMBS BACK HER WET HAIR WITH OPEN FINGERS.
She is still groggy from the shot, barely aware of the whispering
voices that seem to ooze from the cages that surround her. She sits
up straight, her back against the hard wall.*

*"So what is it you want to talk about?" she says, looking down
at the floor, watching what's left of the water run down into the wire
drain. Water that came from a metal bucket that they splashed in
her face. To wake her up out of her enforced sleep.*

*"I want to know what you're doing here," says the mustached
man.*

She laughs, although nothing is funny.

"You brought me here," she says. "Remember?"

*"Don't play games with me," he says, his voice more strained
now, impatient. "What business did you have in the desert with
those Contreras sons of whores?"*

"Getting at the truth."

"What truth?"

"I'm a writer," she says. "I write about the truth."

The water, dripping down into the drain.

*"I know what you are," he says, reaching into the pocket of his
suit jacket, pulling out a paperback copy of her novel,* Godchild.

*"I see you have good literary taste," she says. "For a guy with a
cheesy mustache."*

"*You are Renata Barnes,*" he says, replacing the novel in his pocket. "*The method writer.*"

"*Righto,*" she says.

"*Now tell me,*" he says, bending at the knees, looking at her from eye level, as he had done earlier before injecting her. "*Who were you writing the story for, and for what purpose?*"

"*You asking me if I'm a spy?*"

"*I'm asking who you work for and why.*"

"*I work for myself, asshole.*"

He stands up, crosses his arms. He calls out for a soldier named Juan. A man walks in. He's the same soldier from before. He is carrying a tray with a syringe and vial on it, just like before.

"*Great, you're gonna put me to sleep again. That's gonna get all your questions answered in a real hurry.*"

The soldier begins preparing the syringe.

"*Oh, no,*" he says. "*Nothing like that. This time we inject you with something quite different. Something to stimulate your memory.*"

Heart valves pounding.

Mouth going dry as sand.

She knows they mean business. These crazy Mexicans. As the soldier sticks the syringe into the top of the vial, she begins backing up into the corner of the cell, as if it offers her some protection. Slowly at first, but then faster. "*What the hell are you doing to me?*"

"*We're going to have a nice chat,*" the mustached man says.

"*Please do what they tell you,*" comes the voice of Roberto.

CHAPTER FIFTEEN

TONY INSISTED THAT I FOLLOW HIM IN HIS PORSCHE while he drove my 4Runner to the Albany Medical Center.

Rear entrance.

The morgue.

He gave me strict orders to wait in the car.

I did. No arguments from me.

From there we crossed the bridge into Rensselaer to reach the huge strip of no-man's land between the north-south, high-speed Amtrak line and the Hudson River.

We crossed the tracks and parked along the barren riverbank. An exchange of keys was made. Then Tony asked me to get back into the 4Runner and pull the front end up to the river's edge where a concrete dike wall secured and protected the flood plain.

The task took only a few seconds to accomplish.

"What's this all about?" I asked as I stepped out of the 4Runner. "Part of your preventive maintenance program?"

But Tony wouldn't answer.

The Albany skyline loomed on the horizon, directly across the river. The city looked dead. The sky was heavy and gray.

So was the river.

With his navy-blue fedora pulled over his eyes and his matching blue overcoat, Tony looked sorely out of place standing along the deserted stretch of shoreline in the cold, damp air of midday with illegally discarded refrigerators, washers, and dryers scattered about. He opened the trunk of the Porsche and retrieved an Uzi submachine gun. He reached inside again and pulled out a set of black ammo clips that had been taped together with gray duct tape. He popped the double clip into the gun and stepped away from the car, careful to rest the butt of the gun against his forearm, barrel aimed high toward the sky.

When he was about five feet away from the 4Runner, he lowered the Uzi into position and started firing into it. He fired into the metal side panels, into the windows and windshield, blowing out most of the glass and plastic. He fired into the wheels so that the truck bucked and heaved when the rubber tires popped.

The *rat-a-tat* explosions of the multiple rounds bounced off the sides of the Albany skyscrapers just across the river. I just stood there staring. Feeling nothing. Other than the thunder of the gun and the small, rapid-fire shockwaves that passed through my chest. As though the 4Runner meant nothing to me. And maybe it didn't.

Sometimes, when the world appears to be slipping out from underneath your feet, you don't ask questions. You just go with the flow, place your trust in gravity.

When the clip was empty and all we heard was the *click-click-click* dry-firing of the firing pin, he pulled it out, turned it over, and slapped in the adjoining fresh clip. Then he repeated the process again, shooting the hell out of the 4Runner.

When that clip too was empty, he once again raised the barrel toward the sky. On his way back to the Porsche, he stopped for a moment, met me face to face, set his free hand on my shoulder.

"With the money you make on this job," he said, "you can buy another."

Don't ask questions.

After he placed the Uzi into the trunk of the Porsche, he made his way back to the shot-up 4Runner. He pulled up the tailgate (there was no use unlocking it, since the lock had been shot out) and began sliding out a black plastic body bag. He slid the body all the way out so that it plopped down on the ground, splattering the wet snow. When he unzipped the bag and exposed the cadaver's nearly bald head, I wondered why he had chosen to do the dirty work himself. Why he hadn't employed one of his henchmen or Guinea Pigs to do the job. But then it dawned on me that this must have been an intensely personal job. One that involved cadavers, Uzis, and plenty of bullets. If he wanted to handle the dirty work himself, there had to be a reason.

The odor of formaldehyde was intense, even in the open air.

It was a clean smell.

Tony proceeded to smash the dead man's teeth in with the butt end of the Uzi.

"We don't want them looking up dental records," he said, straining to get out the words while he worked on the old man's face.

A minute later he stood up, took a deep breath, exhaled a white cloud that dissipated into the sky. He asked me to help him lift the body into the driver's seat of the 4Runner.

No questions.

Last, he retrieved a can of gasoline from the trunk of the Porsche. He doused the body with the gas. The clear liquid just poured over the dead man's bald, tight skin. It drained out onto his naked lap. There was some ritual to the process. Respect, almost. I felt it even more when Tony folded the dead man's hands in his lap, one carefully over the other, the fingers looking somehow gentle and thin. As though you could just snap them off the hand like twigs off a dead branch. It never dawned on me until then that I had never touched the hands of a dead man before. One that had been dead that long, anyway.

Tony asked me for a match.

I handed him my Zippo.

The two of us stood side by side.

We watched the fire burn. Like those Indians used to do on the plains before we ruined their lives. Before America became one big Walmart.

There was the smell of burning rubber. Of plastic and leather and human flesh. The smell was acrid and toxic and sometimes sweet. It depended upon where you were standing at the time. And the way the wind blew off the river.

The flames that touched the sky were beautiful. You could almost reach out and touch them, if they wouldn't burn you all to hell.

When the fire was all burned out and all that remained was a sort of carbonized skeleton sitting inside the smoldering shell of the truck, Tony tossed me a brand-new pair of brown garden gloves. Like the kind they sell beside the register at the Mobil. He gave me a wave, and together we pushed what was left of the Toyota over the dike wall.

The front end hit the river hard, making a hollow-sounding splash. It bobbed for a second or two in the chop before finally disappearing below the surface.

Tony took his gloves off.

I did too.

We tossed them into the river. They floated away like dead leaves.

The wind coming off the river was razor-sharp cold. I hadn't really noticed it until then.

Tony stuck out his hand. I took it in mine. We shook, like old pals. It was all very strange.

He congratulated me.

"Why?" I said.

"You have to ask?" he said. He laughed then and walked away, whistling the tune to no song in particular.

PART TWO

LIFE GOES ON
AROUND AREA OF GRIM SEARCH

MONTERREY, Mexico (AP) - Lena Fuentes clutched her infant daughter in her arms and stared at the masked men in black with automatic weapons dangling at their sides. Not far beyond them, masked forensics experts dressed in yellow rain gear and black rubber boots waded through the decaying bodies trapped in an unearthed mass grave.

"This is so hard to believe," Lena said in broken English, verging on tears. "Imagine all this death occurring in such a peaceful place."

CHAPTER SIXTEEN

I UNDERSTOOD MORE WHEN I WAS ON THE PLANE, cruising at thirty thousand feet. Flying will do that to a person. Give him a whole new perspective on life (or in my case, death) impossible to achieve on the relative safety of solid ground. Or maybe it was because I was never much for flying. Or, more accurately, was never much for crashing.

The man sitting next to me wore cotton pants, a blue blazer, and a blue-and-white shirt unbuttoned at the collar. On his right wrist, a gold chain; on his left, a gold Rolex. He wore pink-tinted, horn-rimmed glasses. He hadn't been strapped into his seat for more than five minutes in Albany when he pulled out some papers from his briefcase and began working on them, using a gold-plated ballpoint. He said nothing to me. Didn't even look at me. I could tell it would be that way for the entire flight. Him just looking at his papers, crossing things off, not saying a word, as if I didn't exist. I wondered if he sensed my fear of flying. Maybe he could smell it. Like some people swear they can smell death the minute she walks into the room. Maybe I scared the hell out of him.

As soon as we were airborne, I reached under my seat, pulled out the morning edition of the Albany *Times-Union*. All around me, Mexicans and South Texans on their way home, along with a scattering of tourists. There was a man dressed in a bright, Hawaiian-print shirt. He was swigging whiskey from one of those miniature bottles they pass around. I looked at his face. If the face glowed or gave off some kind of angelic aura, I knew we'd be doomed. But the face was just that: a face. Nothing special. I felt safer suddenly.

Until I read the headline.

FORMER WARDEN FEARED VICTIM OF HOMICIDE.

The headline dwarfed the one not far below it. The one that read, LIFE GOES ON AROUND AREA OF GRIM SEARCH.

The two-column article began by stating that a burned-out, fire-engine-red 1996 Toyota 4Runner registered to Jack Harrison Marconi of Stormville (Dutchess County) had been discovered washed up on the bank of the Hudson River, just south of the Port of Albany.

While the body recovered from the driver's seat had been burned beyond recognition, DNA tests would be scheduled for later that afternoon to aid in the determination of the victim's identity. The 4Runner, which DMV records indicated had been in my possession for nearly three years, had been riddled with dozens of 9mm hollow-point rounds, the type of ammunition typically fired from a semiautomatic assault weapon.

"It is our suspicion," said Detective Mike Ryan of the APD, South Pearl Street Division, "that Mr. Marconi died as a result of the intense barrage of bullets. Until the body is properly identified, however, we cannot be certain of anything."

When asked the nature of the foul play involved, Ryan commented that Marconi, who had not shown up for his own wedding on the previous Saturday, had been seen drinking at Bill's Bar and Grill on Watervliet Avenue until late that afternoon, when suddenly, all traces of him seemed to just disappear.

"Why he hadn't shown up for his own wedding, we can only speculate," Ryan added.

When pressed by reporters, Marconi's fiancée, Valerie Antonelli of Albany, refused comment.

I put the paper down, for now. No photograph of me. No mention of the black Buick. No mention of the walk Ryan and I took through the cemetery on the snowy afternoon of my wedding day. And I had no idea why. Other than the fact that Tony may have requested a little favor of Ryan. To keep his mouth shut. To put a lid on this thing. Maybe to protect me from the black Buick. But if he wanted to protect me from the Buick, he must believe my story about seeing the battered car on Saturday inside the Albany Rural Cemetery. Or maybe he simply wasn't taking any chances. In the interest of saving Renata. In the interest of two hundred thousand dollars. Cash.

I pictured the wiry Ryan talking to reporters on the concrete steps of the South Pearl Street APD headquarters. I didn't know if his testimony had come from the evidence at hand or from a script prepared and delivered by Tony. But since the staging of a mock murder in the State of New York was considered a felony, the payoff would have to have been pretty huge.

My Colt, it had been locked away in a safe below decks.

FAA rules are FAA rules.

I felt naked without those two-and-a-half pounds of pressure against my rib cage.

The plane bucked. My heart lodged itself in my throat.

A gentle chime sounded. The PLEASE FASTEN YOUR SEAT BELT sign lit up.

I had never taken my seat belt off to begin with.

The man sitting next to me had put away his work. Now he had little black headphones stuffed inside his ears and plugged into the common armrest between us. Instead of viewing a movie or in-flight CNN, he was tuned into a channel that broadcast the same exact view the pilot had from the cockpit. If we suddenly nose-dived, we could get an excellent visual of the solid ground as it met our faces at a thousand miles per hour.

I picked the paper up, kept on reading.

I was at the part of the article that stated Marconi had last been seen exiting the law offices of a Mr. Tony Angelino, formerly of Council 84, now running a private practice on the corner of Pearl and State Streets. When asked the nature of the visit, Angelino stated that never, at this or any other time, would he compromise the client-attorney privilege, even if the worst were to happen and the body discovered in the 4Runner were to be identified as Marconi. However, Mr. Angelino did say the visit had been primarily social in nature and that he would be happy to cooperate with the APD to the fullest extent that the law and professional ethics allowed. He also made a point of extending his prayers to the loved ones of his good friend and client, Mr. Marconi, in the hopes that he turned up soon. Alive and otherwise unharmed.

Good old Tony.

What a great friend and a gifted liar he was.

I decided to be a good neighbor. I tapped the man beside me on the shoulder with the folded newspaper.

He pulled the headphones out of his ears, looked at me through those horn-rimmed glasses, saying nothing.

I held the paper up. "Interested?"

He shook his head, plugged the headphones back into his ears, went on watching the view from the cockpit.

Nothing but blue sky.

I tossed the paper onto the cabin floor just as a stewardess came by with a drink cart. The man beside me ordered a Vichy water.

I ordered a small split of champagne. The stewardess poured the drinks for us into small plastic cups. But what the hell was there to celebrate? If the public thought I was dead, then Val thought I was dead. We hadn't left each other on the best of terms. On the other hand, what man doesn't want to trade in his old life for a brand spanking new one?

I picked up my champagne, held it out as if to make a toast.

The man next to me got the message. He lifted up his cup.

"Cheers," he said, a little too loudly since he still had the headphones jammed into his ears.

I tapped the rim of his plastic cup with mine and drank.

"Long life," I said.

He raised his right hand, pointed to his right ear. "Can't hear you," he said.

CHAPTER SEVENTEEN

THIS TIME WHEN THE SOLDIER INJECTS HER IN THE ARM she doesn't get sleepy.

This time she doesn't feel her eyelids getting heavy and the warm concrete floor beneath her turning to mud.

She doesn't dream.

But she lives a nightmare.

The burn shoots through her muscles like a swarm of stinging bees caught inside her veins and desperate for a way out; she feels her brain buzz like it's swelling to twice its normal size. If her brain gets any bigger, it will start oozing out her ears and nostrils.

Her skin tingles, her synapses vibrate.

She doesn't want to move.

It's painful even to be alive.

It doesn't take her long to realize they've shot her up with some kind of drug that enhances normal pain to the point of excruciating.

It all makes sense too.

Because the mustached man is approaching her.

He's got something in his hand. A long needle. The longest needle she's ever seen. Like an ice pick, only thinner, with a wood-grip handle.

She's in too much pain to be frightened.

The mustached man is smiling. He's a happy man. Enjoys his work. The soldier who injected her is standing off in the distance, his back pressed up against the iron bars of the cell, hands folded at his crotch. The sweat runs off the soldier's brow, onto his red lips.

He wants the visual effect. She knows the scoop.

Like the Chinese soldiers who used to whip the shit out of bad prisoners with bamboo reeds. The soldiers who stood around in their green uniforms, smiley faced. She'd been there to write about it not long ago, until the country expelled her for doing what she does best. Writing the truth.

Her hands and feet have been duct-taped together at the ankles, at the wrists.

A piece of tape covers her mouth. She can't fight back. She can't run. She can't even scream.

Her nose is running.

"Are you OK, miss?" she hears Roberto ask from the cell beside hers. "Please do what they tell you, miss. Please tell them what they want."

What she wants to tell the man is this: What fucking choice do I have now?

She's going to tell the mustached man anything he wants to know. Even if she has to make it up.

As he unzips her jumpsuit, pulls off her black lace bra, brings the tip of the needle to her ripe nipple, inserts it, slowly, she knows she's ready to talk.

When the fiery red pain will insist upon it.

CHAPTER EIGHTEEN

I DESCENDED THE ALUMINUM STAIRCASE-ON-WHEELS onto the hot, sandy blacktop.

Monterrey International Airport.

More like an airstrip. A ratty collection of three or four buildings surrounded on all sides by desert.

To my right as I got off the plane, an old hangar covered in wavy, dull metal siding with a long, concave roof. Something Howard Hughes would have loved. Bolted to the tin facade just above the wide, sliding doors was a faded wood sign depicting the giant wheel and swirling wing of the old Pan Am logo.

Dead ahead, the airport terminal: a two-story, flat-roofed job with a series of wide picture windows and plenty of plastic that might have had a little color to it once upon a time but that now had faded to a sort of puke-gray in the hot sun. And yet another structure with a second floor made entirely of green-tinted glass. A revolving satellite dish was mounted to its flat roof and surrounded by an array of antennae.

Weather equipment, I guessed.

In a place where the weather was always the same.

Surrounding the buildings on all sides, an assortment of propeller and jet-driven planes. Some commercial liners, some freight jobs that looked as though they'd been hanging around since before World War II.

There were tractors and wagons and dozens of men in overalls and the occasional woman dressed in a blue pantsuit with a matching blue cap and white gloves on her hands, Pan Am patches sewed to the breast pocket of her blazer.

They were beautiful.

I hadn't slept on the flight. Not at all.

My skull felt wired together.

I hauled my carry-on bag over my shoulder and walked toward the terminal, where I was supposed to meet up with my contact and retrieve my gun, which had been packed for the trip below decks inside a lockable aluminum case.

Once inside the terminal I waited for the bag, my eyes fixed on both the conveyor belt and the people who never broke their pace as they deplaned, snatched up their luggage, and headed for customs. It went on like that for some time—me standing there in the heat with the mechanical humming of the conveyor belt drowning out the scattered voices of the travelers and my pistol case not making its anticipated entrance.

Then, after a while, the trail of luggage began to thin out in proportion to the passengers who had already grabbed their bags and bolted. I hated the feeling of waiting, wishing my bag would appear and it just not happening. At first I thought I might be imagining things. But soon I realized that the young Mexican man who suddenly appeared next to the conveyor belt seemed just a little bit too curious, just a little bit too quick to fix his eyes on me.

That is, unless he was my contact.

He was a medium-sized man. Thin, if not wiry. He wore baggy Levi's jeans, the old stiff kind you could get in the States when I was a kid, and a clean white T-shirt with a pack of cigarettes rolled up in the left sleeve. His thick black hair was slicked back in a sort of greasy ducktail, while a pair of cheap, oversized aviator sunglasses covered his eyes.

At first I hadn't paid any attention to him, what with people coming and going. But then the people stopped coming. So did their bags, just a few scattered and battered bags left behind or long-ago forgotten, circling on the conveyor belt.

A hard glare coming from Mr. Sunglasses. Maybe more than just idle curiosity.

Maybe he was the contact, I thought. But if he was the contact, he would have identified himself by now.

Instead of introducing himself, Sunglasses pulled a toothpick out of his jeans pocket, began chewing on it with his front teeth.

On cue I started back-stepping slowly, one careful step after the other, travel bag clutched tightly to my shoulder.

Then Sunglasses opened up his mouth. "I have a gun," he said, in perfect, plain English.

I stopped, made an about-face.

He held a Colt .45 in his right hand. My Colt .45. Aimed at me.

"The bag," he said.

He thumbed back the hammer on the .45.

I set the carry-on bag down on the terrazzo floor.

He started for me then, stepping away from the conveyor belt, not bothering to pick up the bag but stepping right over it.

I turned and ran for it.

When the shot hit the wall above the exit, I hit the floor.

Shards of plaster and cinder block rained down on me.

But it was then, with my chest pressed flat on the floor, that I saw a man coming in through the double doors. He was carrying a revolver. He fired from the hip, in the direction of Mr. Sunglasses. Within a split second, he placed three shots at Sunglasses's feet.

That did the trick. Sunglasses was so shaken up, he just dropped the .45 and took off through the small, square-shaped conveyor belt opening. Welcome to Mexico.

Some ten seconds later, a policeman arrived on the scene. He was dressed in a brown military uniform and jackboots, sidearm stored in a hip holster, his automatic weapon slung over his right shoulder and draped across his belly. He just came walking in, casual as hell, like nothing had happened. No guns pulled, no shots fired.

By now a small crowd had gathered at the doors that led out to customs.

I brushed the plaster dust off my shirt and pants while our rescuer spoke to the cop. My man smiled, slid the revolver back into the belt on his pants. He said, "Just a schoolboy playing with a toy gun. Nothing to worry about."

"That was my gun that kid was playing with," I said. "And it isn't a toy."

My rescuer, whoever he was, spoke once more to the cop in what sounded to me like some kind of border Spanish. But what the hell did I know? When he appeared to be finished, the policeman turned, looked directly at me with wide eyes. He shook his head, laughed some more, and left the same way he had come in. Through the double doors, leading out to customs.

All in that order.

"What did you tell him?" I asked the man as he retrieved my .45 from where Sunglasses had dropped it beside the conveyor belt.

"That the American is easily frightened…like a timid dog."

"Son of a bitch," I said.

"Listen," the man said, handing my pistol to me. "Before you get into it, I think there's something you should know."

"What should I know?" I said, slipping the piece into my shoulder holster.

"First of all, Mr. Marconi," he said, "I am your contact. Second of all, I just saved your ass."

CHAPTER NINETEEN

THE PAIN IS SO GREAT, HER BRAIN HAS NO CHOICE BUT to shut down.

Their plan backfired. She had passed out after all. Before she had the chance to talk.

Some people just can't be tortured.

Now, alone in her cell, she dreams.

She is back inside her Albany apartment. The one her husband rented while their house was being built. She is walking alone, along the center hallway, feeling her cold bare feet on top of the dirty wood floor.

There is a light on in the bathroom. The light spills out onto the hall floor.

The closer she comes to the light, the more she can make out the little voice of a baby.

There is the baby's laughter and the gentle sound of water being splashed. Bathtub water. The sounds are the sounds of pure love.

But when she comes to the open door and looks inside, the room is suddenly silent.

She sees the back of a man. The man is on his knees, dressed in black suit pants and a white shirt, the sleeves rolled all the way up to the elbows.

His arms are outstretched. He is holding something down in the water.

The baby.

Charlie.

Oh, my Christ!

When she wakes up again, her entire cell is filled with soldiers. They stand around in a semicircle, staring at her. In the center of the semicircle stands the mustached man. His arms are crossed at his chest.

"No more games," he says.

One of the soldiers turns, says, "What do we do now?"

"Get her ready to travel," says the mustached man.

CHAPTER TWENTY

UNDERNEATH SHAW HUDSON'S DAY-OLD BEARD, YOU could find a pleasant-enough face that looked as though it had been no stranger to the sun or the wind. His eyes were blue and his cheeks were hollow; his hair was cut close to the scalp and choppy, with patches of gray at the temples. He had as much as three or four inches on me but probably weighed in at about the same one hundred sixty-five. As for his voice, it was baritone and rough.

A pack-a-day smoker, maybe.

He wore brown lace-up work boots, tan chinos, a button-down work shirt, and a faded black, waist-length leather driving jacket. He carried a revolver. An old, black-plated .38 service revolver like the cops in New York used to pack before they replaced them all with 9mm automatics.

He held out his hand.

We shook.

"My apologies back there," Shaw said.

We were walking past the rows of taxis; cars; motorcycles; trucks; hawkers selling little toys made of wood and paper and string; women dressed in long, colorful print dresses standing behind carts filled with fruit and vegetables, kids with round, tan faces clutching at their apron strings.

It was hot as hell.

We were on our way to a general parking lot located directly in front of the airport terminal. Me with my travel bag slung over my shoulder and my one small suitcase clutched in my left hand.

"That whole thing back there inside the baggage claim," Shaw went on while he walked. "You're the second traveler he's accosted in as many months. What they do is bribe a baggage handler for a passenger list. They then pick what they assume will be a man or woman going it alone. As soon as the plane lands, they are quick to scour the luggage."

We passed a fruit stand set up on the edge of the parking lot. He stopped for a moment, picked out a small orange from the bin, sniffed the skin, and then placed it in the pocket of his leather without paying for it.

He moved on, explaining how Mr. Sunglasses must have waited me out at the baggage claim, knowing full well I was going to be the only person left after all the others had come and gone, because naturally my bags weren't about to show up.

"That's when they decide to mug you for your money and your jewels," Hudson said, his back to me. "Not a bad system when you think about it."

I asked him why the little son of a bitch hadn't been arrested.

"He has been arrested," he said, squinting his eyes in the hot sun. "Been arrested a whole bunch of times. Problem is, no one wants to keep a kid like that in jail because of petty theft. Jails are overcrowded as it is, and what space they have left goes almost exclusively to the mules."

"Mules," I said like a question, moving past a woman standing behind a cart filled with squash plants.

"Yes," Shaw said. "Mules, burriers, drugs runners, whatever."

Then Hudson stopped in his tracks.

He turned.

"There is, of course, another, more important reason that kid is not in jail," he said.

"I'm all ears," I said.

Shaw tucked the thumb on his right hand into the wide, leather holster while he propped the other on the hammer of his revolver. "No one presses charges."

"I'll be happy to press charges," I said. From out of the near distance, the thunder of a jet taking off.

"You're sure you want to do that, Mr. Marconi?" he said, a little louder, over the noise of the jet engines. "The Mexican police would be happy to detain you for a few days. After which they won't hesitate to send you back to the States once they determine your accusations to be wholly unfounded and symptomatic of an American bias toward little old uncivilized Mexico."

I thought about it. If I made a fuss, any kind of fuss at all, the police would step in and send me home. No job done, no rescue of Renata, no answers about the Bald Man.

"I suppose you're right," I said, and let it go at that.

The noise of the jet engines had all but disappeared, along with the plane itself.

Hudson raised his hands in the air as if nothing could be done about law and order—or the lack of it—south of the border.

"We'd better get moving," he said. "We have much to do."

The guide, guiding.

CHAPTER TWENTY-ONE

HUDSON DROVE A WHITE LAND ROVER DISCOVERY. Equipped with oversized tires, back and front brush guards, two extra five-gallon cans of gasoline mounted to the rear wells, a short-wave radio, quad stereo, halogen lamps, and a sawed-off twelve-gauge Savage pump set inside thick plastic clips mounted to the dash.

Easy access.

He was driving us over an unpaved road on our way toward Monterrey and the prison located about twenty miles past the town's perimeter. Open desert surrounded us on both sides of the dirt road. I rode shotgun. On occasion we'd pass a squatter's shack that had been cobbled together out of plywood scraps or corrugated tin or pea-green plastic siding. On occasion we'd bounce our way past a collection of four or five shacks that seemed always to surround a water spigot, as if this were the reason for the shacks and not the other way around.

I leaned into the space between the front bucket seats in order for him to hear me over the engine noise and the wind whipping against our faces. I asked him if he had been filled in on Renata's situation.

"Entirely briefed," he confirmed. "In fact, I am familiar with Richard Barnes. He often visits when he is down this way on business. And I've seen many photos of his wife."

"So you won't have any trouble recognizing her when you see her?"

Hudson shook his head.

"But do we have a plan?" I asked.

"I've got an idea or two, Mr. Marconi," he shouted as the Land Rover engine strained to make the climb out of the desert and up a steep grade covered on both sides with heavy brush and flowering cactus. "But in a case like a prison breakout, you rely less on planning than you do on simple firepower and who you know on the inside who will take a bribe."

The road dipped, then suddenly ended, the brush all but disappearing. We came upon a level plain, the edge of which finished off in a sheer cliff about a hundred yards away.

I thought about all the guards under my command for so many years who'd never had a problem with taking a bribe from the more wealthy inmates (usually drug pushers). And why not? So long as it kept the peace inside the iron house and weight in their pockets.

"I'm sure you had no trouble finding a guard who could be bribed," I said, not without cracking a smile.

"It's more of a challenge deciding which man best suits our collective needs." Shaw motored straight for the cliff's edge as if it didn't exist.

"But that doesn't mean a breakout will be easy, Mr. Marconi," Shaw said a minute later. "It simply means it will not be impossible. Remember, regardless of her intentions, Renata Barnes broke the law. And regardless of the guards who I assume will be working alongside us, there will be many, many more who will want to see her stay exactly where she, by law, belongs. In a cage."

❖

We lay on the gravel- and sand-covered floor of the flat-topped bluff, Shaw on my left. I was viewing the entirety of Monterrey Prison through a pair of Hudson's compact Minolta binoculars. I was pretty surprised at how the setup of the prison resembled some of our own prisons in the States. Namely Attica State Prison.

"An absolute fortress," I pointed out, the binoculars glued to my eyes.

"That's because it is," Shaw said. "In Mexico, prisons are designed to keep people out as much as they are designed to keep criminals in. Perhaps more so."

"And who would they want to keep out?" I said, running the lenses of the binoculars all along the pentagonal exterior wall, hesitating only long enough to examine the stone guard towers that occupied each of the pentagon's five points.

"People like you and me," Shaw said. "Rescuers and irregular armies in the paid employ of the drug traffickers and their families."

I moved my glasses from tower to tower.

Each had a spotlight and was occupied by three guards, all of them packing sidearms, semiautomatic weapons slung over their shoulders. Perched in the tower directly above the front gates, a belt-fed, tripod-mounted machine gun—.30-caliber, if I had to guess. A real spoiler if you got too close.

This was the prison's basic setup: The front, triangular portion of the pentagon-shaped exterior wall faced the open valley to the east, while the back, squared-off portion had been set inside the crotch of the L-shaped cliff face to the west. Inside the stone and razor-wire walls, there was what appeared to be an administration building comprised of four floors and made entirely of dark brown stone. There were a dozen or so freestanding buildings on the inside, four of them serving as the prison's cell blocks.

Long and rectangular, the cell blocks had been laid out at ninety-degree angles to one another to form a perfect square with an open space in the middle. The inside walls that faced the large square of open space were branded with large white letters identifying which unit was which. From where I lay at the top of the cliff, I could identify units A and B only, C and D being hidden by the angle.

The open interior space itself had been segregated into four smaller yards (again, just like at Attica) by a stone wall shaped like a cross, the very center of which supported a separate guard tower and a second .30-caliber machine gun. From where I lay on my stomach on the cliff top, I could see that the tower supported at least six guards. All the guards were armed to the teeth (more like soldiers than guards), with yet a seventh inside the Plexiglas-enclosed hut who manned a telephone and switchboard that I was sure controlled the gates into and out of the four yards.

Aside from the cell blocks and towers, there was a laundry building located near the back west wall. Beside it, a powerhouse. The four major cables that supplied the power were connected to a series of steel-frame, high-voltage towers running parallel to an unpaved access road that spanned the flat desert landscape for as far as my eyes (and binoculars) could see. Until the road just disappeared below the horizon.

And as for man power?

The entire compound was crawling with guards all done up military style in olive-green pants and combat boots. Unlike their American cousins, however, these guards carried both sidearms and automatic weapons slung over their shoulders while working *inside* prison walls.

Barnes had informed Hudson that Renata had been jailed in the basement of A Block, which, as luck or providence would have it, was one of the two blocks located closest to the prison's front gates.

Hopefully they hadn't moved her.

Even from the relative safety of the cliff top, I pictured Shaw and me busting through the gates in his Land Rover, shotguns blasting, pulling up to the front door of A Block only to be met with .30-caliber machine gun fire.

I set the binoculars down flat on the ground, rubbed my eyes with the backs of my hands. I asked Shaw how he planned on getting beyond the gates without getting all shot to hell.

"By utilizing three tried-and-true tactics, my friend," he said.

"And what are those?" I said, feeling the heat of the desert floor against my belly.

"Number one," he said, raising the index finger of his right hand, "we rely on the trickery of diversion."

I nodded.

"Second," he said, raising the middle finger, "we use the power of heavy armor and equally heavy artillery."

He put his arm back down in the dirt and began making his way back to the Rover on all fours.

I propped myself up on my elbows. "Hey," I said, looking back at him over my left shoulder. "You said *three* tried-and-true tactics."

Shaw stopped.

He got up on his knees and smiled. "How could I be so forgetful," he said. He raised his right hand once more, raised three fingers side by side. "Number three," he said. "If number one and two do not work, we will pray to the good Lord very, very hard."

"That's the plan." A question.

He bobbed his head. "For the most part," he explained. "But don't worry so much. Tonight we'll enjoy a little fiesta, and tomorrow morning we'll settle the plans." He got up off the ground and headed, on foot now, toward the Land Rover.

Fiesta, I thought, as I turned my attention back to the prison. Barnes is paying us to break into Fort Apache, and the expert guide wants to have a party. I was reminded of the old saying about eating and drinking until you drop because tomorrow you're as good as dead. Maybe that was the point. Or maybe that's how Shaw led his life in the first place. As for me, I had something to live for, and it wasn't Renata Barnes and it sure as shit wasn't her husband's two hundred Gs or Tony Angelino's orders, for that matter. What I had to live for came in the guise of a bald man who drove a black Buick. I had to keep myself alive long enough to find him. Once I killed him, I'd leave the rest to fate.

I picked up the binoculars, set them against my eyes once more.

There was something going on now in the vicinity of the prison's front gates. The gates were opening up. Some guards were running out of the gates, machine guns balanced at their hips. The guards scanned the immediate area with their gun barrels.

I had no idea what the hell was going on, what they were so jumpy about.

A few seconds later, I found out.

A truck was pulling out of the gates. A one-ton truck, with a front cab and a fully enclosed cargo area. Like a Ryder rental, only instead of yellow, the vehicle had been painted olive-drab green.

The truck stopped. While one of the soldiers got inside the cab, another opened up the back and hefted himself up inside. I tried to get a look inside the truck with my binoculars. But it was impossible to make out anything other than total darkness.

When the soldier was inside, he closed the door.

Then the truck took off, heading due east along the access road parallel with the power lines.

For a moment I thought about asking Shaw to follow the truck for a while. I don't know why I wanted him to do it. Instinct, maybe. My intuition banging against the interior of my skull. But then I thought better of it. Besides, Shaw had already fired up the Land Rover.

If I had to describe it, I would say there were two different sort of looks on his tight face. The first was a pinched expression that said, Get your ass back in the truck.

The second was a wide-eyed smiley face that roared, Let's party!

CHAPTER TWENTY-TWO

SHE HASN'T EATEN IN THREE DAYS. NOT THAT THEY haven't tried to feed her. A tin plate filled with a kind of meatless stew has been set beside her on the concrete floor. Water and bread sits there too. She doesn't eat not because she won't eat, but because she can't eat. She doesn't have the energy or the strength. In the windowless basement cage, she has no idea if it's night or day. She has no way of telling time, no way of knowing how long she's been down in that dungeon. She wants so badly to shout something out, to connect with someone else.

The old man in the cell beside her own has stopped talking to her.

Somehow she finds the strength to crawl up to the front of the cell. She whispers, "Roberto," three distinct times, but all she hears is nothing.

She has no idea what the old man looks like or if he really is an old man. But she suddenly feels a terrible hollowness in the pit of her stomach, like he is dead.

Dead at her expense.

In a moment, she hears the loud banging of the basement gates opening up. She hears the heels of the jackboots slapping against the concrete floor. They appear suddenly at the floor of her cell. The mustached man and his ever-loyal guard.

When the mustached man gives the signal, the cell gate slides open.

He enters the cell, grabs her by the hair, takes a fistful of it. Yanks it.

He leans down, into her ear. "We're going for a little ride," he says.

She's too tired to protest. The soup of drugs running through her veins has poisoned her blood. She's so messed up, in fact, she can hardly feel it when the mustached man lifts her up by her hair.

Next thing she knows, the soldiers are dragging her up a flight of metal stairs. It must be a back stairwell. They drag her by the arms, so fast the tips of her toes bang along the edges of the metal treads and risers.

At the top of the stairs, they pull her into a garage of some kind. A huge, echoey, open place with three or four trucks parked inside and all sorts of mechanic's tools hanging on the walls and sitting on the floor. They cuff her hands behind her back. They lift her up and set her down inside the bay of the first truck. One of the soldiers follows her inside. He has one of those hoods in his hand. A black hood. He sets it over her head and pulls the drawstring on the bottom to secure it.

She hears the sound of an engine starting, feels the movement and bucking of the truck, tastes the hot wool against her lips and tongue.

"Where are you taking me?" she inquires. She is slurring her words, like a drunk. "Tell me…please."

But the soldier sitting across from her says nothing.

Maybe he can't understand English.

"No habla Ingles?" she asks him, in that same slurred voice.

"I can speak English perfectly well," he says.

She realizes he's not about to tell her anything.

The truck stops suddenly and then she hears the doors opening and a second soldier hopping up inside.

"Were going to the pit," he volunteers in a Latin-accented voice.

It's the answer she's been looking for, whether the soldier knows it or not.

She might ask more questions, but she knows in her heart that it is answer enough.

CHAPTER TWENTY-THREE

LIKE MONTERREY PRISON, SHAW HUDSON'S RANCH WAS nothing less than a fortress. From the Land Rover, I could make out the tin roofs of the structures set on what I guessed to be about six or seven acres of desert. A high stone wall topped with bands of razor wire surrounded the property. Video surveillance cameras were mounted on the wall every ten feet or so. Two additional cameras were mounted on the entrance gates, one over each corner of the metal frame that supported two solid, steel-plated doors on sliders.

The armed guards were taking no chances.

When Shaw pulled up to the gates, a Mexican man signaled for us to stop. He was a wiry man in dirty jeans, with a Fu Manchu mustache. He wore boots and a faded leather vest with no shirt underneath, so that the sunburned skin appeared way too tight for his muscles and veins. On his head, he wore a narrow-brimmed cowboy hat with a peacock feather sticking out of the leather band. Slung over his shoulder, a black M-16, the trigger of which he caressed with the index finger on his left hand. He glared at me with wide, intense eyes as he spoke something in Spanish to his *jefe*.

Slowly the gates opened.

I turned to Shaw as he threw the Land Rover into gear. "Cautious," I said.

He turned to me. "You ever hear of the Trojan horse, my friend?" he said.

I nodded. "*The Iliad*," I said. "Or was it *The Odyssey*?"

"I thought it was the Bible," he said.

Then he drove on in.

The buildings inside the compound had been constructed with plenty of stucco and plaster. Toward the far wall, there were a dozen tall aluminum towers topped with windmills that spun slowly but steadily in the breeze. Heavy wires were attached to the windmills and ran to each of the buildings. There was an old-fashioned water pump set in the middle of a very sparse lawn. A wooden trough beneath the pump caught the water that dripped from the spout. I looked around for some horses while Shaw took it slow along the long gravel drive. There were no horses. But five Harley-Davidsons equipped with leather saddlebags were parked side by side, at an angle, in front of the main house.

The main house had been positioned in the center of the wide-open property at the very end of a driveway turnaround. It also was constructed of adobe plaster that had faded to tan. A wide porch wrapped all around the front and sides of the two-story farmhouse. The massive wooden front door was flanked by two sets of French doors spaced equidistantly along the front exterior wall. These doors opened onto the front porch, probably more for ventilation than easy access.

The compound was a busy place.

There were women in long, colorful dresses walking in and out of the house and guards stepping out of their way, all of them wearing jeans and cowboy boots and hats. Rifles hung at their sides; sidearms were mounted to their belts or set inside shoulder holsters. Many of them smoked cigarettes, and they stared at me as I drove in with Shaw, smiling and sometimes laughing at me.

Like I was the brunt of some bad joke.

Set to the immediate left of the house was a three-bay garage with a wooden double door secured with chains and padlocks. Parked beside the garage were a brand-new John Deere backhoe, a good-sized core drilling machine, and a trench digger. Equipment as familiar to me as the old photos of my father I still had lying around my apartment in Stormville. Such are the memories of a construction family.

To the right-hand side of the garage, partially hidden by the main house, was a built-in swimming pool and a pool house with a thatched roof and walls made from dried palm leaves. A long, open bar was connected to the pool house, with the thatched roof extending over it. Hanging from the rafters of the bar were lots of colorful Chinese lanterns.

From where I sat inside the Land Rover, I spotted a small crowd of young women sunning themselves poolside, dressed only in thong bathing bottoms, no tops. They carried tall drinks in their hands. As Shaw stopped the Land Rover and we got out, one of the women took notice of us and came to the end of the wooden pool fence. She was a tall, long-haired beauty, and she wore narrow black-framed sunglasses that covered her eyes. I tried like hell to look only at her face. But under the circumstances, the eyes tended to wander south.

"Don't be shy," Shaw said as he pulled the shotgun off the dashboard clips.

"*Hola,*" I said, feeling a wave of embarrassment spill over me like the pool water that dripped from her long black hair. *Hola!* How silly did that sound?

She smiled and laughed a little and said something to Shaw. "She wants to know if you'd like to take a swim a little later."

"I would," I said.

He told her.

The woman touched her lips with the tip of her index finger. Sexy. And then she turned back to the group. That's the beauty of a thong. When a woman turns her back to you.

I thought about telling Shaw how much I was going to like it here.

But he was already heading for the house, the stock end of the shotgun resting against his right forearm.

This was no time to let down my guard.

Back at the Land Rover, a stocky old man dressed in a Hawaiian shirt, shorts, and sandals began unloading our bags and carrying them into the house.

"Why all the security?" I asked Shaw. "I thought you collected antiques."

As I said it, I noticed a group of people attending to an open pit dug out of the front lawn, laying out wood and coals for a fire, while a separate group of women began preparing three enormous tables with tablecloths, plates, glasses, and silverware. Not far from where the women were working I noticed a tall pole embedded into the ground—it was like a flagpole, only shorter. Instead of a flag flying from its mast, a dozen or more colorful straps hung down from a heavy bolt screwed into the very top of the beam.

Shaw put his arm around my shoulders while we walked up the wooden porch stairs.

"In Mexico a man must take care of his property, no matter what his occupation," he said. "I am simply taking care of mine."

Inside the dimly lit vestibule, he peeled off his leather jacket and hung it up on the rack behind the door. He picked up the mail that had been stacked for him nice and neat on the wooden table next to the coat rack. He quickly flipped through the letters, checking the return address on each until he'd examined each one, then set the entire stack down on the table.

As the old man in the Hawaiian shirt squeezed past and headed up the long center-hall stairs, a small, middle-aged woman emerged from the room at the very end of the center hall.

Shaw bent at the waist for her while she reached up on her tiptoes, embraced each side of his face.

"This is my aunt Angela," he said. "She will see you to your room."

I nodded to her.

Shaw unbuckled the belt on his leather holster and set it down on the table beside the stack of unopened mail.

I asked him again about the plan.

He put his hand on my shoulder. "Patience, Mr. Marconi," he said. "In a short while we'll discuss everything. In the meantime, why not see your room, perhaps have a drink, take a nap and a shower. Then we'll sit down and talk after dinner." He patted my back.

Angela was waiting for me on the stairs.

I was dead tired.

I started up the stairs.

"And Mr. Marconi," Shaw said from the bottom of the staircase, "if there's anything you need—anything at all—just give Angela the word."

I turned. "Antiques collector, huh?" I said to Angela.

She turned to me while taking the stairs. "*No comprendo.*"

"That's what they all say," I said.

❖

Fully clothed, I lay back on the heavy mattress. The late-afternoon breeze blew in through the open, double-hung windows. Warm wind. The walls of the bedroom were painted dark green. Hanging on the wall to my left, a gilt-framed mirror reflected the red setting sun.

I lay as still as possible, listening to the soft foreign voices that mixed with the wind. Gentle voices. You just couldn't get any further away from Stormville or Albany than this place. I tried closing my eyes, to allow the sleep to settle in, to avoid the little thoughts that had begun to tap against my brain like the little rodents that live inside the walls. But sleep never settled in quite the way I wanted it to. Or when I wanted it to, for that matter.

I stared up at the ceiling and the Casablanca fan that revolved slowly, steadily—you guessed it—hypnotically. Five spinning blades slicing through the hot air.

After a time, I saw Tony's face. I couldn't shake the feeling that he was hiding something from me. Some crucial bit of information that might give some sense of order and meaning to this entire mission. To this entire week! I couldn't help but think that maybe this so-called rescue might actually be a diversion for something else. But for what and for whom? I knew what the hell I had been hired for, knew why Tony had chosen me for the job.

So why the persistent questions?

No concrete reason other than a feeling—an intuition that went against the grain of all I'd ever known about Tony. All I'd ever come to believe of him as an honest friend. This is what bothered me (aside from the fact that he had felt it necessary to make me dead): he had kept the news of the Buick from me.

Maybe, in the end, he was trying to protect me.

As my lawyer and friend, maybe he was attempting to keep me out of harm's way. To protect me not only from some person or persons who wanted to see me hurt, but also from myself. Because he knew what I was capable of if I actually found the Bald Man. But all this did not change the fact that he had deceived me. That in itself was a letdown.

On the other hand, maybe I was looking too deeply into too shallow a pool of water. Maybe the job had no other meaning than getting Renata out of that prison, alive. Get her safely across the border and back up to New York, collect my money. Then, and only then, would I attempt to find out exactly what Renata knew about the Bald Man. If there was a real connection between her family and the son of a bitch who killed my wife.

❖

In the dream I feel the cold air. March in upstate New York. Not bright and pleasant with a blanket of freshly fallen snow covering the foothills. But cold and gray and damp with patches of filthy snow and mud. I walk the paved road that leads through the gates of the Albany Rural Cemetery. Move without effort past the nameless gray markers and the leafless trees tipped with melting icicles. As I walk, I feel the damp cold seep into my skin, into my bones. I feel the wet cold scrape the back of my throat.

Up ahead, the figure of a woman.

She is standing at the foot of a gray marker, dressed entirely in black.

Black shawl, black veil, black gown.

The fear burns in my stomach like a flame. I try to pull back, but it's impossible.

The closer I come to the woman, the more clearly I can make out her face. Fran's face. I don't have to see it to know it. It is a face I feel more than I see.

A car pulls up beside me. A battered black Buick. The car takes off again, blows past me. The car runs Fran down, drags her body across the road until it settles on a dirty snowbank.

I try to scream.

No words will come.

The face of the Bald Man. I see it staring out at me from the open driver's-side window in the Buick. He smiles at me, winks, just as he throws the car into drive, speeds out of the cemetery.

Now I am kneeling over the body. The body lies face first in the melting snow, the long hair matted with blood until the red coloring is almost black and I am floating up above my own body, watching myself watch my wife.

I reach out for her, roll her over.

Her head is gone.

❧

Sitting up, getting out of bed, catching my breath.

Sweat dripping from my forehead, into my eyes, down the ridge line of my nose.

The taste of salt on my lips. My salt.

I looked at my watch face. Two solid hours of uninterrupted sleep. Not bad. Even for me.

Out the open window, the afternoon sun had settled deep into the desert horizon. The ranch was lit up with the firelight of dozens of stake-mounted torches dug into the perimeter of the front yard.

I saw the women and the men attending to the picnic tables with plates of food covered in tin foil and large plastic tubs full of ice and bottled beer. I smelled the fresh meat that roasted on a skewer in the open pit. I knew I couldn't stay in the room all night. There was a job to do, plans had to be made.

Shaw.

I needed a little face-time with Shaw.

A drink would be nice too.

CHAPTER TWENTY-FOUR

SHE IS DOWN ON HER KNEES, HANDS CUFFED BEHIND her back, face hanging over the edge of the pit. Over the dead bodies, the stench of the rotting flesh infiltrating her nasal passages like the gas in a gas chamber.

The night is dark and windy.

The cool air is already settling in.

A half-dozen soldiers, dressed in green fatigues and plain green baseball hats, stand all around her. Two more stand guard on the perimeter.

Behind her stands the mustached man. He is holding a pistol on her, pressing the barrel to a soft spot she never knew existed just behind her left earlobe.

"Who sent you here?" he demands. It's the third or fourth time he's asked. She's not sure. She's lost count. Just like she's lost count of the bodies stacked three and four high in the pit.

"Jesus Christ sent me here," she says.

He grabs a fist of hair, jerks her head back violently.

"Once more. Why are you spying?"

Her eyes are tearing. The pain of her hair ripping away from her scalp.

"I...told...you. I'm...a...writer."

He lets go of her hair. With his free hand, he caresses her cheek suddenly, wipes away a tear.

He pulls the pistol away. "Perhaps," he says, "I am being too harsh. Perhaps I am not handling this the correct way, señorita. Perhaps I'm not asking the right questions."

She feels his rough hand on her skin. It is like an insect. A wasp she has no way of shaking off.

"Did Richard send you here? Does Richard Barnes no longer trust his partners?"

His fingertips, now brushing up against her full, moist lips. The wasp about to sting.

That is, unless she can sting first.

She opens her mouth wide, catches his finger in her mouth, bites down on it with all the strength she has left.

He screams in agony, drops his pistol into the pit.

The soldiers cock their weapons, aim them at her.

"No, no, no!" screams the mustached man. "We need her alive!"

There's blood all over her lips, on her tongue. She can taste it.

He falls back. "Oh, my God. Oh, my sweet Jesus."

He holds up his right hand. The tip of his middle finger is gone. From the third joint up.

"Look what you did," he cries. "Look what you did. Look what you fucking did."

Real tears pour down his cheeks, soaking his mustache.

The soldiers stand around, looking at one another, like, What the hell do we do now?

"You bitch," the mustached man says. "You horrible bitch. You'll pay for this."

That's when Renata smiles, opens her mouth, just slightly, spits the tip of his middle finger onto the sand. "I'm rich, asshole," she says. "I can afford it."

CHAPTER TWENTY-FIVE

TORCHES LIT UP THE OPEN-AIR PARTY, ALONG WITH countless red and green lanterns that hung from the porch rafters. A roasting pig revolved on a metal skewer over a pit filled with fire. The brown-baked skin on the pig glistened with the drippings that the old Mexican cook had used for basting between stirs of the black bean chili. The chili bubbled in a heavy black kettle that had been placed on a charcoal-filled fifty-gallon drum cut down the middle and supported horizontally with sawhorses.

By seven I was standing on the porch of the main house, a cold bottle of Corona in my hand. I soaked in the warm but breezy night in my Levi's jeans, Tony Lama boots, and denim work shirt, sleeves rolled up to the elbows. There was the sound of Latin music and all the nameless people who passed by me in pairs or one by one. Older, heavyset women in loose, flowery dresses and long hair, some with fresh carnations pinned just above their right ears, their lively dark eyes lit up all the more by the firelight and the colorful lanterns. And men—most of them from Hudson's little private army—who had set their automatic rifles aside but who would not give up their sidearms.

But soon came an odd collection of men whose faces I did not recognize from my initial visit to the compound just a few short hours before. Big men, dressed in suits and wing-tipped shoes, a couple of them wearing sunglasses in the night, as if to block out the moonlight, or their identity, which was probably more the case. One of them sported a thick, Pancho Villa mustache. A thin, angry-looking man dressed in a charcoal suit. The thing that made him stand out above all the others was the thick white bandage wrapped around his right hand, the very tip of which showed traces of blood. He was drinking tequila from a quart bottle. Not to get drunk, I imagined. More likely to kill the pain in his hand.

The men stuck together in a sort of tight semicircle that shifted from one end of the front yard to the other and back again. They passed that bottle around and they laughed at one another's jokes and nearly fell on the sandy ground when one of them pinched the backside of an old woman as she went about placing big bowls of food on the picnic tables.

They were having one hell of a time.

All except the mustached man with the bandage. He seemed to be in a hell of a lot of pain, not all of it coming from his injured hand.

Shaw was nowhere to be seen.

I knew he would show soon enough.

In the meantime, I leaned back against the porch rail and considered tracking down someone with a pack of smokes. But cigarettes were suddenly the last thing on my mind when the woman walked out onto the front porch.

She was the same woman I'd met earlier by the pool. Now she was dressed in a black, thigh-length cocktail dress and black stockings, and she was coming my way.

When she was close to me, she ran the tips of her fingers gently down the left side of my face. I stood very still and stared at the strand of white pearls that wrapped around her neck and the way they shimmered against her black dress in the soft overhead porch light. I watched the way her hair hung down over her ears, how it seemed as alive and on fire as her brown eyes did.

I knew that if I gripped the bottle of Corona any tighter it might explode in my hand. I breathed and set what was left of the beer down on the rail, reached my hand out for hers. She laughed a little. She never had to say a word. She simply took my hand in hers and closed in on me. I brought my face to that special place just between her neck and shoulder and I breathed in her smell. Gently I brushed back her long black hair with my fingertips, brought my mouth to her ear, and kissed it so softly I barely touched it with my lips.

For a time we stayed close like that, our arms wrapped around each other's waists. I smelled her sweet smell and felt her body heat and the slow, steady pace of her heart. Before I knew it, we were dancing to a slow Latin rhythm, doing these smooth turns on the porch floor, her light body in my arms.

When the music stopped, everything else seemed to stop along with it.

I kissed her.

❖

A few seconds later, Shaw made his entrance onto the porch. He was wearing a pressed white button-down along with matching white pants and a thick black holster to support an ivory-handled six-shooter. On his feet, black snakeskin Tony Lama boots.

Judging from the smile on his narrow face, it must have pleased the hell out of him to see his guests enjoying themselves.

My new girlfriend had taken her place among the crowd. I took hold of my beer from the rail and approached Shaw.

"Considering what's going down tomorrow," I said, "you throw one hell of a pig roast."

He wrapped his left arm around my shoulder while surveying the crowd from the vantage point of the porch. "My business is my pleasure," he said. Then he slid his arm off my shoulder and jogged down the porch steps. He was making a beeline toward the group of well-dressed Mexican men who were now calling out his name, like he was their big buddy. All except the man with the bandage wrapped around his right hand. He was drinking from the tequila bottle again. And the closer Shaw came to him, the more pain he appeared to be in.

For hours we feasted on chili and freshly sliced pork from the skewer and washed it all down with Coronas. And for a time I forgot all about the reasons for crossing the border in the first place. I sat at the end of a very long picnic table, beside my nameless girlfriend, a full bottle of beer set beside a few empties.

Between the girl and the stars that lit up the night sky, I almost felt content, as though I'd never seen a battered black Buick the Saturday before, as though I'd never missed my own wedding, as though I'd never had to be peeled off the beer-soaked floor of an Albany gin mill. None of it mattered. Not my relationship with Val or her son, Ben. Not the short, happy life Fran and I had had together, not the long, happy life we got gypped out of. Not the Bald Man I never found nor the probability that I would never find him. Not Renata Barnes or her imprisonment, not her husband, Richard, or their dead kid. Not Tony and his reasons for giving me this job in the first place. Not my sleeplessness nor my memories nor the children I never had nor the children I never would have. Not my life.

It just didn't matter anymore.

I'm not sure exactly when or how it happened or if there was a point to it at all, but after a time a group of seven men appeared. Boys *and* men, who sort of emerged from out of the desert. Little men—not a single man over five-foot-two or a hundred and ten pounds—dressed in white pants with little bright red bandannas wrapped around their necks.

Barefoot men with dark, rugged faces.

Like the faces of ancient Indians.

At first I thought I must be hallucinating. Then the smallest of the seven began to climb the flagless pole embedded in the middle of the yard with all the ease and grace of a monkey on its favorite tree. He just scaled the vertical pole without an ounce of effort, using both his hands and bare feet to grip the smooth, narrow surface.

I thought that maybe somebody had slipped something into one of my drinks when each man followed the little boy up the pole, just like that. Even when I turned to my nameless girl, she had this wide-eyed look of wonder on her face, as if she was absolutely getting a kick out of the whole thing but at the same time was thoroughly perplexed.

But if drugs were available at the hacienda that night, I hadn't seen them. Besides, the display was no hallucination. If it had been, then the entire party had to be caught up in the subliminal trance. Because by now the entire crowd had gathered around the pole, even the well-dressed men. (Except for the man with the bandage on his hand. He was up on the porch with Shaw. He seemed to be in a fit over something, waving his bandaged hand in the air as if using it to make a point. And all the time Shaw just nodding his head, as though in complete agreement.)

The crowd clapped their hands to the natural rhythm the little boy made when he slipped his bare feet into the topmost strap, reached out with one hand into the night, began twirling himself around and around. Until the momentum he gathered was enough to let himself go completely from the pole, relying only on the strength of the leather strap to support his weight.

As the little boy spun in a clockwise direction, the other six men began to spin around the pole also, each one in the opposite direction of the men above and below him. Their movements seemed effortless and graceful. Like gravity never entered the picture.

It wasn't until a few minutes had gone by that I realized I was clapping like a crazy man, pounding boot heels on the bare ground. I felt my heart beat and my lungs fill with the sweet desert air, and there was the sweat that had built up on my brow. From across the table I spotted the girl and she spotted me.

She got up first and came around to my side of the table. And while the men in white spun away on the pole and the crowd continued to cheer them, she took my hand in hers and pulled me away from the picnic table. She led me across the front yard past the garage and the digging equipment, to the in-ground pool behind the main house.

Without saying anything we took our clothes off and jumped into the cool water of the deep end. We kissed underwater with the lamplight sparkling and gleaming all around, and it wasn't until we came up to the surface that I realized we weren't alone.

Another woman had already been swimming before we jumped in. She was a beautifully built Mexican woman of about my own height with long black hair that went all the way down to the center of her back. She had brown eyes that glistened in the lamplight and full red lips from which pool water dripped. At first I thought my girl might be embarrassed or that the Mexican woman might feel invaded by our sudden intrusion. But after only a few seconds of slightly self-conscious giggling, the two women and I discovered some strange sort of chemistry together.

As the party grew louder and the water that surrounded our bodies grew warmer (it was March, after all, even in the desert), I picked my girl up by her waist and set her down gently on the smooth wooden deck that wrapped around the pool. I kissed her lips, neck, breasts, and stomach. Then I went down on her thighs and moved in slowly, until I began to kiss something else entirely. I knew she couldn't help herself when she wrapped both hands around the back of my head, pulled me farther into her as if it were possible for me to go all the way through her body.

I stayed like that for as long as she could stand it.

When finally I lifted my head, opened my eyes, and looked up at her, I could see that she was kissing the Mexican woman. The two saw me looking at them and they both giggled like schoolgirls. That's when my girl moved me away from her angel space.

To make room for somebody new.

I watched them make love to each other and to themselves and to me for more than an hour. The three of us rock 'n' rolled for a while more, until the Mexican woman and my girl joined hands and helped each other out of the pool. They slipped towels around their waists and torsos, took turns reaching down to me, laying one final kiss on me apiece. Then, hand in hand, they slipped into the house together by way of the back door off the kitchen for what I assumed would be a cozy desert nap.

I laughed, more out of a strange pride for the girls than myself, and hopped out of the pool. I dried myself with one of the towels from behind the open bar and put my clothes back on. Then I rejoined what was left of the fiesta.

CHAPTER TWENTY-SIX

IN DREAMS SHE CAN SEE THE PHOTOS. THE ONES SET UP on the mantel above the fireplace. Inside the old apartment.

There is the one taken the day she first brought Charlie home from the hospital. It is the photo that always catches her attention first. Before all the others.

Even in dreams.

This is a happy photo.

Looking at it now, she can see how nervous she was with Charlie in her arms. She can still feel the nerves affecting her stomach— muscles constricting, tightening. Charlie was brand new. Charlie's head was round and fuzzy on top, his skin dark but flushed (yellowed with jaundice). His eyes were closed, his face scrunched up (like a skinned rabbit, her husband said). His hands were already opening and closing into fists.

That's how strong Charlie was.

She's smiling in the photo.

But she's also holding on tight.

This was not a pose.

She was acting natural.

Charlie was so smooth, so tiny, she thought there was nothing to prevent him from falling right through her arms.

The expression on her face told the whole story.

Looking at her face in the dream, she can see how happy she was back then. But scared too. That kind of photo.

For Charlie, the fireplace mantel was like This Is Your Life!

The photographs were everywhere back in those days.

There was Charlie swinging, Charlie crawling, Charlie rolling helplessly onto his side, Charlie playing in an early snowfall with his father. There was Charlie eating spaghetti, Charlie covered in spaghetti, Charlie soaking in the bathtub.

Eventually, there was no more Charlie.

CHAPTER TWENTY-SEVEN

THE MEXICAN MAN WHO GUARDED THE ENTRANCE TO Shaw's first-floor office was passed out on the floor, his back pressed up against the wall beside the door, his head lolling on his neck, an empty bottle of tequila set between his knees.

All it took to get past him was gently removing the key from the clip on his belt, slowly and quietly unlocking the door, replacing the key on the clip. Then slipping inside, locking the door behind me.

A foolproof plan.

So long as Shaw didn't decide to pay a visit.

A clarification of sorts: I might have simply asked Shaw if I could use his office. He might have said, By all means. But then, he might have placed one of his guards in charge of accompanying me. To make sure I had no intention of rummaging through his personal affairs, of attempting to uncover any information that might lead me to believe his relationship with Richard Barnes was anything other than it appeared to be: a hired gun and his very hands-off employer.

How would I be expected to snoop, if I couldn't do it on my own terms?

Square-shaped and paneled in mahogany, the office had a working fireplace with a railroad tie mantel mounted on the floor-to-ceiling stone hearth. The exterior wall behind the large wooden desk was composed mostly of French doors that opened onto the porch. For now, the doors were partially covered with heavy navy-blue drapes with gold rope drawstrings.

The interior bearing wall opposite the desk was filled with television monitors, one for each of the six cameras mounted to the stone and razor-wire fence that surrounded the ranch. There was a set of fireproof file cabinets placed up against the wall between the television monitors and another wooden table that housed a Xerox color copier and a Brother fax machine.

I went behind the desk, pulled back the curtain to get a look outside.

Shaw was a safe-enough distance away, sitting on top of a picnic table, sharing cigars with the well-dressed men. The mustached man with the bandaged hand was still there too, although he did not smoke a cigar. He just stood off to the side, staring at the little group, observing them, rubbing the tip of his bandaged hand with the fingers on his good hand.

I set myself on the corner of the desk and used his cordless phone to dial Tony's New York number. After a series of electronic beeps and rings, he picked up.

"You awake?" I said, as if the question needed answering.

"Keeper," he said, his voice dry, cracking. "What's wrong?"

"Everything's OK," I said while glancing at the television monitors. Nothing to view in any of the six, other than a black, empty desert and the occasional winged insect lit up by the white perimeter spotlight.

He asked me what I needed.

"A reduced blueprint of Attica State Prison," I said. "A schematic of a typical cell block basement. Get a hold of it, condense it, and fax it to me here at Shaw Hudson's place outside Monterrey."

I gave him the fax number and the number for Hudson's private telephone line.

"Shaw Hudson," he said while jotting down the information. "Barnes's man?"

"My contact," I said.

"He mind you using his private line?"

"He doesn't know."

"Risky."

"I thought I'd take a little look around."

"Thought I told you to keep your nose where it belonged."

I didn't answer him.

The head of a coyote suddenly appeared in the lower right-hand monitor. The animal looked up at the camera, let off with a silent fang-filled bark or two, then turned and ran off, disappearing into the blackness.

"Can you get the layout?" I asked.

"Won't be easy," Tony said. "Even for the Guinea Pigs. You know department rules. Once a prison's construction is complete, all blueprints are destroyed, other than the original as-built. And even that's stored inside a Department of Corrections safe."

"How long?" I asked.

"Could take a while," he said.

"You're slipping, Tone," I said.

"I'll call you back in a couple of minutes," he said.

"I'll be here," I said. Then I hung up.

Another peek outside, through the glass doors behind Shaw's desk.

The men laughing, shouting. One short man with a paunch pressing up against his white shirt, goose-stepping around and around in a circle like some mad Nazi leftover from World War II, his cohorts laughing like crazy, about to fall over. Shaw laughed too, but not like them. His laughter seemed faked. As for the mustached man, he drank from his bottle and sneered at the goose-stepping man.

The phone rang, caller ID displaying Tony's number.

I hit the TALK button before it had the chance to sound off a second time.

"Give me a half hour to get you the layout," Tony said.

"OK," I said.

No choice.

"This guy Hudson," Tony said. "Can you trust him?"

"No way to tell yet," I said, my eyes once again glued to the real-life Hudson and his little private party. "But he's definitely running something, and you can bet your ass it's not antiques."

"Dope," Tony said. "Or immigrants. Both, I can bet."

"I'm beginning to think Barnes wanted me strictly as a transport man," I said. "To accompany Renata once we managed to get her out."

"He needs you for more than just transport."

"Yeah, well, I'm a little bit suspicious of this guy Barnes and his connection with Hudson."

There was a pause in the connection.

I asked Tony if he was still there.

"I know what you're trying to do, Keeper," he said finally. "And I understand it."

Do you? I thought to myself, knowing full well he was referring to the black Buick and the Bald Man. But I said nothing about it.

"Your job is to get that woman out of prison," he said. "Get her home safe and sound. Nothing more, nothing less. You start poking around into Barnes's affairs, it'll get us both hurt, understand?"

"What do you mean, hurt?"

"It'll keep us from getting paid."

I looked out the window once more. Shaw Hudson in the near distance, laughing his ass off. Not fake laughter now. The man with the paunch was down on his back on the grass, pretending to snore, his stocky chest heaving and constricting.

"The article in the *Times-Union*," I said.

"Still no positive ID on the body. But they think it's you."

"Val knows?"

"I went to see her about it."

"You told her the truth. About the deception, I mean."

"I told her *a* truth."

I knew what that meant.

Val thought I was dead. Like everyone else.

I wondered if she cared.

I decided not to press the issue any longer. None of it mattered.

"I'll call you tomorrow," I said. "After it's over. From the airport. Or from the air."

"I'll fax you the layout," he said. "Soon as it comes in."

I pictured Tony standing inside his home office, a silk robe wrapped around his stocky torso. His office more like an English smoking room, furnished with a leather couch, original oil paintings, antique wooden desk. But also furnished with powerful computers with enough RAM to wage a small war. And not just one but three separate flat-screened monitors bracketed to the ceiling above the desk.

"Stick to the job at hand," he said. "Then get out. This one is strictly about money. Not about playing hero."

"I'm no hero, Tone," I said. "You should know that by now."

"It's why you're still alive," he said.

"Correction," I said. "It's why I'm dead."

CHAPTER TWENTY-EIGHT

SHE WAKES UP ON THE COLD CONCRETE.

Head pounding.

She reaches up with her right hand, touches the tender bruise the pistol made when the mustached man jammed the barrel behind her left earlobe. The bruise is round and protruding, like a lump. She can't resist pressing down on it with her fingertips. When she does, it causes her right eye to water.

But the pain and her shallow breaths tell her she's alive.

She sits up, presses her back against the wall. On the floor, a tin pail filled halfway with water. She reaches down for it, lifts the semi-heavy bucket with two hands, brings it to her mouth, takes a long, deep drink. The water is warm and smells faintly of rotten eggs. But she doesn't care. She is parched.

When she's had her fill, she sets the bucket down and dips her hands into the water. She brings her wet hands to her face, rubs the moisture into her skin, into her eyes. She allows herself to drip dry.

All around her come the groaning voices of the caged and the corrupt. The drugged-up bodies awaiting their own personal tortures for their own personal reasons.

But of the many voices, one stands out above the rest. It is a crying voice and it comes from the cell directly beside her own. It is Roberto. She hears him sobbing.

She slides up to the front of the cell, presses her face against the narrow vertical bars.

"*Are you all right?*" she says, half whispering, half out loud.

He does not answer.

She asks again. "*Are you OK, Roberto?*"

"*We should not talk,*" he says after a time. "*It is very dangerous. They will hurt us.*"

"*What's wrong?*" she asks him. "*Something must be very wrong.*"

"*We should not talk, miss,*" he repeats. "*We must do what they tell us.*"

"*I'll make a deal with you,*" she says. "*You tell me what's wrong, and I'll shut up. Deal?*"

The old man lets out a breath that seems to linger in the stale, damp air, like the moans and groans of the prisoners who occupy the surrounding cells.

"*This morning,*" the old man says, his voice shaking and rattling. "*This morning they told me the news.*"

"*What news?*" she says.

"*About my son.*"

She knows what he's going to say before he says it. But she asks him anyway. "What about your son?"

"*He's dead. My Juan is dead. A soldier shot him, they said. Over drugs.*"

"*Don't you believe it,*" she says. "*Don't you believe any of it.*"

"*Believe it,*" says the voice of another man. This one a soldier. *He is carrying a tray of food, which he sets down on the floor and slides under the gate. "I was there myself. They caught him with a truckload of cocaine. Caught him at the border a few days ago during a deal with a beautiful burrier.*

"*They hauled his ass out to the pit, made him go down on his knees. Then they shot him in the back of the head!" He makes like a pistol with his right hand, brings his thumb down fast. "Bang, bang,* just like that. His brains spattered all over the sand. Then they tossed his body in the hole with the other scum. It was a sight to see, old man. A beautiful sight."

Now the old man is openly weeping.

"You bastard," she says, now picturing the two men she dealt with in the desert. But not believing any of those creeps were Roberto's son. "You evil bastard."

"Eat," says the soldier, standing. "Eat and shut up."

That's when she gets the idea.

She calls out for him.

"What is it now?"

"There's something in my food," she says, staring down at a bowl of rice and a second bowl filled with a watery, yellow-colored potato salad, as well as a Styrofoam cup filled with red Kool-Aid.

"So what?"

"So I want you to look at it, tell me what it is."

The soldier takes a deep breath, releases it. He turns, makes his way back over to her. He bends at the knees, looks directly at the tray. "What is it?" he says.

She flings the food in his face.

He stands fast, wiping the food out of his eyes.

"Bitch," he says, slimy potato salad and Kool-Aid dripping off his face and chin. "Fucking bitch."

She slams the tray down, slides back against the far wall, as though it will protect her from the inevitable.

"Open up two!" the soldier shouts, wiping what's left of the food from his eyes.

There is a loud buzzer and the gate opens with a solid bang.

"Close two!" the guard shouts again.

The gate closes with a resounding slam.

As the soldier comes for her, he unbuckles his belt, unzips his zipper.

"Don't you scream," he says.

She lets out a resigned breath. "Who would want to hear me anyway?" she asks.

CHAPTER TWENTY-NINE

THE FIESTA WAS ALL BUT DEAD. NOW ALL THAT COULD be heard above the hum of swarming insects were the voices coming from Shaw's little private party on the front yard.

I didn't have a lot of time.

I tried the top desk drawer first. When that didn't work, I went for the side drawer.

Both locked.

The file cabinet too.

But when I looked through the stack of mail laid out nice and neat on the desk, one letter stuck out at me above the bills and correspondence from people and international organizations I had no way of recognizing. A letter from Richard Barnes in an envelope bearing the tin-reel-and-celluloid logo of Reel Productions.

I folded the letter in half, stuck it in my pants pocket.

It was time to get the hell out.

I knew I could always retrieve the fax first thing in the morning under less suspicious circumstances. But when I turned to leave, the door to Shaw's office opened for me.

Standing in the doorway, the shadowy figure of a man. He stood there, stiff as hell, blocking my path. Not a figure with a recognizable face and clothing, but a dark silhouette.

Then the silhouette took a step inside the office, and the little bit of porch light that leaked in through the glass doors revealed Hudson's face.

"Calling home?" he asked, the thumb on his left hand jammed into his belt buckle, the fingers on his right tickling the hammer on his ivory-handled six-shooter.

An innocent smile. "My man in New York, if you want to know the truth."

"Who might that be?" He walked over to his desk, sat down behind it, turned on the desk lamp. In the lamplight that poured down out of the lamp shade, I could make out the hard contours of his face, now made harder by the thin layer of black stubble.

"Tony Angelino," I volunteered, standing still and stiff—non-threatening—in the middle of the office floor.

"Oh yes, Tony Angelino and his famous Guinea Pigs," Shaw said, taking me a little by surprise at the mention of the Pigs. He sat way back in his chair, setting the heels of his boots up on the wood desk. He unlocked the drawers using the keys on his key ring. He set the keys down, slid out the bottom right-hand drawer, and pulled out a bottle of Jose Cuervo along with a large plastic sandwich bag filled with some pretty heavy-duty-looking marijuana buds. "Don't look so surprised," he went on. "Mr. Barnes has told me much about his lawyer. In fact, he discusses him very specifically in that letter you have in your pocket. A letter that also contains, among other monies, my advance for services rendered in the eventual rescue of his wife, Renata."

My heart jumped then.

"Go ahead, Mr. Marconi. Open up the envelope. See for yourself."

I was caught between a rock and a hard place.

I knew that if I just picked the letter out of my pocket, laid it back down on his desk without having read it, I'd never have the satisfaction of knowing what it might tell me. But then, if I called his bluff, actually looked it over, and it truly turned out to be a personal check for services rendered and nothing more, I'd come off looking like the sneaky, suspicious son of a bitch that I was.

A no-win situation. Either way.

I pulled the envelope out of my pocket, tossed it back onto his desk.

I tried to work up a smile. Penitent as hell. "Can't blame a guy for trying, can you, Shaw?"

"No. But I can blame him for sticking his nose where it does not belong."

I sat down in one of the wooden chairs in front of Hudson's desk.

He waved his right hand over the plastic bag. "Smoke?"

I shook my head.

"Too bad," he said. "Very high grade. The best. Rarely acquired north of, say, Amarillo."

"I get crazy," I said. "Paranoid."

"So I've heard," he said, tapping his right temple with his index finger.

There it was: the old internal organ slide. The lower abdominal pain that made me feel like my insides were going to spill out onto the floor.

"I know all about the Buick that killed your wife," he said. "And how you might have seen one just like it on Saturday. I know all about the wedding you skipped and the little tantrum you had at that bar up in Albany. And now it appears you're dead."

I swallowed something hard and bitter.

He opened up the bottom whiskey drawer, pulled out a folded copy of the previous day's *Times-Union*.

"Can't…blame…a…guy…for…trying," he mimicked, a fake contrite smile plastered on his face.

Shaw had been running his own little investigation into me.

That much was obvious now.

"Right now I'm safer dead than alive," I said.

"Aren't we all?" he said.

I stuck my hand out, waved it over the newspaper. "But all this is strictly a personal matter," I added.

He put the paper back in the drawer. "Yes," he said. "Death is a private affair for us all. In the end." He held up the bag with his fingertips. "Sure you won't reconsider?"

"What do you know about the black Buick?" I asked.

"Not a goddamned thing," he said. "Other than what I've been told by Mr. Barnes. Which is nothing more than what I just told you."

He replaced the bag in his desk drawer and brought out two clear sipping glasses.

"You don't smoke, either?" I asked him.

"Never touch the stuff," he said, reaching over the desk with the tequila bottle, pouring us a single shot apiece. "Like you, it makes me lose all semblance of reality. And when you're in the business I'm in, it is important to keep your head firmly in place."

I took a couple of steps forward, reached for the drinking glass on the desktop. I lifted it up to chest height, tipped it in his direction, downed it in one quick swallow. Then I set the empty glass back down on the desk.

"And what business is that, Shaw?" I asked, feeling the slow but soothing burn of the tequila.

He pulled back his own shot and immediately poured us both another. "I'm surprised Mr. Barnes has not informed you about my business ventures."

"He told me you collect antiques or buried treasure or some such shit," I said. "And that on occasion, when the treasure business gets a little slow, you act as a—let's say—travel guide."

"You don't believe our employer?" This time he handed me the drinking glass from across his desk.

First I looked down into the golden-colored tequila. Then I looked back at him, at his face in the white lamplight. "I guess it doesn't matter what I think or what I suspect about you or your business. What matters is that you have something planned for our little daylight raid."

He laughed a little and rolled the glass around in his right hand.

"You assume that because I live south of the border and that because I have a protected ranch and a few connections, I am a drug dealer. Or perhaps an agent for the Contreras Brothers." He downed his shot while maintaining that smile, then ran his open hand through his cropped salt-and-pepper hair.

Now I was rolling the empty sipping glass around in my right hand. "Like I said, it doesn't matter so long as you do your job."

"You're forgetting that Mr. Barnes is the boss, Mr. Marconi," he said, pouring yet another shot, setting the bottle on the far edge of the desk, for me to help myself. "The man who is paying not only me but Tony Angelino *and* yourself." His face went taut in the lamplight as he pulled the six-shooter out of his holster, aimed it directly at my face. "And if I ever catch you sneaking around my office again, I'll blow your fucking brains out all over the ceiling. Am I clear on this?"

"Crystal." I know when it's time to surrender.

I stood up gently, held out my hands, even with my waist. "Take it easy, Shaw," I said, gently taking hold of the tequila bottle by the neck with my right hand, my empty sipping glass in my left as if to pour another drink. "Don't you know when a man is trying to protect his ass—"

I tossed the glass at his head and smashed the tequila bottle on the edge of the desk.

He fired off a round into the ceiling just as I slipped around behind him, bringing the jagged edge of the bottle up against the soft underside of his neck.

The office door shot open.

The Mexican guard wearing the old leather vest came rushing in.

Did the son of a bitch sleep?

He gripped a black-plated 9mm in his right hand. He aimed it at my forehead.

I could feel Shaw tensing up in my arms. I could feel his heart beating, could feel his Adam's apple pressing up against the inside of my forearm when he swallowed. He spoke something to Old Leather Vest in a gentle voice and set the six-shooter down flat on the desk, pushing it away.

I guess he knew when to surrender too.

Because he held up his hands.

Old Leather Vest in turn looked at me with boiling black eyes. He wasn't about to surrender. Unless Shaw ordered him to do so. Which was my only hope.

"Tell him to get the hell out, Shaw," I said, pushing the jagged edge of the bottle even harder against his throat. "Do it now."

"You going to cut me open?" he said. "You need me to help you break into that prison tomorrow."

"Try me," I said, applying so much pressure the bottle verged on breaking the skin, if it hadn't already.

"Take it easy, man," he said, his voice reduced to a scratchy whisper.

"Tell him," I shouted.

He whispered something in Spanish.

The vest man aimed the piece at my head. His hand was shaking. His index finger was wrapped around the trigger. He might take me out, but Shaw was going with me.

But after a second or two, he eyed me up and down the same way he had when I'd first arrived at the entrance gates that afternoon. A sour, disgusted look. He replaced the 9mm back inside his belt and walked out, closing the door behind him.

I pulled the bottle away from Shaw's neck and tossed it inside the fireplace, where it shattered.

Then I grabbed the six-shooter before he had the chance.

I moved around to the front of the desk, pulled up a chair, sat down.

"Now," I said, setting the piece on my lap, "what the hell is your plan, Mr. Hudson?"

CHAPTER THIRTY

WHEN IT IS OVER AND THE SOLDIER IS GONE, SHE LIES on her back on the concrete floor, her jumpsuit in a crumpled heap beside her. She is listening to Roberto's sobs.

She, on the other hand, does not cry.

Unlike the man in the cell beside her, she doesn't care.

She doesn't care that she's naked; she doesn't care that they hurt her for answers she cannot possibly give them.

She sets her mind to thinking about other things. About the future. A possible future.

The new book, for instance. She is thinking about the new book she has been working on that resides in a secret place inside her home office. A book so secret not even Richard or her editor knows about it. She won't even write it on a computer for fear it will get into the wrong hands.

The book is about Charlie. The book that will tell the true story about his death, about how it really happened. About who is responsible, and why. The book she lives for now.

Now she doesn't care if she lives or dies.

But what she does care about is staying alive long enough to tell her story. Charlie's story. No matter who it will hurt in the end. No matter who it will destroy.

The real story.

CHAPTER THIRTY-ONE

"TO BE PERFECTLY HONEST, MR. MARCONI," SHAW SAID, breaking the label on a second bottle of tequila, "I don't really have a solid plan."

There it was again.

The old intestine slide. In just a few short hours, I was expected to break into a major maximum security prison, and my guide—the man I was supposed to entrust my life with—had no solid plan.

What he did have was a talent for throwing parties.

He shook his head and laughed.

"Everybody down here likes to laugh at everything that's not funny," I said.

"You have completely misunderstood me, Mr. Marconi." He poured another shot. "In a real way, this plan, as you call it, has already begun." He drank the shot. "What do you think this little party was all about tonight? To welcome you to Mexico?"

Laughing.

"I have no idea."

"Those finely dressed men whom you surely noticed standing in my yard tonight, drinking my liquor, eating my food. They were not my friends." He made quotation marks with his fingers when he said "friends."

He poured some more tequila.

"They were, in fact, your kind of people, Mr. Marconi. Half the support staff of Monterrey Prison, including Warden Castillo himself. The man with the bandaged hand."

I pictured the man with the injured hand. The one with the heavy mustache, who drank tequila directly from the bottle. He was a warden. Just like me.

Once upon a lifetime.

Maybe I assumed Shaw had just wanted to have a good time tonight at the risk of blowing the operation. But if he was telling the truth (and let's face it, I had no real reason to doubt he was telling the truth), then it was entirely possible he'd already secured our way in and out of Monterrey Prison the easiest and safest way possible: not by bribing the guards, but by bribing the hell out of their bosses—the corrections staff.

I stood up, set Shaw's six-shooter back down on his desk, held out my right hand.

Shaw took it.

"My apologies," I said.

"No harm done," he said, slipping the piece back into his holster. "At least not to me."

What he meant by that, I had no idea.

Sitting back down. "So what did these men promise you?"

"The short of it is this," he said. "In the morning, I will have a team of excavators on the west end of the prison, supposedly in search of an old Huichol Indian find supposedly buried at the base of the cliffs. For this operation, I have full permission from Warden Castillo. In the meantime, I will have gun emplacements set along the cliff top—sharpshooters with their sights set on the prison guards who we suspect will remain true to their cause should the worst begin to occur."

"What do you mean by 'the worst'?"

"If all goes sour and we are forced to shoot our way out."

"That could be a problem."

"Indeed, but then, it should not be a problem, because we are guaranteed access to the prison administration building."

"And how are you planning that?"

"One of my men will cut his hand and demand to see the prison doctor, who is located in the basement of administration. Since the buildings and cell blocks are connected by a series of underground tunnels and concrete passageways, we will make our way over to Cell Block A, grab Renata, bring her back through into the medical unit, dress her in workmen's clothes, make her out to be one of our workers. From there we simply walk her out through the front gate, slip her into my Land Rover, and get her the hell out."

"And the warden knows about our plans for breaking Renata out?"

"Not exactly," Shaw said, waving his hands in the air. "But I suspect he has his suspicions—suspicions he's willing to overlook, so long as the price is right. These men will do just about anything for money, you see."

"Price," I said, "as in the money you're paying him to look the other way."

"Not my money." He lifted the now slightly mutilated Reel Productions envelope from off his desk, waved it in the air like a small flag. "Barnes's money, of course."

Shaw sat back in his chair, stared into his sipping glass. "There are, however, two problems that bother me at present."

"What's that?" I said.

"First of all," he said, "we could have some trouble navigating the underground tunnels of the prison compound. After all, Mr. Marconi, there are no maps or plans available."

The ringer on Shaw's fax machine going off.

"Correction, Shaw," I said. "A blueprint *does* exist."

From where I sat I spotted the first page of Tony's fax now appearing.

"You can't possibly have a plan of Monterrey," Shaw said, sitting up in his chair, elbows on the desktop.

"Not exactly," I said. "But I do have a layout of Attica State Prison in upstate New York."

"I don't follow."

"Yesterday afternoon I noticed that Monterrey and Attica were nearly identical in their construction and setup. Which leads me to believe that the Monterrey people commandeered the actual design for their own purposes. It doesn't mean the basement layout is the same, but there's a pretty good shot that it is. So I had Angelino round me up a layout of Attica's basement."

Shaw smiled, filled his glass with more tequila, set it on the edge of his desk. "One last drink, in the name of renewed friendship."

I took the glass in hand. Together we drank down the tequila while the last page of the fax appeared. A small beep followed, indicating the transmission's end.

Out beyond the French doors, a hint of a rising sun on the horizon.

I stood up. "Maybe we should try and get some sleep," I said.

"Sleep would be good," Shaw said, standing up from his chair, coming around the desk, "if it weren't for that second problem."

"What second problem?" I asked.

"Remember I told you there were *two* problems that had me bothered?"

"What's the second problem?"

"Let's take a walk upstairs," he said. "Perhaps you can tell me."

CHAPTER THIRTY-TWO

HOURS LATER, SHE IS DRESSED.

She has washed herself as best she can with the water that came from the bucket in the far corner of the cell. She still has not eaten. Nor will she. Not until she is allowed to go free. If she is ever allowed to go free.

After a time, she hears the familiar sound of the metal gates opening in the distance and she knows the men are back.

She swallows her fear, trying like hell not to cry or shake or shiver but to just sit there, her back against the wall, like nothing affects her.

But, of course, it does.

When the mustached man appears at the bars, he raises his right hand high in the air.

The buzzer sounds and the gate opens.

The same two soldiers are standing behind him. The one on his left holding an automatic rifle, the black barrel aimed at her head.

The soldier on his right is carrying a tray.

Time for another shot.

She swallows, clears her throat. "You should know by now," she says, trying to hold back the trembling in her voice, "that I have nothing at all to tell you."

She breathes.

In and out. Not too fast, not too slow.

The mustached man approaches her. He is smiling now, the bandaging on his right hand changed to something fresh and clean. He no longer appears to be in any kind of pain.

He bends at the knees, brings his face to within inches of her own.

There is liquor on his breath, and cigarette smoke.

"There's been a change of plans," he says, while the soldier to his left sets the tray on the ground, begins prepping the syringe.

"Please don't inject me again."

The soldier depresses the syringe just a tad, so that a bit of the clear liquid comes spurting out.

"Don't worry," says the mustached man, running his good hand gently, coldly through her hair. "This will put you to sleep. Peacefully."

She looks at the soldier. He is smiling, coming toward her with the syringe.

"I don't want to go to sleep," she protests. But what she means to say is, I don't want to die. Not now, not this way.

Suddenly, when death is upon her, she chooses life.

But then, she has no choice in the matter.

The mustached man is already rolling up the sleeve on her jumpsuit. "And when you wake up," he says, "you will no longer be with us."

She feels the sharp prick of the needle.

It's not that she's afraid to die.

It's just that it's happening way too soon.

CHAPTER THIRTY-THREE

THEIR THROATS HAD BEEN SLICED FROM EAR TO EAR, the cuts so deep their yellow-white vertebrae were visible in spots through the blood.

Necks violently snapped back over blood-soaked pillows. Like twigs.

Mouths wide open.

Gaping.

You'd think that a man who'd spent the better part of his life in the Department of Corrections might be used to blood when it spills so fast and deep that it appears more black than red. You might assume that just because I've seen men gutted from neck to navel with a piece of glass no bigger than a man's palm or a skull crushed with a canvas sack filled with five-pound weights, I'd have no trouble stomaching a pair of sliced necks.

Listen: You might think that a man who witnessed his own wife's decapitation might not be affected by another woman's blood.

But killing wasn't anything like that for me.

Killing never would be.

How could any man go from doing the tango with a couple of girls in one breath to standing over their mutilated bodies the next, staring into their wide-open eyes as though in death they were somehow more alive than ever—eyes that didn't stare back at you but through you, until you felt the squeeze of a fist around your heart and your brain, felt your stomach being wrung inside out.

And what made you even sicker is that you couldn't help but stare at the naked bodies, from head to toe, careful to keep a distance between you and the flies that had already begun to make nests out of the sex parts.

"Who did this?" I asked, my voice hardly more than a whisper.

"Funny," Shaw said. "I was just about to ask you the same thing."

It took me a few seconds, but after a time I turned, caught Hudson's eyes with my own. "Go to hell," I said.

Behind me, Old Leather Vest took a step or two forward, ever at the ready.

Shaw crossed his arms at his chest. "I understand your distress, Mr. Marconi," he said. "But I think it only appropriate to mention that in all my years of living in Monterrey, I have never had a death to contend with inside my home."

"Why do I find that hard to believe?" I said, ever conscious of the vest man breathing down my neck.

The blood dripping over the silence.

"Did you enjoy your swim with those girls tonight?"

I went for his neck.

But not before the vest man jumped on my back, the barrel of his pistol pressed up against the back of my skull.

I pulled back.

"That's enough, Chico," Hudson said. "Let Mr. Marconi go."

It was the first time I'd heard him say anything to the man in English.

Chico's breath was sour and hot. It coated my neck like a mist. He removed the pistol and backed up against the far wall. From out the second-floor window, the orange hue of dawn was clearly visible while the sun rose over the Monterrey desert.

Shaw cleared his throat. "I'm sorry, my friend," he said, his voice reserved, his eyes averted from my own, peering down at the floor like a guilty child.

"Sorry for what?" I said.

"Sorry I had to reveal the bodies to you in quite this manner." Shaw's remorse seemed to grow deeper with every word. He seemed suddenly gentle, resigned, sad.

"No one deserves this," I said, nodding in the direction of the bodies.

"Quite simply, Keeper," Shaw went on, "I needed to evaluate your reaction."

"And if you didn't like my reaction?"

"It's not a question of *liking* your reaction. It's a matter of believing in it."

"If you didn't believe in it," I said, "what then?"

"Then I would have been certain that you were the responsible party."

"And you expect me to believe that shit?"

"You don't get as far as I have—no, allow me to rephrase that. You don't stay *alive* as long as I have without the talent to recognize guilt when it stares you in the face."

"But there's one thing you're forgetting, Shaw," I said. "You're going to be wrong from time to time."

"You mean what if I thought you were guilty?"

I nodded.

"Then I would have dealt with you in a manner I felt appropriate."

"And what's appropriate?"

"In biblical terms, a punishment that fits the deed," he said, rubbing the stubble on his chin with forefinger and thumb. "I'll show you."

He took a step forward, toward the place I occupied at the foot of the king-sized bed.

"Chico," he said, holding out his hand, palm up. "The gun, please."

Chico's eyes went noticeably wide, the tanned skin on his tight face suddenly pale. He handed the 9mm to his boss, as ordered. Shaw gripped the weapon, pressed the barrel against Chico's forehead, thumbed back the hammer.

"Pay close attention, Mr. Marconi," he said.

And then he pulled the trigger.

The explosion blew off the Mexican's cowboy hat, along with the entire back of his skull.

My body turned to ice in the desert.

The air in the room was thick with blood. The floor was covered with it.

Holy Christ, Shaw! I wanted to shout, but I couldn't work up enough voice to say it.

"Before you assume I acted wholly inappropriately, Mr. Marconi," he said, "let me tell you this. From the moment I walked you up here, I harbored a suspicion that my old and trusted employee, Chico, may have been responsible for the murder of those women."

"Jesus Christ," I said, trying to get my breath back.

"I spotted him coming out of their room about an hour ago," he explained. "He locked the door behind him." He paused only long enough to take a breath, the smoking 9mm still in his right hand. "However, I could not be certain."

"Until you confronted me."

"Perhaps *consulted* is the better word," he said.

We were silent for moment while the blood drained from the bodies and the new morning sun lit up the room. I looked down at Chico's face, the collapsed hollow cheeks, the three-day-old stubble, the now-hatless, blown-away head.

Now I knew why it had been so easy to get into Shaw's office undetected. It might not have been the old passed-out Mexican's job at all to oversee the room so much as it had been Old Leather Vest's responsibility.

Shaw tossed the pistol onto Chico's stomach. "Look, Keeper," he said, the slightest evidence of a yawn in his voice, "it is already day-light. My digging team left for the prison an hour ago. It will take them some time to set up the equipment and to position the gun emplacements along the cliff top. Why don't you catch some sleep while you still can. We'll meet out at the pit for breakfast in exactly one hour."

Breakfast.

Shaw was thinking of breakfast while the blood of three people flowed all around him. But then, if you can believe it, nabbing an hour's sleep along with putting a little something in my stomach did not seem like an insane idea. Maybe all the death was finally settling in. Maybe I was getting used to it after all. Anyhow, it didn't matter a whole lot how I felt about it. What mattered was getting Renata out of prison.

Then getting the hell away from this bloodbath.

I took my hand away from the bed's footboard, tiptoed around the blood to the head of the bed, reached out with my right hand, brushed it over the faces of both girls, closing their eyelids.

"Please, Mr. Marconi," he said. "Sleep."

"I heard you the first time," I said.

I stepped over Chico's body on my way out.

CHAPTER THIRTY-FOUR

IN THE DREAM, SHE IS ONCE AGAIN INSIDE HER OLD apartment.

Once again walking the center hall.

Slow motion.

The bright white light spills out of the open bathroom door, makes a halo on the wood floor.

There are the pleasant sounds of little hands and feet splashing in the water and the baby giggles that go with it.

Until she makes it to the open door and the light turns into water, spilling out of the bath onto the floor, while the hands of the man who kneels by the tub hold her little baby underwater.

CHAPTER THIRTY-FIVE

BUT HOW COULD I SLEEP OVER THE SCRUB BRUSHES, over the voices of the old women on their knees wiping away the blood in the bedroom beside my own? One sleepless hour later found me up and out of bed, fully clothed in jeans, boots, fresh work shirt, and leather jacket. I was drinking a cup of cowboy coffee that one of Shaw's loyal Mexican servants had prepared in a huge black pot set over a fire built inside the open pit. To say that breakfast was being served to the crowd of workers and servants would have been putting it mildly.

Four mammoth skillets were set on the black grate beside the coffeepot.

One skillet to fry eggs so fresh they lay steaming from birth inside a straw basket on the picnic table. Another skillet used for cooking whole chunks of bacon (not store-bought strips). In the third and fourth, refried beans and a Mexican dish called *cholo*, made from corn and green and red peppers, sizzled away.

I sat on the edge of a picnic table farthest away from both the fire and the crowd of people. I smelled the fresh breakfast food as it cooked and listened to the morning people laughing and playfully arguing in a language I did not understand.

I had no appetite.

Not only did I have the breakout at Monterrey Prison ahead of me, but my stomach hadn't had sufficient time to get over the murdered girls or the way Chico's brains had spattered all over the bedroom wall when Shaw shot him.

Stomachs tend to rebel at the sight of wasted brain matter.

Mine was no exception.

Maybe in the end, the killings had been used to relay some kind of message to me. A simple warning not to play around with Shaw, now or in the future. Whatever the case, I knew the ugly deed had presented one hell of an opportunity for him. An opportunity for demonstrating his supposed powers of reason, his powers of delineating the guilty and the sinless.

But then, I wasn't planning on sticking around long enough to find out just how much power Shaw wielded in Monterrey or anywhere else in Mexico, for that matter. Nor did I plan on sticking around long enough for him to kill more people just to make that power known. In just a few hours' time I would have custody of Renata.

Alive. Or so I could only hope.

Shaw joined me at the picnic table.

He asked me if I'd slept well.

I told him that I hadn't slept at all.

"Stupid question," he said, a smile planted on his ruddy face. "Even for me."

He laid out the maps of Monterrey Prison's basement along with our arsenal du jour, which included my Colt .45 with three extra ammo clips to stuff into the interior pockets of my leather bomber. As far as I could see, Shaw had strapped on his favorite six-shooter for the occasion. But then he placed the heel of his work boot up on the bench of the picnic table. He lifted the cuff on his khaki pants up above his knee in order to adjust the small leg-mounted Velcro holster that supported a two-shot derringer.

There wasn't a whole lot to view on the four reduced pages that Tony had faxed from Albany. But what they did reveal was this: If the sublevels of Monterrey were similar to Attica's, then we could easily reach the basement cells of A Block by following a narrow plumbing chase that connected directly to the basement of the administration building. *If* we could get into the prison hospital. *If* the warden took the bribe. So far, there were an awful lot of "ifs" hanging over our heads.

But the plan—if you could call it that—was simple.

Acquire access to the hospital by faking an injury. From there, gain access to the tunnel and then the basement of A Block. Uncomplicated, safe, and, according to the ever-confident Shaw, effective.

But when I asked what he planned to do if we got down to the basement only to find that Renata wasn't there, he just raised his hands in the air and smiled.

"In that case, we're S.O.L.," he said.

❖

Eight o'clock on a bright Wednesday morning.

Shaw at the wheel of his Land Rover, driving us over a bumpy dirt road that cut through the desert. Past the cactus and thorn bushes, past pecan trees and cotton fields manned by raggedy peasants and small children.

Besides our pistols, Shaw had locked and loaded his twelve-gauge Savage pump and set it in the thick plastic clips mounted to the dash. Placed in the open space between the two all-weather bucket seats was an additional box of ammo.

Two-shot magnum loads.

Shaw asked me if I was nervous.

"Wouldn't you be?" I said, nodding.

"Most of the danger is imagined," he commented. "I believe we have sufficiently covered our tracks with each individual bribe." Patting his breast pocket with the palm of his right hand. "And I've also taken the precaution of bringing along a few additional cash prizes, just in case."

"What if your bribed guards decide to double-cross and shoot on sight?" I said.

"We won't give them a reason to shoot," he said. "There's nothing suspicious about an injured man who requires immediate medical attention."

He was right and he knew it. Hell, I knew it. But I still couldn't find a way to squash the suspicion gnawing at my gut. As if my best instincts were raising their separate red flags. I wasn't scared of breaking into Monterrey Prison. I wasn't scared of breaking out Renata or stealing her out of the country. In a word, I was scared of Shaw, scared of his secret agenda. And after all, I could still smell the stench of those two women in the upstairs bedroom. Chico or no Chico, I had no real clue as to who truly ran that blade across their necks.

We said nothing for quite a while, until Shaw reached over with his right hand, opened the glove box, and pulled out a fifth of tequila. He broke the tab on the bottle while managing to maneuver the Land Rover by steering with his elbows. He tilted his head back, took a long swig, capped the bottle loosely and, without looking, handed it to me.

"ETA just five minutes," he said.

I took hold of the bottle, drank a shot, felt the cool, hot booze cut the dust in my throat. I took a second hit off the bottle and handed it back to Shaw.

He took another, longer drink and returned the bottle to the glove box.

Not ten seconds later the massive concrete and razor-wire-topped walls of Monterrey Prison came into view on the horizon.

CHAPTER THIRTY-SIX

THE DIGGING CREW WAS ALREADY BUSY AT WORK tearing up a portion of the desert by the time Shaw and I passed by the powerhouse. We pulled into the prison turnaround just outside Guard Tower Number One and crossed over into a nearly empty parking lot between the concrete walls and the cliff faces to the west.

The excavation crew consisted of a handful of men armed with pickaxes and spades, while the trench digger mined a narrow swath out of the desert floor.

Shaw hopped out of the Land Rover and approached the dig site.

The ever-concerned boss.

I followed close behind.

He spoke to a man who was operating a transit—a thin, wiry old man in a canvas coat whom I immediately took as the foreman for the phony digging project. In the meantime, I tried my best to eye the three gun emplacements Shaw had supposedly set up on the cliff top.

It was impossible to make out a single gunner. But then, if I could see them, the guards inside Monterrey Prison manning the towers could see them too.

For a while I eyed Shaw and the foreman as they spoke, each of them raising their hands in the air while surveying the surrounding desert, really putting on a show for the guards in the towers. I tried my best to catch what they were saying. But the engine on the trench digger was drowning out their incomprehensible Spanish.

At one point Shaw walked up to the machine operator and told him to cut the engine, an order he gave by running his right hand across his throat. The engine was cut, but the mechanical noise lingered, echoing across the valley, reverberating off the cliff faces. Shaw went down on his knees at the edge of the trench. He reached inside with his right hand, pulled out what looked to be a plain everyday rock but what to Shaw and his foreman appeared to be something else entirely.

As Shaw stood up, I glanced up at the guards. All eyes from all six men were planted on the scene, as expected. They continued to eye Shaw as he shook the hands of each and every man on his digging crew. They, in turn, let loose with wild cheers, triumphant fists raised in the air. Christ, even I had to smile, because I knew goddamned well that Shaw hadn't discovered anything other than a rock. It was all just a part of an act for the guards in the towers. An act that continued with the foreman now taking his turn at the trench, going down on his knees just like Shaw had done only a few seconds before.

Only this time, something went wrong.

This time the operator of the digger mistakenly started the machine back up when the foreman decided to reach down into the trench with his right hand.

From where I stood I could see the blood coming from the gash in the old man's forearm, just above his wrist. For a split second or two, I could have sworn it had all been a major mistake, that this old man in dust-caked jeans, loose-fitting canvas jacket, and work boots with the steel toes worn through the old leather had actually come close to losing his right hand to the claw of the trench-digging machine. Don't think I didn't feel the slight jolt of panic blast through my veins when Shaw grabbed the old man by his good arm and shouted, "Keeper, help me get this man inside."

I took hold of the old man's apparently damaged arm as gently as I could, placed it around my shoulder so that Shaw and I both were supporting him, acting as his legs. As we began leading him toward the front gates, I couldn't help but look up at the number one tower and the three men who manned it. They were standing at the edge of the parapet, elbows planted firmly on the chest-high wall. Maybe the reflective aviator sunglasses they wore shielded their eyes, but from where I stood with an injured old man in my arms, their smiles were clearly visible.

Of course, I had to believe it was all a part of Shaw's original plan to fool the guards of Monterrey Prison into thinking we had a real injury on our hands. As far as I could see, we did. One of his workers appeared to have sustained a wound severe enough to require immediate medical attention. The most accessible place for the treatment was inside the prison hospital.

I had to give Shaw credit.

So far the plan was working.

Shaw left me alone with the old man while he attended to business inside the prison gates. The gates themselves consisted of a large set of steel doors embedded into the pentagonal wall. Surrounding the double doors was an elaborate, cathedral-shaped stone arch and keystone set into the solid concrete. Two guards stood outside the open steel doors, both of them dressed in standard olive-green uniforms—short-sleeved shirts, tight pants tucked into tall black combat boots, matching baseball caps, sidearms at their hips, and vest-mounted radio transmitters and receivers.

The guards were smoking and talking, leaning their shoulders up against the solid concrete door frame.

Shaw approached the men while I held up the injured foreman. I got a good look at the two guards as they slowly turned away from each other and stared into Shaw's face. They were about the same height, with dark complexions and black hair that stuck out from underneath their prison-issue baseball caps. Could they have been guests at Shaw's party the night before? Tough to tell in the daylight.

But when he spoke to the guard on his left-hand side while slipping a single, number-ten business envelope to the man on his right side, I knew for sure these men had partied up the night before at Shaw's ranch. In turn the guards stepped aside, allowing us to pass on through. The area was guarded by yet another man who sat inside a booth hewn out of the twenty-foot-thick concrete wall and shielded with special bulletproof Plexiglas.

Shaw reached into his jacket, pulled out another envelope, slid it through the mail-slot-sized opening in the transparent shield. The guard never gave us a first or second look. He simply took the envelope, slipped it into his breast pocket, issued a backhanded wave that gave us the green light to proceed on down the hall, no registering our names, no surrendering our weapons.

Easy, just like Shaw insisted the operation would be.

Maybe too easy.

But then, I had no way to gauge my experience against another operation of its kind. After all, I had spent the better part of my life keeping men from escaping prisons just like this one. Here I was, the Keeper—the former warden—involved in a breakout, and I was completely at the mercy of Shaw and his experience.

He turned away from the Plexiglas shield, faced me. All the blood seemed to have drained out of his face suddenly. In a low voice he told me we'd been granted access to the prison hospital for twenty minutes only. No more. "That money I just distributed, all the favors I called in last night, that's all they're worth. Twenty fucking minutes. Then they come after our asses. So I suggest we move."

"It's your party," I said.

"And everyone else's ass," he said.

I dragged the foreman into the elevator.

The door closed behind us. Shaw hit the button for the basement. There was the jolt of the car and the sinking-gut feeling that let me know we were on our way down. The heat inside the elevator was stifling.

Shaw looked at his watch once more.

"Eighteen minutes, forty-five seconds," he said. "Not enough time."

"Enough time," I insisted. I didn't believe it either. But what choice did we have?

I looked at the ceiling for a closed-circuit TV camera. I saw nothing. My cue to take a quick break from holding the foreman. "Shaw," I said. "Tell the old man he can relax."

The foreman groaned when I released him. He would have fallen to the cab floor if Shaw hadn't caught him.

"That's part of the problem, Keeper," he said, his eyes going from the overhead light-up floor indicators to his watch and back again. "He can't relax. Nor can he stand on his own. Not with that injury."

I looked at the floor. A puddle of the old man's blood.

"I thought the point was to make it *look* like an accident," I said, taking hold of the man once more.

"He was supposed to just graze his hand, maybe break the skin enough to bleed," Shaw explained. "Instead the old bastard nearly severed the limb."

"The old man is willing to lose a hand for money?"

"You see, Keeper," Shaw explained, "in an operation like this, one must rely on realism."

The old man was growing dead heavy on my back in the overheated elevator car, his blood now warming my right leg as it soaked through my jeans and spilled out onto the rubber-covered floor of the cab. "How much money?" I said.

"Two thousand dollars," Shaw said. "American."

"Two grand to lose a hand."

The elevator abruptly stopped. The doors opened up onto a corridor filled with pipes and ductwork mounted on the concrete ceiling and walls.

"Two thousand dollars is more money than this man or his children and grandchildren have ever seen in their lives."

"That makes it right?" I said.

"Save the moral lecture for later on, amigo." He pulled out his six-shooter, stepped out into the hall. "Now do you want Renata or not?"

I dragged the old man out into the basement corridor of Monterrey Prison. What I really wanted was the Bald Man. But Renata would have to come first. "I want her," I said.

Shaw looked at his wristwatch once more. "Good," he said. "You're not back in fifteen minutes, you find your own way out."

CHAPTER THIRTY-SEVEN

I SHOT DOWN A NARROW CORRIDOR THAT I HOPED would connect the basement of administration to the basement "cage area" of A Block. In my right hand, poised at shoulder height, my Colt .45.

Both walls of the low-ceilinged corridor were lined with metal conduits and cast-iron pipes stacked horizontally along metal racks. The caged lightbulbs mounted on the ceiling lit up the place in an iridescent half light, the air damp and clammy, the moisture beading along the surface of the pipes and dripping to the concrete floor.

It took only about thirty seconds to sprint the entire length of the shaft. But what difference did it make, since the access to A Block was secured with a steel door padlocked from the inside?

I took a step back from the door, positioned the barrel of the .45 an inch away from the padlock, triggered off a round. The bullet blew the lock into three pieces.

That was the good news.

The bad news was that the explosion surely served as one hell of a wake-up call for the guards on the other side.

I stood shielded by the metal door, both hands clasped around the .45, my breaths coming and going more rapidly than the beating of my heart. I tried to swallow. I wiped the sweat from my eyes with the backs of my hands, filled my lungs with the warm, wet oxygen, and exhaled only half of it. Then I raised my left foot, pressed the heel of the boot flat against the metal door. I let go with the rest of my breath and kicked the door open.

I put two rounds into the Plexiglas guard shack. The man inside dropped his sidearm, fell forward onto the electronic panels. I immediately went into a crouch, waved the .45 from left to right and back again.

The area was clear.

I took a few steps inside. When I got a better look at the guard shack, I could see the man sprawled out on top of the control panel. The same mustached man I'd seen at Shaw's the night before. The one with the bandaged hand.

The warden.

I'd killed the warden, for Christ's sake.

The six cells were arranged piggyback style, with three facing in a northerly direction, another three facing south, all six cells sharing a common sanitary pipe chase. I set about making a check of each cell. The search didn't take very long. By the time I'd reached the number two cell, I'd located Renata. She was alone inside an iron box, curled up on her left side on the concrete floor—fetal position   facing the wall that separated her cell from the number one cell beside it.

I called out for her.

No response.

What I mean is, not only did she say nothing, she didn't make a move. Not a jolt of a leg or an extension of her arms or a mumble-filled rollover. Not so much as a twitch of her little finger. I thought for sure she was dead. Seeing her lying there, perfectly still, no evidence of even the slightest expansion and contraction of her lungs, it was as if she had died in her sleep and all this had been for nothing.

But I wouldn't know for sure until I broke into the cell, felt for a pulse.

Or some other sign of life.

Monterrey might have resembled Attica in layout and construction. But that's where the similarities ended. It was a prison like no other. At least none that I had ever experienced before. The place was silent. No sound. Not even when the inmate from cell one pressed his soiled face up against the vertical bars. He said nothing. The old, gray-bearded man just stood there like a zombie, staring at me with wide black eyes and a pale face, his naked, sack-of-ribs torso drowning in the overhead sodium lamplight.

When he opened his mouth, it nearly scared me to death.

"She's dead," said the old man. "The poor girl is dead, don't you see, mister? It's me you want now. She's a good girl, but they shot her up with too much shit and now she can't go nowhere. Take me with you, mister."

I did my best to ignore him.

"Renata!" I shouted once more. "Renata Barnes!" Still no response.

"I'm telling you she's dead," the old man repeated. "She's gone, don't you see?"

"Shut up!" I screamed at the old man. "Shut! Up!" I was panicking.

"Go to hell," the old man said, his voice suddenly no more than a resigned whisper. "But what am I saying? You're already in hell."

I took a deep breath, tried to calm down.

I was a former warden, after all. I knew prisons, how they worked.

I knew the cell doors were controlled electronically, via the control panel located inside the guard shack. I peeled the warden off the panel, dropped him to the floor. A quick scan of the controls revealed the trigger release for each of the six individual cells. I thumbed the round red button for cell number two. An electronic buzzing shot through the concrete cage. There was the unmistakable sound of the cell door sliding open along its iron tracks.

I shot around the corner into Renata's cell. Collapsing to my knees, I brought the middle and index fingers of my right hand to her carotid, my ear to her mouth. I felt a pulse, however slight, and her warm breath against the skin of my ear.

"There's no helping that poor girl," the old man insisted.

I rolled Renata onto her back, took hold of her hands, swung both her arms over my right shoulder, hefting her up in a fireman's hold. She was as light as air. I carried her out and made a beeline for the open tunnel. I didn't have to look at my watch to know that no more than nine minutes could possibly remain before Shaw's deal with the Monterrey Prison guards went bad.

The old man called out for me, just as I made it to the steel door. "Take me," he pleaded. "You can't leave me here. My son died. Yesterday. I must see my wife. You can't leave me here."

I felt the light weight of Renata draped over my right shoulder. I sensed what little time I had left slipping through my fingers like so much desert sand. "Goddammit," I said to myself.

"Please," the old man shouted. "For God's sake, they'll kill me too. Please."

For a few more seconds than I could spare, I stood there at the opening to the tunnel, hesitating. I didn't want anything from anybody anymore. Why should I give out? Until I finally said, "Screw it," to myself and headed back to the guard shack with Renata slumped over my back, stepping over the dead guard, coming down hard with a clenched fist on the general switch that would release every single cell door.

The place exploded in alarms and the violent clanging sound of iron against iron as the doors on all the remaining five cages opened up.

"May God bless you," came the voice of the old man as I turned once more and carried Renata into the tunnel toward Shaw and, God willing, our getaway.

CHAPTER THIRTY-EIGHT

SHE DREAMS OF RIDING A HORSE ACROSS A BUSY CITY street.

A horse, of all things, in New York City.

It's hot. Summer. But raining. The rainwater pouring out of the gray clouds that hide the tops of the skyscrapers…

But then she is awake.

Not completely. Half-awake.

She opens her eyes, just a crack.

She swears she is being carried. Not on a horse but on a man's back. Through a brightly lit tunnel, warm water dripping from the ceiling onto her head. She can feel the warm wetness on her hair, on her scalp.

Maybe she's not awake at all. Maybe she's dreaming again.

The next thing she knows, she's cradling Charlie in her arms. She has him dressed in a pair of little overalls and a T-shirt that says Baby Gap and little white sneakers and ankle socks. She stands all alone, holding her baby in the wide-open cemetery with the green grass and the leaves shaking on the trees in the wind. She knows this day. She has lived it and died on it once before.

The warm spring day they should *have buried Charlie.*

CHAPTER THIRTY-NINE

RENATA SLUNG OVER MY SHOULDER, SPRINTING THE tunnel from A Block to the administration building, praying to Christ that Shaw would still be waiting.

There he was when I reached the end of the passage.

Standing inside the open elevator car, holding the sliding door open.

"How we doing on time?" I said, stepping inside.

"Less than six minutes." He released his hold on the button, the elevator doors sliding closed. "Tell me she's alive."

"A little," I said, shifting Renata's dead weight on my shoulder.

The elevator, rising.

A bucket placed in the far right corner of the square car. A small, bright yellow bucket with the words HAZARD: MEDICAL WASTE printed on the side in orange Day-Glo letters.

"What about the old man and his hand?" I said. "We're gonna just leave him?" The upward thrust of the elevator pushing against the inside of my stomach.

"It's too late for him," Shaw said, forever glancing at his wristwatch.

"What's the matter with you?" I said, now grabbing his right arm with my left hand. "The goons will kill him."

Shaw broke my hold.

I nearly dropped Renata.

"If the old man's not dead now, he will be any minute," he said. "The proof is right there."

"Where?"

"In the bucket."

The elevator, approaching the first floor.

I steadied Renata while, bending at the knees, I peeled the lid off the bucket. Inside, the old man's hand, severed at the wrist. Jagged edges of the white bone sticking through the red and white flesh. Like it'd been hacked away with a dull hatchet.

Hot bile shot up from my stomach, filling my mouth.

I tossed the lid back on the bucket, turned away, swallowing.

The car came to an abrupt stop.

The doors slid open.

"Emergency amputation," Shaw said.

"You let the doctor do that?"

"Not a doctor. Just some jerk, works in the clinic. Part of the price we're paying for Renata."

"Part of the price," I said. "What price?"

"I didn't let the drunk bastard do anything," he said. "I was standing out in the hall waiting for you." The doors of the elevator opened wide. "We have to move," he said.

My hold on Renata, tight. Solid.

"We've got about five minutes," Shaw said, stepping out onto the empty administration corridor. "Maybe less."

"What if we don't make it?" I said, following him toward the front gates, Renata suddenly growing heavier on my shoulder.

"We die," he said.

CHAPTER FORTY

I CAN'T SAY EXACTLY WHEN THE FIRST SHOTS WERE fired or who fired them or if the guards began shooting at us before our negotiated twenty minutes were up. Or maybe the entire plan had been bullshit from the very beginning.

But the guards were already shooting at us when we bolted out the front gates. Shooting to kill. As if Shaw had never made a deal with them to begin with. Maybe he hadn't.

At least half a dozen Mexican guards, all of them down on one knee, combat position, spread out in semicircle formation atop the grassy prison turnaround. Some sporting prison-issue .38s, others using black M-16s, all of them firing on cue as soon as they saw the whites of our pretty little eyes.

How they missed us was a miracle.

But as I threw Renata into the back of the Land Rover and hopped into the passenger seat, it dawned on me that no miracle whatsoever had been involved. As soon as Shaw got behind the wheel and calmly turned the engine over, I knew there was no other explanation for it: they missed us on purpose.

Which was why the gunmen set on top of the cliff face hadn't returned their volleys.

The guards had given Shaw a break after all, held fast to their bargain while pretending to perform their sacred duty. Except for the one bastard who either decided not to play fair or was such a bad shot that he managed to nick the back of my left thigh. Despite the pinprick sensation of the bullet, I didn't feel the pain right away. Just a prick, like a bee sting, and the telltale wet warmth trickling down the back of my leg.

As soon as we were on the road, I reached into the backseat, pressed the index and middle fingers of my right hand up against Renata's carotid. Her pulse was still weak but somehow steadier. Like her condition had actually improved during the craziness!

What's more, she had begun to mumble in her unconscious state. "Charlie," she said, over and over again, like a chant. "Charlie."

"Who's Charlie?" Shaw asked, while I turned to see if we were being tailed.

I turned back around, slipped down into the bucket seat. "Her son," I said, trying to catch my breath.

He reached across my legs for the glove box and the fifth of tequila he had opened earlier. "She wrote a book about it, am I right?"

"*Godchild*," I said.

"Yes, of course, *Godchild*," Shaw said. "I haven't read it." He took a swig of the tequila and handed the bottle to me. "She must have loved him very much to have written an entire book about him."

"You could say that," I said, bringing the bottle to my mouth.

I closed my eyes against the wind and the sand and took a deep drink. I knew I was bleeding on the seat. But I said nothing about it. The tequila cut through the dry soreness in the back of my throat. Adrenaline was still shooting through my veins. That's when it hit me like a brick. Only harder. Maybe I hadn't had the chance to think about it before. Or maybe I hadn't wanted to think about it. But suddenly, at that very moment, sitting in the Land Rover, I had to wonder just what the hell I was doing there. Just what the hell had transpired in my life since my wedding day that would have led me to the desert, to the breakout of a woman I'd never laid eyes upon until a few moments ago.

While Shaw Hudson sped over the dirt road, it hit me that I had just pulled off the impossible. No, that wasn't exactly right either. What I meant to say was this: Renata's rescue had gone off too easily. Regardless of who had died, who got shot along the way. Regardless of the flesh wound in my thigh. As if every move had been choreographed, planned out by someone much more important than Shaw or Tony Angelino or maybe even Richard Barnes.

But then, I had to wonder. Just who the hell was pulling the strings?

And for what cause?

What was Barnes's intent? To get his wife back? Simple as that? Because if that's all he wanted, this was no way to go about it. Unless, of course, he wanted to risk her getting shot in the process.

And just what had been Renata's cause in the first place? Why would she have risked her life to come down here? Had she been running away from the memory of her drowned child? Just like I had tried to run away from the persistent memory of a murdered wife? But then, what the hell was my cause? Why had I agreed to the job in the first place? Let's face it, my cause had nothing to do with Renata or money or getting my feet back on the solid concrete. It had everything to do with finding the Bald Man. Finding him once and for all. Then killing him. That was my cause. And that was all that mattered to me.

It was while wrapping a torn-away section of my shirttail around the flesh wound on my thigh that Shaw asked me to hand over my Colt. At the same time, I felt the barrel of his six-gun pressed up against my left temple.

"Son of a bitch," I said.

"The Colt, please," he repeated. Eyes peeled to the road.

I reached for it, handed it to him, butt first. He set it down by his feet on the floor.

We rode for about another half mile until we were completely surrounded by empty desert on all sides. Then Shaw suddenly pulled off onto the side of the road and stopped. "Now," he said, "out of the car, Mr. Marconi."

I got out.

He then asked me to help him remove Renata from the backseat.

"No," I said.

"Do it," he said, the barrel of the pistol in my face.

No choice.

I took her legs. He took her arms. Together we laid her out on the desert floor.

"I assume you would like an explanation," he said, shifting his aim from my face to Renata's. "But I am not in the position to give you one."

Shaw bent at the waist, pressed the barrel of his six-gun against Renata's head, drew back the hammer, averted his face—just slightly—as though to avoid the inevitable spatter.

"Shaw," I said. "Don't do it."

"Stay out of this," he said. "This isn't about you and me."

"Then what is it about?"

"What the hell does it matter?" he said, grinning. "So long as the money's right?"

CHAPTER FORTY-ONE

THIS TIME WHEN SHE OPENS HER EYES, SHE IS IN THE middle of the desert. She can still see her boy, Charlie. The memory of his little round face is ingrained in her brain. But at the same time, she is remembering the pit.

The mass grave.

All those bloating bodies covered in white powder, stacked up like piled logs, their stench sweet, overwhelming, floating up into her nose like vapor.

She doesn't want to go back to the pit. She can't go back to the pit. She's not ready to die.

She cares now. Suddenly. About life. Her life.

The book. She has to write Charlie's book first. She has to have the chance to tell the truth.

She hears some men talking. Arguing.

She has no idea who they are. They speak English.

If only she could wake up, get her wits about her.

If only she could move a muscle.

She could run away.

CHAPTER FORTY-TWO

ONCE, WHEN I WAS CAPTAIN OF THE GUARD AT Coxsackie Prison, I found myself in the middle of a lover's quarrel that had erupted between cell mates. At some point around midnight, one of the inmates—a big, burly, tattooed man who went by the name of Ricky Too-Sweet—had pulled a screwdriver out from under his mattress and slid the sharp end of the foot-long shank just inside the ear canal of his lover—a slight, effeminate man known around the iron house only as Skinny.

By the time the guard sergeant had awakened me and called me onto the scene, big Ricky was crying like a baby. "He don't love me no more," he groaned between sobs and sniffles, Skinny trembling under the weight of his thick arm and the pressure of the screwdriver against his eardrum.

I stood directly outside the then-open door of the cell, a gang of five or six corrections officers behind me, standing at the ready, batons in hand. All around us came the sounds of inmates who'd been awakened from a sound sleep. "Waste him, Ricky!" they shouted. "Kill the fag!"

"Listen, Ricky," I said, my two hands raised in the air in a kind of mock surrender, "don't do anything you'll regret later on."

But he looked up at me with big brown eyes inside a round face made all the rounder by a clean-shaved head. "Regret shit," he said. "I already doin' life."

He gave the tool just a little nudge.

Skinny yelped like a dog that's just had his paw stomped on. "Oh Christ, help me," he said, a small stream of blood running from his ear down his sweat-soaked cheek.

"What is it you want?" I asked Ricky.

He looked at me with those eyes. "You wouldn't know what I want," he cried. "You don't live in here with me. Only he lives in here with me. Only he knows what I want, what I need. And now he wants to take it all away from me...from us."

He was right. I had no way in hell of knowing how he felt. But the point was to stall him, keep him talking, keep the big man tuned into me while I bought precious time.

"Skinny is going to get parole with or without you," I said. "He's going home. You can't stop it, Ricky."

"He don't love me no more," he said. Just another slight nudge of the screwdriver, another squeal from Skinny, along with five or six separate breaths swallowed by the five or six COs standing behind me.

Ricky's eyes seemed about to explode out of their sockets. Those wide, glassy eyes that told me there'd be no talking him out of what he wanted or what he needed to do with that screwdriver. Words alone would have no effect, since he'd already made up his mind long before I'd come onto the scene.

But that didn't give me the right to give up. As the captain of the guard, it was my job to protect society from the likes of Ricky Too-Sweet. But it was also my impossible job to protect the inmates from one another.

I took another step inside the cell, held out my hand. "Give me the shank, Ricky," I said. But the gesture was useless. I took two more steps forward, but in all reality I might have taken five steps back. A split second later, Ricky plunged that metal shaft through

Skinny's brain just like I knew he would right from the start, right from the second I'd stepped inside the cell. The chrome-plated, foot-long screwdriver plunged in one ear, sticking out the other, the silver shank now coated with blood and brain fluid.

Call it a blessing, call it a curse. But it was a talent I had. An intuition or an instinct I'd developed after years spent inside the walls of an iron house as the *other* inmate: the corrections officer.

Knowing a man had made up his mind was never evident in his words or in his actions or even in his threats. It was evident in his eyes. If you learned how to read a man's eyes, you could save yourself a whole lot of time and trouble trying to talk him out of something or attempting to negotiate a settlement. Because there's no negotiating anything when his eyes get that glazed over, that red, that wide. If he wanted to kill somebody, then you could be damned sure that that somebody was already dead, already buried, already decayed, long before the shank got thrust or the trigger got pulled.

It was no different for Shaw.

When I looked into his blue eyes I had no doubt he intended to kill Renata without hesitation. The eyes were wide, red, glazed.

I had only one option available.

I lunged at him, shoulders square, using my legs as springs, my head as a battering ram. I caught him square in the face, exploding his nose like a water balloon.

We went down together.

Shaw on his back, me on my stomach, clawing for the pistol he still held in his right hand.

His six-gun.

I reached out for it. But that was when he thrust the heel of his palm up against my forehead. The blow tossed me onto my back. But the collision caused him to lose the pistol.

We both went after it.

At the same time.

The crowns of our heads collided, the sun going down on me for just a split second, the sound of breathing replaced with a loud, interior buzz.

The quick flash of blackness.

❖

Shaw laid out on the sand, eyes rolled up into the back of his head. But somehow still with it, still holding on to consciousness. The two of us crawling on our hands and knees toward the pistol just three or four feet in front of us in the sand, like a bad dream.

"Who wants her dead, Shaw?" I shouted, voice dry and raw. "Is it Barnes?"

Shaw said nothing. He just turned to me, looked me in the eye, spit a mouthful of blood into my face.

I woke up then.

The dizziness drained from my head while his blood dribbled down my lips and chin. I got up on my knees and let him have it where it hurt: in his broken nose. He fell back, the pistol still barely out of reach. I knew if I lunged for it, I could get to it before he did.

Which is exactly what I did.

I cocked the hammer on the revolver, pressed the barrel against his forehead.

"Who ordered the kill?" I said.

He smiled and rolled over onto his hands and knees, eyes glazed and wide but somehow happy. "Go to hell, Mr. Marconi," he said.

I fired a round over his head, cocked the hammer again.

"Maybe, Mr. Marconi," Shaw said, as calmly as he had spoken to me in his office the night before, "I just want to kill her for the fun of it."

I could see it in his eyes.

The look that told me he would rather die than give away any information at all, meaning I could either shoot him dead or simply let him go.

While Shaw vomited his breakfast onto the desert floor, I opened the chamber on the six-gun, spun the cylinder, spilled out one round at a time—one by blessed one—onto the sand. Then I tossed the piece as far away as I could.

I limped my way over to Renata.

She was rolling around on the ground now, still mumbling something about Charlie when I picked her up, cradled her in my arms, laid her once more in the backseat of the Land Rover. As for Shaw, he was finished heaving his guts. He had turned onto his left side, propped himself up on his left elbow during the time it took me to hobble back into the driver's seat and fire up the engine.

"Hey, Marconi," I heard him say above the engine noise. "You're not going to just leave me alone in the desert like this?"

"You got feet," I said, pulling my .45 out from under the driver's seat where Shaw had stored it, setting it on the empty seat beside me.

"How can you be sure I'll make it, amigo?" he said, the creases of his face filled with blood both wet and dry. "You've inflicted one hell of a beating on me." He smiled.

"Walk," I said, pushing on the clutch with my left foot. But not before seeing him reach down toward his right ankle.

"Now that's heartless," he said, ripping the derringer out of his ankle holster, firing off a shot that made a nickel-size hole in the windshield.

It was then that Renata sat up straight. It was then, just as Shaw got set to let off that second round, that she blew two holes into his chest with my .45.

Shaw rolled onto his back, mouth and eyes wide open as if his soul had taken off for hell before his body knew it was dead.

"Miracle of miracles," I exhaled.

Without a word Renata handed me the piece, grip first, then fell back onto the seat.

This time I slipped the pistol into my holster and threw Shaw's Land Rover into gear. I felt a throbbing in my left thigh when I depressed the clutch. The first time I noticed the pain coming from the flesh wound.

"Not bad for a dead woman," I said, looking at Renata by way of the rearview.

I saw her run both hands through her short hair while lying flat on her back. "If you don't mind," she said, "I'm going to pass out now."

She did.

I pulled the truck onto the dirt road. It was already ten o'clock in the morning. I had to haul ass. The resurrected Renata and I had a plane to catch in less than an hour.

PART THREE

NO INTACT BODIES FOUND AT SITE AS FORENSICS EXPERTS CONTINUE SEARCH

MONTERREY, Mexico (AP) - In cooperation with Mexican authorities, the FBI has established a command post in downtown Monterrey, where it is expected to begin analysis of over 196 remains recently uncovered in just one of what are suspected to be at least a half-dozen as-yet-undiscovered mass graves located along the vast Mexican border.

Nearly all the missing have disappeared after having been detained by Mexican Federal Police and Monterrey Prison officials. Evidence compiled by the association suggests that in some cases the victims were arrested and later tortured and/or killed by Mexican police or soldiers hired by drug traffickers to eliminate a rival or punish a debtor. In other cases, the victims appear to have vanished when they were detained for questioning by Mexican narcotics agents.

CHAPTER FORTY-THREE

SHE CLOSES HER EYES AT THE VERY MOMENT SHE FEELS the liftoff inside her stomach.

She wakes up then, in a bucket seat.

Her ears pop. The cabin of the plane is warm. There is a blanket covering her lap. The man beside her is asleep. His jeans are dirty. There is a spot of blood on his left thigh. She can hear his snores. She wants so badly to say something to him. This man who came for her in the desert. She wants to wake him. But she can't. She's so exhausted she can't move, can't speak. She can only sleep. And yet she can still feel the weight of that pistol in her hand, feel the solid buck of the shot.

But first, one last look out the window onto the heavenly blue sky.

"I'm flying," she whispers.

But no one hears her. And that's OK with her.

CHAPTER FORTY-FOUR

I WAS ON MY BACK ON A DOUBLE BED INSIDE THE SAME second-floor room I'd rented at Coco's Motor Inn before my excursion to Mexico little more than forty-eight hours ago.

My honeymoon motel.

I was staring up at the red neon light that reflected off the white popcorn ceiling, the dog-eared copy of *Godchild* by my side on the mattress.

Barnes's job was finished, even though I had no cash to show for it. But then, I hadn't exactly lived up to my side of the bargain.

Not yet, anyway.

As far as Barnes or Tony knew, Renata and I were still in Mexico.

My leg ached.

At least I was alive.

Renata was alive too, lying on the bed opposite my own, asleep. My deal with Richard had been to return his wife as soon as I brought her back, no questions asked. But things had changed since then. It had been one hell of a twenty-four hours, the last fourteen of those particularly long. Renata and I left Shaw lying on his back in the middle of the desert. Left him for the buzzards.

For whatever reason, he had betrayed the cause. Maybe he had acted on his own (as he'd indicated while on his knees in the desert), for the benefit of his own pocketbook. Kill Renata, kill me, then call Barnes, tell him he could have his wife back. But not until he raised the ante a bit. Meanwhile Barnes would have no choice but to wire another million or two, and all that time his talented young wife was dust anyway.

Renata could not have conjured a better plot herself.

But then, maybe Shaw had acted on Barnes's direct request. Maybe Barnes *wanted* his wife dead. And if he wanted his wife dead, he could very well want me dead. I had been a witness, after all, to the entire operation. Let's face it, I would have to go. The thing is, why bother sending me after his wife in the first place if, in the end, he wanted her dead? Why not simply let her rot in prison?

The answer was easy.

Because there was always the possibility that she could get out. Always the possibility that she could go public. That the public would find out about her predicament and how her rich husband hadn't lifted a finger to get her out. By rescuing his wife, Barnes could make himself look like the good guy. At the same time, he could make sure, once and for all, that she was dead.

Eight p.m.

The red neon light flashed on and off. My leg throbbed. Maybe my homemade bandage had been applied too tightly. Maybe I needed a codeine. Maybe two codeines and a drink. Another drink would definitely help the pain, help me decide what to do next.

I sat up, slid off the bed, grabbed one of the beers I'd packed on ice in one of the little plastic ice buckets. I cracked the cap, took a swig, sat back down on the bed.

Draped over the desk chair, my leather jacket, the restraining order still stuffed inside. A little worse for wear. I didn't have to read it to know what it said. That I should be treated with extreme caution; that by law I could not place myself within one hundred feet of Val Antonelli.

I picked up the phone, dialed nine for an outside line, and then punched in Val's number. She picked up after the third ring, said hello, a bit flustered, as though I'd caught her in the middle of something.

I swallowed a brick. Then I said, "Val."

She took a deep breath, released it. "Oh, my sweet Jesus," she said.

"I'm alive," I said.

For a full minute or more she just hung on the phone. Not saying anything. Just breathing hard. Until she gathered herself together. "What does that mean?" Voice calm, collected. Holding back. For now.

"I've been asking myself the same question lately."

"Please," she said. "Don't do this."

"Dying," I said. "It was all Tony's idea."

"What difference does it make now?"

"I went to Mexico on a job," I said. "It was better if certain people thought I'd died. But it's over now."

"I don't love you."

"I don't expect you to," I said. "I just wanted you to know."

"What you did…Standing me up…It's unforgivable."

"Can I see you?" I asked, taking a quick drink of my beer, setting it back down on the table.

"I have protection now," she said.

"It's just a piece of paper, Val. At least give me the chance to explain—"

"You don't have to," she said. "I know why you stood me up. So there's no point in talking about it."

"The black Buick," I said. "I saw it in the cemetery on Saturday. Tony's known about it for weeks. It could be the one."

"Fran's dead, Keeper," Val said.

"You don't understand," I said, glancing at Renata, asleep on the bed beside my own. "I'm closer than I've ever been."

"I can't compete with a dead woman," she said.

And then she hung up.

I drank the rest of my beer while Renata slept.

I opened another.

The room was dark, except for the red neon leaking in through the picture window. I lit up a cigarette and smoked it while watching the red light as it flashed against the wall and the ceiling. Sometimes I concentrated directly on the backward letters. Other times I just watched the smoke as it collected in swirling clouds that floated upward and dissipated.

Renata was on her back, breathing regularly now, her mouth opened just slightly, her left forearm stuffed under the pillow that supported her head. She was wearing a black leather jumpsuit that had small tears in the elbows and the knees. Her short auburn hair was mussed, her black boots set on the floor beside the bed. I knew she had a lot of sleeping to do to counteract the junk the Mexicans had been shooting through her veins for days on end.

As soon as we had checked into our motel room, she told me they had injected her with a sedative called Diprovat, which, according to Renata, actually slows the heart rate to a near death-like rhythm. The opiate was made in the US by a company called Zerline Pharmaceuticals. She knew this because she managed to study one of the empty vials her captors had accidentally left behind on the floor of her windowless cell.

But she also knew of the product because once she had assisted Richard in putting together a public-relations profile for Zerline, just a year before their son drowned.

Eventually the proposal was rejected, but she had learned that Diprovat was used mostly as a cardiac anesthesia and that it could also be used as a general anesthesia in MAC patients. When I asked her what MAC meant, she sleepily informed me that Monitored Anesthesia Care patients were generally nuts, psychotic, or just plain wacky, depending upon what side of the psychiatric fence you were standing on. Diprovat was utilized to keep them subdued, which is exactly what the Mexicans had been doing with the stuff. Drugging up their more rambunctious inmates. I had Renata's publicity package spread out all over the bed. The articles on the death of her child were lined up side by side. I had read them over three or four times in the past half hour. The more I read them, the more the words stayed the same.

It was time to contact Tony.

I tried his office. When I couldn't get him there, I tried his house.

"Where are you?" he said.

I told him we were back.

"What about Renata?" he said. "Is she alive? Because if she's not alive, we're dead."

Interesting way of putting it, I thought.

"She's alive," I said. "Sleeping like a baby."

"You were supposed to call me from the plane, *paisan*," he said. "We have a deal with Barnes. You have a deal with me."

"Hudson tried to kill Renata and me this morning."

Dead air.

"Did you hear me? Barnes's ace contact drove us both out into the desert, tried to shoot us in the back. Like that had been his plan all along."

"And you believe that was his plan?"

"Makes sense, doesn't it?" I said. "Barnes wants his wife dead. This Mexican thing provides him with the perfect opportunity. Hire a sap like me to go down and rescue her, give the impression of caring and concern. When she shows up dead, he blames the whole thing on me, says I was crazy over the death of my wife. He should have known better. Bad judgment on his part. And I'm not around to defend myself because I'm lying in the middle of the desert."

Tony said he didn't believe any of this. Not that I would lie. He just had a hard time believing he could be taken for a fool, even by a slick operator like Barnes.

Then I told him about the girls in the pool. About their slashed throats.

He let out all his air. He wasn't saying anything, but I knew how his brain worked. It was either believe me or allow his pride to get in the way of a quick solution.

On the bed beside me, Renata mumbled something and then rolled over.

"Did it ever occur to you that Hudson had a personal agenda? They're all bandits down there."

"What I know is what I believe," I said. "And I believe that Barnes has not played this one straight with you or me, old buddy."

"You don't know that," Tony said. "Not yet."

"He wanted her dead, Tony, and he wanted to blame it on me. Just like he would have blamed the deaths of those two women on me to prove what a psycho I am, and I think you know something about it."

"You don't think for a moment I would have betrayed our trust. For God's sake, I'm your friend, not your adversary."

"I don't know who to trust anymore, Tone," I said. "I don't know who to trust or where the hell to go, for that matter. The guy screwed us over. Do you hear what I'm saying? Shaw screwed me and Barnes screwed you. That's what it comes down to. That's what this is all about now."

I picked up the little article, the one with Renata and Richard walking out of the church, the Bald Man (or *a* bald man) walking out along with them.

"Tell me where you are. We can talk to Barnes together, get this thing straightened out."

"I'll decide when we get together," I said.

"At least tell me where you are."

"I'll tell you when I think you need to know, Tone," I said, my eyes fixed on the Bald Man.

"What about the girl?"

"She stays with me," I said, hearing Renata's deep sleeping breaths. "Until I get a better idea of what's happening."

"Keeper, wait," Tony pleaded.

I cut the connection.

CHAPTER FORTY-FIVE

RENATA AND I HAD TO MOVE.

Other than my apartment in Stormville, Coco's Motor Inn would be the first place Tony looked for us. I knew we had to get the hell out, find a new safe house. Do it quick.

First I packed up our things, set everything by the door. Then I called out for Renata. She stirred and propped herself up on her elbow.

"We have to leave," I said.

She sat up straight, slid herself off the mattress.

No arguments.

I stood by the door, looked out the window. Nothing in the parking lot other than a Ford pickup, a Chevy Malibu, and the Ford Explorer I'd rented at the Hertz counter at the Albany International Airport.

I turned and allowed the curtain to fall back. She was sitting on the edge of the bed now, groggily bending over her boots, zipping them up. Although we had hardly spoken at all on the plane (she slept for almost the entire five hours), we'd spoken enough for her to know I'd been hired by her husband to get her out of Monterrey Prison. But did she know that it had all been a charade, that he may have wanted her dead at my expense?

"If he wanted me dead," she had said from her window-side seat on our flight from Monterrey to Albany, "why would he send you after me?"

"Maybe to make it look like he wanted you rescued," I told her and let it go at that.

She asked me what I planned on doing next.

I told her I wanted to keep her with me. What I didn't tell her was that I was prepared to force her to stay. At gunpoint, if necessary.

"Until you figure something out?" she asked, her words coming slow and slurred, her head bobbing.

"Until I know it's safe," I said. "And that goes for the both of us."

But that's as far as I got before the captain asked us to fasten our seat belts and whatever Diprovat was left in her bloodstream knocked her out cold.

I grabbed my leather, slipped it on. I had a crewneck sweater in one of my honeymoon duffel bags. I tossed it on the bed for Renata to wear.

She asked me where we were going.

"New motel," I said, hitting the overhead light, drowning out the red neon that leaked in through the small space between the curtain and the window.

"So are you like my unofficial bodyguard now?" she asked, her eyes squinty in the white light.

"Something like that."

"Who exactly is it we're hiding from at this point?" she said.

"Like I already told you," I said, "we're hiding from your husband. And another man."

"What man?"

"My best friend."

"Doesn't sound like much of a best friend to me," she said.

I felt my heart sink when she said it.

Doesn't sound like much of a husband either, I wanted to say.

The setup of the second-floor room at the Airport Days Inn was basically the same as the room at Coco's Motor Inn. Same twin beds, same color TV mounted to a black, plastic swivel stand, same bathroom off to the left as you came through the door, same coin-operated bed vibrator, same FREE HBO.

We sat down on the bed beside each other, me in my leather jacket, Renata in my oversized gray sweater. I knew we were running out of time. Even the change of hotels didn't guarantee that we wouldn't be spotted in a day or two, or in the next five minutes, for that matter. Which meant I had to work fast. Find out first why Barnes might want his wife dead while paying Tony and me two hundred Gs to keep her alive. Then find out what Renata knew about the Bald Man. If there was any connection between them whatsoever.

I looked into Renata's eyes. They were blue and glazed over in the dim room light.

She breathed in and out. "You're looking for answers," she said, like a question.

I got right to the point.

I asked her if she could think of any reason in the world why her husband might want to have her killed.

She broke all eye contact with me, choosing instead to concentrate her gaze on the wallpaper directly in front of her. Wallpaper patterned with colorful fruits. Oranges, pears, lemons.

"In all seriousness, Mr. Marconi," she said, "I've always assumed my husband loved me very much."

I grabbed her arm, pulled her into me. Face to face. "I need real answers," I said. "Not some crap about how your husband loves you."

"I saved your life," she said, her voice trembling, verging on tears. "That's got to be worth something."

"I saved yours too. That makes us even."

I let go of her arm.

She put her head in her hands. The skin on her hands was pale—as pale as her face, anyway. Or maybe it was the way the skin looked in contrast to the black leather jumpsuit.

I went for my bag, set it up on the bed. I unzipped it and pulled out the publicity package. I opened the envelope and pulled out the article with the photograph of the grieving Barneses and the Bald Man following them out of the church.

"What can you tell me about this man?" I said.

I handed her the clip. She dried her eyes and sniffled. She stared at the black-and-white photo.

"What man?" she said.

Pressing the tip of my index finger against him. "The bald man with the sunglasses," I said. "What do you know about him?"

She stared at it a little longer. "No idea," she said.

She tried to hand the clip back.

I stepped away from her.

"The man was at your son's funeral service, Renata," I said. "You must know who he is."

I was trying to stay calm. I didn't want to scare her any more than I wanted to force her into admitting something that may not have been true.

She looked at the clip once more, brought it close to her face, as though she could actually see into the photo. Then she set it down on the pile of publicity material on the bed.

"I'll say it again," she said. "I have no idea who this man is or why he was at the funeral service. Perhaps he was a friend of Richard's," she said, waving her open hand in the air. "Or someone working for the governor."

I looked at her.

"The governor attended the funeral?"

"Richard worked for him. For his campaign. Maybe that man is a bodyguard or a driver. I really don't know."

I thought about the Bald Man. About the black Buick. A sedan, not unlike the kind of cars the Albany politicos drive around in with numbered license plates. I felt a slight jolt of electricity in my brain. Whether Renata knew it or not, she was answering my questions. Could it be possible that the Bald Man worked for the governor? And if he was working for the governor, had he been working directly with Wash Pelton, back when Wash was the commissioner for the Department of Corrections? If Wash had wanted me out of the picture because of the way I had come down on the drug trade at Green Haven Prison, it only made sense that he might hire a goon like the Bald Man to shake me up a little. It would have been risky on his part. A real reckless move. But a possibility all the same.

I put the clip back inside its folder with all the rest of the publicity material while I pursued another, not totally unrelated line of questioning.

But first I lit two cigarettes. One for me, one for Renata.

She inhaled hers slowly, with feeling. She exhaled a long, blue stream that floated to the ceiling. She was one of those people who made a cigarette look good.

"You never answered my question," I said.

"Which one?" she asked, taking another long drag.

"About your husband, Richard," I said. "Why he'd want to see you dead."

She smoked for a while longer, once again staring at the wall-paper. Until she looked up to me with those glazed blue eyes. "I assumed he had no idea," she said, the words barely leaving her lips.

"No idea about what, Renata?" I asked. I was pacing the floor now, from one end of the bed to the other.

"About the book I've been writing," she said. "The follow-up to *Godchild*. The true story behind Charlie's death."

"What story?" I said, spinning my right hand around and around, as if to coax her into telling me more.

"Mr. Marconi," she said, her hands set in her lap, the cigarette held between two fingers on her right hand. "Would you believe me if I told you my son's death was not an accident?"

I walked over to the small desk at the far end of the room.

I looked at Renata's image in the mirror. Her pale face seemed swollen now, her eyes filled with more tears.

"Tell me about it," I said into the mirror.

"Richard!" she screamed. So suddenly, I felt the shock of her voice shoot up and down the length of my spine. Like a French knife. Only sharper.

I turned, looked her in the eye. "Richard what?" I said.

"Richard is the key to the whole thing. The answer to all your questions."

She was openly crying now.

Sobbing.

"What key, Renata?" I shouted, slamming my fist against the desktop. "What! Key!?"

She let her head drop, chin against chest.

"I...am...so...tired," she said.

The cigarette between her fingers had burned all the way down. But it didn't seem to matter to her when she raised her head, slowly, and whispered, "The son of a bitch. He killed Charlie."

CHAPTER FORTY-SIX

SHE SEES HIM NOW, IN HER SLEEP.

He is kneeling on the floor of the bathroom, the water splashing against his clothes, as he holds the child down with outstretched arms.

But then, suddenly, he senses someone coming up behind him.

She knows he must feel her presence.

Because he turns fast and spots her. His wife.

Just before she smashes him in the head with the claw hammer.

CHAPTER FORTY-SEVEN

AFTER A TIME, RENATA STOPPED CRYING.

I tried to talk her into ordering out. Burgers, maybe, or a pizza from the joint across the street. Anything. She looked like a bag of rags and bones in that jumpsuit. But she refused ("How the hell can I eat?" were her exact words).

She smoked another one of my cigarettes, then curled herself up and went back to sleep.

An hour later, Renata was awake and sitting on the bed staring into the TV at CNN *Headline News*. Rather than risk leaving the room, I had found a nearby deli that delivered. I laid out a couple of rare roast beef sandwiches with Russian and horseradish and deli pickles, a can of Diet Coke for her and a bottle of Bud for me.

When we were finished I went to the window and checked the parking lot. The lot was full of cars I didn't recognize. But that didn't mean Tony or any of his Guinea Pigs weren't watching us right at that moment.

I lit a cigarette from the pack on the small desk and leaned back against it.

"Tell me more about this new book," I said.

Renata leaned back against the headboard of the bed. Only the wall-mounted fixture above her head had been turned on, bathing the room in a dim half light. Maybe it was my imagination, but she looked better since she'd eaten. A little color had returned to her face.

"There's not much to tell other than what I've already said. Richard killed him and that's what I've planned on writing about."

"Why keep it from the police for so long?"

She inhaled and then let the air out. "For a long time I wouldn't accept the truth, that my husband was capable of doing what he did to our little boy. The only way I could actually deal with it, on a personal level, was to write *Godchild*."

I smoked a little and drank some beer.

"I actually saw myself as a fictional character," she went on. "A woman who accidentally drowns her child." She breathed again, her face flushed. "Don't you see? I was blaming myself in place of Richard. Because I *allowed* him to get away with murder."

We were quiet for a time.

Then I said, "Can you tell me how it really happened and why?"

She twisted her head. "Not now," she said, lighting up another one of my smokes. "It's why I've been writing it down. It's how I deal."

"You can reveal the truth by writing it," I said. "But you can't get yourself to talk about it."

"Something like that, Mr. Marconi."

"Keeper," I offered.

She nodded.

"But if your husband were to find this book, Renata," I said, "if he were aware of its existence, he would want it destroyed and you along with it."

She nodded once more and stamped out the half-smoked cigarette in the little Days Inn ashtray.

"But he couldn't possibly know about it," she said. "I never told him."

"Where's the manuscript now?"

"It's at my home."

"The home you share with Richard in Loudonville." A question I already knew the answer to.

Another nod.

"A hell of a place to keep it," I said.

"It's not like you think, Mr. Marconi...Keeper," she said. "I have a place in the house where it is safely hidden. A place he doesn't know about."

"Is the book backed up on computer, something he'd have access to?"

"No. I wrote it on a manual, for just that reason."

"Carbons?"

"No."

She got up off the bed and went into the bathroom.

"Renata," I said through the door. "Are you certain you haven't told anyone about this book? Not your friends, not your publisher, not anyone?"

"I'm certain," she said, her voice barely audible above the sound of running water.

"Is it possible that your husband simply suspects you are writing this book? That his intuition tells him you're ready to tell the truth to the world?"

She said nothing. Or if she did I couldn't hear her.

I stepped away from the desk, knocked on the bathroom door, asked if she was OK.

Another knock.

Nothing.

I tried to open it. The door was locked.

"Renata," I shouted.

Just running water.

I rammed my left shoulder against the door, plowed it open. She'd opened the bathroom window and managed to squeeze her torso through the narrow slider.

I grabbed her by the legs, pulled her back in.

No resistance.

She sat down on the toilet lid and cried.

"Nice try," I said, slamming the slider closed.

"I'm sorry," she said. An apology not directed to me but to herself.

I was breathing hard. "Just promise me you won't do that again," I said. I put my hand on her shoulder. "Listen to me for a second," I said. "This is what it all comes down to. This is the reality of it all. Your husband has somehow gotten wind of your new book project. Because of it, he wants you dead, and naturally he wants to destroy any evidence of the manuscript. I suspect it's been his plan all along to blame your murder on me. But I'll tell you what, I've been accused of murder before and I don't plan to go through it a second time, understand? So please tell me you don't plan on running off again."

"Then what is it you want from me?" she asked through the tears.

"I want you to help me take your husband down before he gets another chance to take me down. Us down."

"And how do you propose to do that?"

I took a step back, pressed my back against the bathroom wall. "You've already done it for me," I said, "by writing that book."

"It's not done," she said.

"How much *is* done?"

"About half...a little more than half, maybe."

"How much time do you need to complete it?"

She shook her head. "You can't really estimate a thing like that—"

"If you work nonstop."

"Five days, maybe a week. But it won't read very well."

"I'm not looking for a masterpiece," I said. "I'm looking for information, the true story. An accusation strong enough to shift the burden of proof onto your husband."

"What about you?" she said. "What are you supposed to get out of all this?"

"First of all," I said, "I want the money Richard owes me. Second, I want him to admit he set me up, used me as a patsy. But I'll explain more during the ride."

"Where are we going?" she asked.

"Home," I said.

CHAPTER FORTY-EIGHT

BY TEN THIRTY WE WERE SITTING IN THE FRONT SEAT of the Ford Explorer, just outside Renata's Loudonville home. The half-dozen or so lamp lights that edged the long driveway were off. As were the lights in and around the massive center hall colonial. No sign of Richard anywhere. No cars outside the three-bay garage, no nothing.

"What are you going to do?" she said as I stepped out of the Explorer.

"Break in," I said.

"I know where everything is. I should go."

"Richard sees you, he'll kill you," I said. "I can't take that chance." I felt the cold wind blowing against my neck.

"There's an alarm."

"Give me the code."

She did. I repeated the four-digit code in my head until I had it memorized.

"I don't suppose you have a key," I said.

"No key," she said.

I went to close the door. But before all that, I reached inside, in the direction of the steering column, to pull the keys from the ignition, stuff them in the pocket of my jeans. Why take unnecessary chances? Why give her the opportunity to just drive away?

But then I looked at Renata and she looked at me.

Although we never said word one about it, I knew what she was thinking.

Can he trust me?

I took my hand away.

"Just give me a few minutes," I said.

"Whatever it takes," she said.

And then I closed the door.

Maybe it was a stupid move, leaving the keys like that.

But in the end, I knew it would be the perfect test.

I walked over the snow-crusted lawn to the back of the house, over the ice-covered patio to the back door. I brought my fingers to my mouth, blew warm breath on them, and punched the code into the electronic pad. The little red light above the keypad switched to green.

I took off my leather jacket, wrapped it around my right fist, punched out the bottom glass on the six-pane door. Then I put the jacket back on, reached in through the opening, and unlocked the dead bolt.

A second later, I was in.

The layout of the house matched Renata's description exactly, with the kitchen to my left, the family room just off the French doors leading out onto the back patio. Colt in hand, I made my way through the kitchen to the center hall and up the stairs, the stairwell so dark I could hardly make out the pistol in front of my face. But the night-light in the bathroom at the top of the stairs shined brightly enough for me to make out the long hall and the three or four bedrooms it accessed. I immediately made my way down the corridor.

Renata had told me to look for the manuscript in a writing room she had set up in what would have been Charlie's bedroom, had he survived, on the second floor of the house—the room directly across from Richard's home office. A square of wood floor lifted out from under the bed. I would find the manuscript there. All I had to do was get in, get the manuscript, get the hell out. Easy. The famous last word.

Renata's writing room.

I went down on my knees, felt around the floor for the edges of the cutout square. When I found it, I dug my nails into the crack and pried out the small piece of flooring. Laying the piece aside, I reached into the opening, felt the manuscript with my hand, and lifted it out. I replaced the flooring and got back on my feet.

At first I walked out of the room thinking that I had accomplished what I set out to do. But then I couldn't stop myself from drifting into Barnes's home office, directly across from Renata's. I suppose it was stupid. But I turned on the overhead light anyway and nearly fell flat on my back when I saw the three decapitated heads set on top of the wooden bookshelf mounted on the far wall. One head that appeared to have been hacked off by a hatchet with the eyes still wide open, the tongue sticking out red and purple, the face and wild hair spattered with blood. Then another head, this one the head of a woman with long blonde hair and a delicate mouth, her eyes closed as though she was asleep. The last head obviously had served as an exact replica of former New York Gov. Mario Cuomo. Of course, the heads were nothing more than very well-done special effects, the hauntingly real Cuomo head most likely coming from the 1995 and 1996 slash-and-burn campaign Barnes had orchestrated for Cuomo's Republican challenger.

I stood there, eyes closed, breathing hard and deep.

Turning away from the heads, I tried my best to survey the rest of the office without taking a second look. I caught my breath, tried like hell not to be reminded of Fran.

The decapitation.

The place was clean and neat. Too neat, as though it had never been used as an office at all. There was a long wooden desk and a file cabinet and some floor lamps. There was a green leather couch and matching club chair and a coffee table. I walked around the desk, tried the drawer. It was locked. I tried the file cabinet. Also locked.

Toward the back of the rectangular room was a large-screen television that took up the majority of the wall space. Mounted to the floor, about a half-dozen feet in front of the television, a chair with a heavy retractable bottom and thick cushions, like movie-theater seating.

The locked cabinet sat there in front of me.

I thought about shooting away the lock, going through the video library.

But time was getting tight.

I turned the light off in the room.

I felt a dryness in my mouth. There was a buzzing in my head. I had to leave this house. Renata had to get to work on the manuscript. She claimed it would take five days to finish it off. I could give her three days, no more.

I walked out of Richard's office, went back into Renata's room. I picked up her portable typewriter, cradled it in my arms. Like a mother and her godchild.

CHAPTER FORTY-NINE

SHE SITS IN THE PASSENGER SEAT OF THE EXPLORER.

The car is still warm from the heater. But now that it is turned off, she knows it's only a matter of time until the cold sneaks its way back in.

She is staring at the set of keys dangling from the ignition.

As soon as Keeper is out of sight, around the back of the house, she finds herself opening the door. Without even thinking about it, she has her hand on the door handle so that she can get out and get back in. Only this time, in the driver's seat. All she has to do to get out of this mess is start the engine, pull out, and head south. Or west. Or north.

What difference does it make so long as she's far away from this place?

She almost goes through with it.

But then something stops her.

Something makes her take her hand off the door handle.

She doesn't know if it's this man who rescued her—this raggedy, salt-and-pepper man who calls himself Keeper—who claims he is being set up right along with her. This man who insists she knows some Bald Man who just happened to attend Charlie's funeral.

She's never met any Bald Man.

She does not know any Bald Man.

What she does know is that somehow Richard has gotten wind of her new book. And because he knows, he will stop at nothing until he sees her dead. *He can make it look like an accident too. Richard Barnes, marketer extraordinaire, has that kind of power. That kind of connection to the right people.*

Or is it the wrong people?

Maybe that's why she takes her hand off the door handle. Maybe that's why she only stares at the car keys, never bothering to so much as place a fingertip to them.

This is not about her or Richard or this raggedy man who is after the truth.

This isn't about her life or anyone else's life, other than Charlie's.

About telling his life and death story.

And if Keeper Marconi is willing to keep her safe so that she can write the story—if he's willing to help put Richard away for what he did in the bathroom of their apartment—then she'd be dead wrong to stop him or to run away from him.

What she needs to do is stay with him. Work with him.

Not for her sake.

But for Charlie's.

PART FOUR

NO ANSWERS YET IN
SUSPECTED DEATH OF FORMER WARDEN

ALBANY (AP) - DNA tests failed to reveal the true identity of the body recently recovered inside the charred wreckage of a 1996 Toyota 4Runner belonging to former Green Haven warden turned private detective Jack "Keeper" Marconi.

Marconi is best known for having been falsely charged in 1997 in the shooting death of Eduard Vasquez, the convicted New York City cop-killer who escaped Green Haven Prison. But it wasn't until going on the run to produce the proof necessary to acquit himself and convict the true murderer—former Department of Corrections Commissioner Washington Pelton—that Marconi was able to vindicate himself.

Marconi did not returned to public service but chose instead to operate as a private consultant. Pelton was serving a life sentence at Clinton Correctional Facility for the murder of Vasquez when he died of stomach cancer last August.

Marconi, who for two years waged a campaign to locate the man accused of killing his former wife, Frances, in a 1996 hit-and-run, failed to show up for his wedding last Saturday to Albany native Valerie Antonelli. After being spotted at Bill's Bar and Grill on Watervliet Avenue, he disappeared. His badly burned 4Runner was recovered from the Hudson River a day later, riddled with 9mm bullet holes. The body discovered inside the wreckage had been burned beyond recognition, prompting a series of DNA tests that, thus far, have proven inconclusive.

CHAPTER FIFTY

WE WERE GOING ON OUR THIRD DAY AT THE DAYS INN.

It was only a matter of time until Tony and his Guinea Pigs found us. Not that he had even the slightest clue as to how and where to find us. But I'd never known Tony not to find a simple way around that kind of problem. He might check the address I used when I filled out the form for the rental car. He might check out the billing address of the credit card. But the address would have led him to my apartment in Stormville, ninety miles south of the Albany city limits.

Two things were certain: He knew I was somewhere in Albany and he knew I had Renata with me. How long we'd keep out of sight was his guess. Whether or not he had personally acknowledged to Barnes that we were back and that we were hiding out was anybody's guess. It was possible he had kept the whole thing to himself.

For now, while I lay back on the bed watching the early evening edition of CNN, Renata continued to work at the hotel desk, just as she had for the past three days. She worked incessantly, never coming up for air, on occasion breaking into tears or slamming her fist on the table, throwing herself on the bed, stuffing her face into the pillow.

She seemed mesmerized by her work. Transfixed on one hand, agonized on the other, as though recounting the experience of losing her child was not enough. She had to actually relive it in her mind, put herself through all the pain and suffering in order to get it right. Why was she putting herself through the misery? Had she decided to finish the manuscript just because I'd asked her to? Why hadn't she just split? In my mind, I knew she was finishing the job she had started simply because it had to be done. What's more, I knew that deep down she feared for her life. She already knew her husband was capable of murder. But in the end, so what if the manuscript could not be used as admissible evidence against her husband? As long as it got written, it could be used as an accusation. Anyone with a law-and-order background could tell you that when it came to murder, the accusation counted almost as much as the burden of proof.

Until the guilty were proven innocent.

Renata hardly ate or drank. She had been taking time out only to shower (which she did as often as four times a day). She hardly slept, catching only the occasional power nap for an hour or so at a time. She rarely spoke. The life she lived inside the motel room with me didn't seem to matter. It was the life she was living inside her mind that mattered—the past she shared with her two-year-old son and the father who allegedly killed him.

Late in the morning of the third day, I picked up a sheet of the carefully stacked paper and began to read:

When Richard came home from the office that night, his mood was black. He asked for Charlie. I told him that I was getting Charlie ready for his bath and reminded him that it was bath night. Instead of dinner, Richard fixed himself a drink. When that drink was gone, he fixed another, using less soda. Then he fixed another and yet another until he wasn't using any soda at all, rather, just straight whiskey from the bottle...

That's as far as I got before she ripped the page from my hand, looked at me with eyes that weren't eyes at all but mirrors that reflected her pain and hatred. Not for me, but for what she was writing. I realized then that the actual process of writing for Renata wasn't pleasurable. It was a drive, a force, a possession even. It was weird, but just watching her write gave me the creeps, like watching an addict shoot up. I couldn't imagine how anyone in his right mind would want to write for a living. But then, maybe the answer was inherent in the question. Whatever the case, I never dared to read another page. I never even took a chance while she was taking one of her many showers. I knew better than to betray the trust of the dead.

❖

Now I was leaning back on the bed, an open bottle of spring water by my side, the .45 resting on my lap, locked and loaded. I was watching TV to the now-familiar clatter of typing. *CNN Headline News* was running a story about fifteen school kids shot and killed in a peaceful Indiana cow town. Another story on mass graves uncovered in Mexico.

I drank some water.

CNN broke for a commercial. When the live local spot aired for an Albany car dealership in which a young woman was being interviewed by a salesman about her great new Chevy, I thought I could be hallucinating, that maybe in my exhaustion I was dreaming or seeing things. It wasn't the commercial itself that bothered me. It was the man who stood only a few feet away from the woman playing the part of the satisfied customer.

While Renata typed away, I got up off the bed, bottle of water in hand. I crouched before the TV, looked directly into it. There was no doubt in my mind. The man behind the woman was the

Bald Man. The same round John Lennon sunglasses, the same shaved head, the pencil-thin mustache, the tiny silver hoop in his left earlobe. He stood not more than three or four feet behind the woman while she spoke into the microphone.

I never noticed when the water bottle slipped out of my hand and fell to the carpeted floor.

Renata never noticed it either.

I went back to the bed and picked up the telephone.

Maybe the spot wasn't truly live after all. Maybe it simply had been made to look live in the cold darkness of a typical March night.

There was only one way to tell.

I flipped on the lamp, looked up the number for the local cable television station in the yellow pages. I dialed the number and got the woman who worked the night shift. I inquired about the commercial spot. How could I find out if it was live or Memorex?

"Hold on," she said, fuzzy Muzak now pouring into my head.

A minute later she came back on the line.

"Live," she said. "They have three top-of-the-hour spots left, including eleven o'clock."

"Can you tell me who's producing the commercial?"

She let out a breath, slightly exasperated. I could hear the sound of pages flipping. "Reel Productions," she said.

"Bingo," I said.

"Excuse me?" the woman said.

I hung up the phone.

First I grabbed my leather. Then I checked the .45, made sure I had the three extra clips stuffed inside the interior pocket of the jacket. I holstered the weapon once more. Afterward I bent down and spoke softly to Renata.

"I have to go out," I said. "For a little while."

She kept right on typing, pulling out the pages as she completed them, piling them in a neat stack, facedown so I couldn't read them.

"I'm going to lock the door from the outside," I said. "Don't open it for anyone. Do you understand me, Renata?"

She nodded to her typewriter.

But she understood. I knew I could trust her not to leave. But just to be safe, I disconnected the telephone. It felt like the right thing to do under the circumstances.

I locked the door behind me when I left the room.

I was off to check out some new Chevys.

CHAPTER FIFTY-ONE

CAPITAL CITY AUTO CENTER WASN'T ONE OF THOSE RUN-of-the-mill used-car lots with dozens of colorful flags hanging from light poles and bright spots illuminating a lot full of freshly detailed used cars and trucks that didn't work for spit underneath the paint.

Instead, it looked more like a mall for cars. A modern-day marketing marvel. Complete with electronically controlled gas pumps, brushless car wash, five-star restaurant and bar (Drag Racers), specialty shops, and thousands of cars.

Used and new.

Tonight the lot was lit up not with the usual strategically positioned halogens, but with spotlighting for two or three shoulder-mounted TV cameras. Parked in the lot, beside the huge metal-and-glass building that housed the showroom, was a large van with a satellite dish mounted to the roof. Printed on the side of the van were the words Reel Productions.

A man approached me just as I stepped out of the Explorer at the edge of a sea of brand-new Chevy cars, trucks, and vans. A tall, thin man with the face of a rat, who wore a tan polyester suit, loafers covered with black rubbers, and a hooded Kmart parka for an overcoat.

"I'm Bob," he said, bare hand extended, smile plastered from ear to ear on his gaunt rat face. "How can I help you?"

I looked over his shoulder at the mobile camera crew film-ing the same brown-haired girl I'd just seen on television at the

Days Inn, standing between the camera and a brand-new, baby-blue SUV. Although I was out of earshot, I could plainly see her jumping for joy over what a hell of a buy the SUV was. But when the director—a man in a red down vest with black headphones wrapped around his neck—crisscrossed his hands overhead as if to say, "Cut," I could tell they were running through a rehearsal.

So far, no sign of the Bald Man.

"New wheels?" Rat Face asked, as if to snare my complete and undivided attention from the television crew.

"The SUV over there," I said, pointing over the hoods of the cars at the film crew. "The baby-blue one."

"We're running a live promo," Rat Face said, using his left arm as a pointer. "So it's going to be a bit tough to take a good look at that particular automobile." He started walking toward the opposite side of the lot. "But if you'll come with me, I'll gladly walk you through a variety of SUVs we have in stock."

I started toward the film crew, taking the most direct path I could manage between the cars and trucks.

"Sir, I'll have to ask you to come this way."

I ignored him, kept on walking.

Now the director was wearing the headphones over his ears. He held a clipboard in his right hand. "Ten seconds," I heard him say as he stared at his watch, right hand raised high overhead, the bright stand-mounted spotlights aimed at the face of the brown-haired girl.

"Five seconds," the director said, beginning the backward count. When he got to number one, he formed a pistol with his right hand, pointed it at the girl, brought down his thumb.

That's when he came out of the showroom and stepped into view.

The Bald Man. *My* Bald Man. Dressed in black jeans and combat boots, a black turtleneck to match.

"Welcome back to Capital City Auto Center," the girl said in a happy singsong voice.

I made my way up to the edge of the cars and stopped.

Rat Face Bob was on my tail. He grabbed at my leather jacket. "Sir," he whispered in my ear. "I'm going to have to insist—"

"Bob," I said, turning toward him. "Shut the hell up."

The Bald Man turned toward me, caught my glare.

He did a double take.

He breathed white vapor out his mouth.

He took a couple of steps toward me. He must have stepped within range of the camera lens, because the director started waving his right arm violently, mouthing, "Get out of the way, get out of the way..." over and over again.

My heart was beating in my throat.

Brown-haired girl kept on talking into the mike anyway, her face angled at the camera but her eyes most definitely shifting to me. Because suddenly I was the center of attention.

Until finally the Bald Man turned, bolted.

I took off after him, knocking one of the bright, mobile television lamps to the pavement, the huge bulb exploding like a grenade when it hit the frozen blacktop, forcing the director and the brown-haired girl to hit the pavement. Both of us sprinted, dodging around the parked cars and trucks. Until I hopped up on the hood of a green Chevy Malibu, then onto the hood of the cherry red Malibu beside it and the tan Dodge Dakota beside that.

I sucked the cold wind and I ran as fast as my legs would take me and I narrowed the space between us to three cars.

Maybe two.

One more and I could have cut him off before he got to the end of the lot.

I would have made it too, if it hadn't been for the white-hot explosion against the back of my head...and the cold darkness that followed.

CHAPTER FIFTY-TWO

THE FIRST THING I SAW WHEN I CAME TO WAS THE blurry outline of two people standing at the foot of a bed. After a few seconds of blinking and breathing, I was able to get a better fix on them.

Tony Angelino and Detective Mike Ryan.

Four walls surrounded me.

Capital City Auto Center had disappeared.

So had the Bald Man.

My head hurt. A lot.

At least my leg didn't hurt anymore. If it did, it hadn't registered yet.

"Look who's awake," Tony said, as if I were a toddler waking up from a mid-afternoon nap.

He had on his dark blue, double-breasted suit underneath a charcoal overcoat, a matching navy-blue fedora resting back on his head. In the corner of his mouth, a toothpick bobbed up and down when he moved his lips.

"Two hours," Ryan said, not to me, but to Tony. "Not bad." He crossed his arms at his chest, a gold claddagh ring visible on the third finger of his left hand. He was still wearing his leather blazer, even indoors, his thin black tie pulled down a few inches on his chest.

When I tried to lift my head, it felt like it had been run over by a squad car. I decided not to lift it again.

"You got one hell of a lump," Tony said. "You've been unconscious for a couple of hours."

"Baseball bat," Ryan said. "Some guy named Bob. Salesman at Capital City."

I breathed a little.

"They also took care of that little flesh wound in the back of your left thigh," Tony said. "They had to reopen it."

"As a lawman you should know better than to attempt aggravated assault in front of so many witnesses," Ryan said. "And you should also know better than to fake your own death." He tossed a folded newspaper onto the bed. "I can get you two-to-five for that little charade. Or maybe a nice little stay in the nuthouse. I'm not even gonna ask where you appropriated the cadaver."

I looked at Tony.

He was looking at the floor. Apparently Ryan hadn't guessed his role in the staging of my sudden and unfortunate passing. I suppose it all made a hell of a lot of sense.

No doubt about it, I had to suck this one up.

A nurse walked in. She slipped a battery-operated thermometer under my tongue.

I looked at Tony and Ryan while the plastic thermometer did its job. They both gave the nurse a couple of up-and-down looks.

When the thermometer beeped, she pulled it back out, stared at the readout, and set it beside the sink in the little alcove near the bathroom. "Good," she said.

"Are you going to be giving him a sponge bath?" Tony said. "We can step outside if you like. Or perhaps it would be better if we just averted our eyes?"

Ryan couldn't keep from laughing. He brought his fisted right hand up to his mouth to hide his smile.

The nurse ignored Tony. She went out into the hall and came back with a little paper cup, which she handed to me. Inside the cup were two bright red, sugarcoated caplets. Tylenol, I assumed. It hurt to look at them. I swallowed them while she filled up a plastic jug with water from the sink and then set it on a portable stand beside the bed. She began filling a cup with the water. But I grabbed the pitcher right out of her hand, taking a long, deep drink. When I'd had my fill I wiped my mouth with the back of my hand and set the pitcher back down again on the portable stand.

"Oh my," she said. "Aren't we thirsty."

"Lady," I growled. "You have no idea."

She turned to Tony and Ryan. "Gentlemen," she said, "I suggest you make your conversation a quick one. Mr. Marconi has suffered a mild concussion and he needs his rest."

When the nurse was gone, Tony pulled a hip flask from his right-hand overcoat pocket. He unscrewed the little sterling silver cap, took a deep drink. Then he handed the flask to Ryan. Ryan drank and passed the flask to me.

I decided to pass.

Tony took the flask back, shoved it into the side pocket of his overcoat.

In my head I pictured Renata. I prayed to Christ she was still safe and sound inside the motel room. I looked at Tony. "The Bald Man," I said. "I saw him."

Tony ran the index finger on his right hand across his throat like a knife, stopping me in mid-sentence. "Mike has something to tell you, *paisan*."

"Reel Productions wants to press assault charges," Ryan said.

I pictured Barnes's face. The prominent cheeks, the slicked-back hair, the wireless glasses.

"You tried to assault one of their employees," Ryan went on. "Barnes is convinced you're a madman, that you were trying to kill that man." The cop poked at his nostrils with the forefinger and thumb on his right hand.

I managed to prop myself up on my left elbow. "You stupid cop," I said. "It's him. The Bald Man. The man who killed my wife."

"Keeper," Tony said. "That man's name is Leonard Kauffman. He's forty-six years old and he's been a production manager at Reel Productions for more than five years now. He's married with a wife and kids, lives in the burbs. Church on Sundays; pickup basketball games on Monday nights at the high school; PTA meetings once a month. He's the guy you saw in the newspaper clipping."

"It's him, Tony," I insisted. "I know it."

"You don't know it," Tony said. "Yeah, he's bald; yeah, he's got an earring. So do a hundred thousand other guys going through a midlife crisis."

In my mind, the Bald Man staring at me from the driver's seat of his battered Buick on the warm spring morning. Before he turned around, peeled away from the scene of the crime.

"It all makes sense," I said. "You said yourself the Buick's been spotted around town. The Bald Man suddenly shows his face. He works for Barnes. Barnes tried to have me killed."

Ryan looked cross-eyed at Tony. "What in the world is he talking about?"

"Must be the head injury," Tony said.

I sat up straight. "You listen to me," I said. "That Bald Man killed my wife. He drives a black Buick." I looked into Tony's eyes. "He recognized me, Tony. Don't you get it? That's why he ran away. He recognized me when I showed up at the lot."

"Maybe you should calm down, Keeper," Tony said. "You've had a tough—"

"It doesn't change what I saw!" I shouted. But what I really wanted to shout out was how Barnes had hired me to find his wife, how he most likely had attempted to have the both of us killed. And now that he knew I was in town hiding his wife, he wanted to have me busted. But I couldn't say a word about it. Not a single word. All in the interest of preserving the Tony Angelino Experience.

"You know what I'm getting at, Ryan," I insisted. "Because you were there. You took my testimony. Your man took a description of the car."

Ryan crossed his arms at his chest. He wasn't looking at me. He was looking at the floor. His expression was the same one I recognized from the cemetery a few days before when I first spotted the black Buick. It was a tight-lipped smile. More like a smirk I would have gladly knocked off his face, if I'd had the energy and if it wouldn't get me busted.

"Obsessive-compulsive disorder," Ryan said, with a shake of his head. "That's all this is. Severe O.C.D. It causes people to be unable to distinguish between actually witnessed events and things they just imagined. It's nothing to be ashamed about. I once worked on a case about a guy who got fired from his job because he was always late for work. At this specific spot near his home, he imagined himself running over a little kid. I mean, the crazy bastard would drive around the block something like twenty-five times to make sure he hadn't made roadkill out of some innocent kid who existed only in his mind. Eventually he killed himself. And that's what worries me more than anything. The mock staging of your death this time can simply be the prelude to something slightly more real and certainly more permanent next time."

"You've been under a lot of strain, Keeper," Tony said, eyes wide, taking a step forward, once again holding out his hip flask for me. "You need some rest."

I knocked the flask away, onto the floor.

"Barnes is behind all this," I said, lying back on the bed again, my head on the pillow, a distinct dizziness settling in. "Just like he's behind the attempted murder of his own wife. Barnes is behind everything. He owns Reel Productions. This isn't rocket science, and you can't go around protecting him just because he's your client."

"What attempted murder?" Ryan said. "What the hell is he talking about?"

"He's delirious," Tony said, looking at me with wide, shut-the-hell-up eyes.

Then the bed-spins started kicking in.

"Look, it's not that we don't believe you," Tony explained, bending over, picking up his flask from the terrazzo floor. "It's just that there's no evidence to suggest the man working for Barnes is the same man who killed Fran."

"You can find him in the employ of Richard Barnes," I said.

But it was no use. If Tony, my advocate, didn't believe me, then you could bet Ryan wouldn't believe me either. So what was the point? And besides, the room had begun to spin like crazy, my head getting suddenly heavy. The red pills, I thought. The red pills weren't Tylenol after all. The red pills must have been sedatives.

Ryan took another step forward, closer to the bed. "All we know about Barnes's wife is that she is officially reported missing. Richard seems to believe you know of her whereabouts. Now why in the world would he make such an accusation, Mr. Marconi?" He slid his thumbs inside his black belt. "We have witnesses at the airport and at the Hertz rent-a-car who claim they saw two people matching your descriptions only three days ago. We have what looks like your signature on the credit slip."

"Now just a moment, Detective Ryan," Tony said. "There's no reason in the world to believe my client has any knowledge whatsoever as to the location of Mr. Barnes's wife."

There, I thought. Finally Tony said something I wanted him to say. No, that's not right either. For a change, he said what I needed him to say. Maybe he was covering for me after all. He knew goddamned well I was hiding Renata. And yet there was still the possibility that he was going to bat for me. Maybe in the end he was playing Ryan like a well-tuned fiddle, sometimes stroking him lightly, other times playing him hard as hell.

Despite my trouble focusing, I kept my eyes on Tony, as though he were running a shell game. And in a way, he was.

"I've personally managed to persuade Barnes to hold off his dogs on the assault charge for now, Keeper," Tony went on, his voice sounding as though he were talking through a cardboard tube. "But I won't be able to keep him at bay for long. There are time limits to these things." He turned to Ryan. "But as far as your accusations on the location of Renata Barnes, Mike, I find them outrageous and unfounded."

"We'll see," Ryan said, in that same through-the-tube voice. "Until Barnes presses charges, you're off the hook, Keeper. For now I've asked Tony to stay on your ass. Until whatever is going on with you calms down a little."

"Perfect," I mumbled, but I couldn't be sure if I was dreaming the words or not.

Ryan started for the door. But then he stopped.

"Oh," he said, "and there'll be one more thing."

I stared up at the ceiling. I felt like I was falling. But not afraid to fall.

"I'll need your weapon and your license."

The wall-mounted lights behind the bed reflected off the smooth white surface of the ceiling like two shiny circles. Out of the corner of my eye, I saw Tony walk over to the closet near the door to the room. He reached inside, grabbed my shoulder holster and the .45 it held from the hook. Then he approached the bed and the nightstand beside it. He opened the drawer, pulled out my wallet, slid out the laminated pistol permit, and shut the drawer. "Why don't I hold onto this stuff until this blows over," he said to Ryan. "There's no reason to make this official until we have to *make* it official, *capisce?*"

Ryan thought about it for minute. "OK," he said. "But if anyone asks, it's your ass I'm gonna point my finger at, Angelino."

"Fair enough," Tony said, giving me a wink.

I was too tired to wink back. But not too tired to see Tony go through the pockets of my leather jacket, taking my car keys, stuffing them into his pocket along with a book of matches that had "Airport Days Inn" printed on it. He made eye contact with me, coughed into his hand, and gave me a telltale wink. I became convinced then that he was playing along, going as far as he could to keep Ryan amused and satisfied. I was also convinced he had to play the game as delicately as possible in order to save his own ass and, in the long run, mine.

He turned to the young cop. "Look, Mike," he said. "This is just a temporary setback for Keeper. You have to understand all he's been through. For instance, did you know he wasn't even eighteen years of age when he survived the Attica uprising..." He went on and on, just like that, explaining and detailing the more violent portions of my life—from the four-day-and-night Attica Prison siege in 1971, to Fran's hit-and-run, to my trouble with former Commissioner for Corrections Wash Pelton only a few years ago. He started in on it all as though it would explain why I'd officially gone off the deep end. But as Tony's voice thinned out and trailed off into silence and the circles on the ceiling joined together, I fell off the edge of the world.

CHAPTER FIFTY-THREE

IT'S HOURS BEFORE SHE REALIZES HE'S GONE.

No.

That's not right either.

It's hours before she actually misses him.

She knew he was gone from the moment he left. From the very second he claimed he saw the Bald Man on the television, then grabbed his jacket and his pistol and left the room, locking the dead bolt behind him.

What is it, this obsession with a bald man?

She is nearly done with the manuscript. Just a few fleeting pages away from the ending of her story. Charlie's life-and-death story.

Just in time too, because she hears footsteps now, coming down the exterior hall. More than one set of footsteps. It's two in the morning. It's got to be Keeper. But who else could be with him? At this hour? She knows she should get up from the desk, walk over to the window, pull back the curtain just enough to get a glimpse at them. But she's got only a page to go.

One more page.

The page on which Charlie dies.

All over again.

CHAPTER FIFTY-FOUR

THIS TIME WHEN I WOKE UP, I WAS IN A COMPLETELY different room.

This room colder than the last.

Smelly.

Like a pile of rain-soaked worms.

A big, narrow room full of beds, like an infirmary.

The head of my bed was pressed up against a wide window. A sunbeam shone in through the uncovered glass, making a bright yellow parallelogram on the floor between my bed and the one directly to my right. In the near distance, the voice of a man begging for a cigarette. "Gimme a cigarette," the man repeated over and over. "Gimme a cigarette."

My head wasn't hurting anymore.

It just felt heavy, like my brain had been replaced with wet cement.

But no real pain to speak of.

I moved my hands, my feet, my legs. I breathed in and swallowed. When I sat up and turned to look out the window, the bright sun stung my eyes. But then my eyes adjusted and I could make out a wide piece of glass reinforced with chicken wire. I also made out the vertical iron bars that covered the window on the outside. Because I'd been placed on the top floor of the building, I saw only the highest level of the concrete parking garage directly across from the lot and what I immediately recognized as New

Scotland Avenue, the main north-south artery that ran smack-dab down the middle of what had to be the Capital District Psychiatric Center campus.

The bastards must have transferred me overnight while I was passed out.

I knew that they kept us here under lock and key and constant observation.

House arrest.

In the loony bin.

"Excuse me, sir," came a voice from beside my bed. A meek, mousy voice.

I turned back around. The man to my right was sitting up. "Do you know what time it is?" A middle-aged man with a round, clean-shaven face, thin lips, and a hooked nose. His hair was thin if not balding, cut over stick-out ears, parted with precision on the left-hand side of his round skull. He was rubbing his left wrist where a wristwatch should have been.

I went to look at my own watch.

The watch was gone.

All my things were gone—clothes, watch, jacket, shoes.

All of it.

The only things I had left were my boxer shorts and a white dressing gown that tied down the front. I remembered Tony taking my gun and my license. But what I had no recollection of was him taking the clothes off my back.

"Time," the man said again. "Do you know what time it is?"

I turned back to him. "No, pal," I said, "I don't."

"What would you say then?" he asked. "If you had to guess. The time, I mean."

A slight sickness bubbling up from my stomach.

A distinct nausea that went with waking up in a nuthouse.

I had to breathe and get my bearings.

I tried to turn off the Mickey Mouse voice of the little man and concentrate on the dozen beds pushed up against the hospital-white wall directly across from me, the half-dozen or so beds to my left, and the equal number to my right. Dozens of men laid out either on their backs, snoring away, or curled up in fetal position. All of them still caught up in the midst of some drug-fed sleep.

"Please," the mouse said again. "The time."

I turned to him. "For all I know," I said, "it could be four in the afternoon." But I knew it had to be early morning.

"Oh my," said the man, "I have to be getting to work." He swung the sheets and covers off his bed, revealing a pair of skinny white legs peppered with curly black hair. "You're new here," he said. "But where are my manners?" He reached inside the opening of his gown. He pulled his hand back out, his little fingers pressed together, as if pretending to hold something in them. "Edward Pukas," he said. "That's P-U-K-A-S. My card."

Poor bastard. With a name like that, no wonder he went nuts.

I pretended to take the pretend card in hand and stuff it into the pretend pocket of my pretend suit jacket.

"I'm a stockbroker," Pukas said, lifting a pair of eyeglasses set in heavy black frames from the table between our beds. He slipped them on.

"What's yours?" he asked, the muscles in his face doing all sorts of contortions, constrictions, and contractions, as though to get used to the weight of those glasses.

"What's my what?" I said, now searching the entrance and exit ways for who might be manning them. As far as I could see, no one. But mounted on the walls, in the corners, video surveillance cameras.

"What's your game? You know, what do you do?"

Suddenly the four televisions mounted high up on the opposite wall, set between the video cameras, spontaneously turned on to the *Today* show. The bright face of the mannequin-pretty broadcaster beamed live, directly to the psycho ward. "I'm self-employed," I went on, trying to shrug him off. "Securities."

"Securities," he said, "as in stocks and bonds?"

"Securities as in life and death," I said.

"Oh, that sort of securities," he said, bobbing his head, half-smiling, half-frowning, not at all sure which emotion he wanted to go with. "Great business. Wave of the future. Going to be ten billion people in the world in the next ten years. Ten billion, my friend. Do you have any idea what that means? Do you have any idea the amount of security each individual is going to require as his personal space becomes more and more confined? Do you have any clue as to the demands all those people will have on the food supplies of this nation, of the world? Not to mention the pestilence and the disease, the infestations that will attack the starving little children in the night, eating their eyes out like maggots? Yes, sir, securities is the business to be in."

I felt like slapping Mr. Pukas.

But then the double doors crashed open to a small gang of men and women dressed in white, pushing carts and carrying black plastic trays, shouting, "Good morning, people!"

As they approached us with their carts, I had to wonder how *I'd* gotten here in the first place. I figured that Ryan must have ordered it. But then, had Barnes gone ahead and pressed charges? Whatever the case, I knew that it would take at least a day for Tony to counter the order, get me released on bail or my own recognizance or whatever they do inside the nuthouse. In the meantime, I had to wait it out. I had to hope and pray that Renata stayed put. I had to hope and pray that no one, save Tony, found her.

Two orderlies—the first a short white man with a goatee and long sideburns, the second a very large black man with tattoos running down the length of his right arm—stood at the foot of my bed.

"Nice to have you with us, Mr. Marconi," Short Goatee said, approaching me with a little paper cup in his hand. The kind used for dispensing meds. "Will you be breakfasting in or out today, sir?"

Funny.

"How about breakfast in bed?" Goatee went on, handing me the cup with a set of red pills identical to the ones the nurse had given me the night before. He bent just slightly at the knees, brought his lips to my right ear. "Now you listen to me, motherfucker," he said. "I know who you are and I know why you're here, and if you fuck up for even a second, even for one split second of time…if you so much as spit, fart, or cough, I'll bust your ass and toss you into the rubber room. Do I make myself perfectly clear, Mr. Marconi? Because if I don't, my pal Leon has ways of making the blind see." He stood up. "Don't you, Leon, baby?"

Leon smiled and flexed the biceps on his right arm. Muscle nearly popped out of the white T-shirt. Nice bedside manner, these two orderlies.

"Everybody understand one another?" Short Goatee said, straightening back up.

"Cozy," I said, tipping the contents of the paper cup into my mouth, chasing it with the cup of water Leon handed me.

I smiled at Short Goatee, winked at Leon.

As they approached Mr. Pukas with the med carts, I rolled over, turned my back to them.

"But I have to be back at work in less than an hour," I heard Mr. Pukas say.

"Sure you do, Eddy," Short Goatee responded as I stuck my left index finger in my mouth, scooped out the meds, stuffed them in between the mattress and the box spring, just like I'd seen someone do in a movie once.

"Please, don't do this," I heard Mr. Pukas say as I rolled over onto my back to get a better look. Out of the corner of my right eye, I saw Leon walk to the head of the bed, saw him hold Mr. Pukas down flat on his back while Short Goatee undid the zipper on his white pants and pulled out his sex. I saw him stuff it into Pukas's mouth.

"And if you bite me, Mr. Pukey Eddy Pukas," he said, not even bothering to muffle his voice, "there'll be no milk or cookies for dessert. Do we understand each other?"

"Gimme a cigarette," came the voice of a crazy old bastard.

"Suck it," came the voice of Short Goatee.

CHAPTER FIFTY-FIVE

FOR ALMOST THREE HOURS, I PRETENDED TO PASS IN and out of sleep.

I snored a couple of times when Leon and his little buddy passed by.

For the sake of realism.

As for Mr. Pukas, he passed out not long after his interlude with Short Goatee. He lay on his side, curled up under his blue hospital blanket, the thumb of his right hand stuffed inside his mouth like the perpetual four-year-old to which these sadistic bastards had reduced him.

On more than one occasion, I thought about just taking my chances. Getting up, heading for the double doors, walking out. But I knew that when those video monitors caught me in their lenses, those men in white would come running. I'd be dragged down, thrown in restraints, tossed into some kind of lockdown.

The rubber room.

Sedation city.

❖

The house doctor made his rounds at a little past noon. Just as the morning meds were wearing off and the orderlies had begun to assist the patients to a small dining area at the far end of the corridor for lunch.

The ones who could walk, anyway.

He was a tall, thin man in his late fifties, with a high forehead and slicked-back gray hair and wide blue eyes. Like most doctors, he wore a long white overcoat. The overcoat had a chest pocket that housed a couple of ballpoint pens.

He took one of the pens from his pocket, pulled the chart that had been hanging on the end of my bed. Depressing the back of the pen, he quickly jotted something down on the chart, then set it back on its hook.

He approached me, a bright smile plastered on his narrow face, introducing himself as Dr. Matthew Pearl.

"How's your head this afternoon, Mr. Marconi?" he said, voice calm, soft, singsongy.

"Why am I here?" I asked.

He fake-laughed. "You're here to get better," he said.

I sat up fast.

"Let me use a phone," I said.

"I'm afraid that's just not possible," he said.

I grabbed his shirt collar. "You can't keep me here," I said.

"We have a c-c-court order." Pearl, struggling to form his words. "I'd be h-h-happy to show you."

Leon and Short Goatee came running.

"Drop him, asshole," Short Goatee shouted.

Leon grabbed me by the hair. He yanked so hard I thought he tore the scalp right off my skull.

I let go of Pearl.

He jumped away from the bed, brushed back his gray hair with open hands, ran them down the front of his white overcoat. He breathed in.

"You want I should shoot him up, Doc?" Goatee suggested.

Beside my bed, Edward Pukas mumbled something indiscernible in his sleep.

"Just bring him to my office," Pearl whispered. "No sedation."

He turned and walked away.

Leon grabbed hold of my smock, pulled me out of bed.

I went down on the floor, hard, onto my side. When he bent over to pick me up, I made a fist with my right hand and clocked him in the mouth.

His lower lip exploded in a haze of red blood.

"You little freak!" he screamed, grabbing on to my throat, picking me up by my neck.

Short Goatee came running.

"Leon," he shouted, gripping the big man's right arm. "Let him down."

Leon tightened his grip. He was breathing in and out with fat, pursed lips, blood and spit spraying in my face. I felt the initial burst of pain. Then I felt my Adam's apple get set to pop. I started to black out.

But just like that, Leon released his hold.

I fell back down to the floor. Leon kicked me in the kidney. The pain shot through my side, through my back. I tried to swallow. My throat felt like it had been scraped with a pipe cleaner. My head was on fire. I vowed never to fight the big man again. Not without a gun.

"You ready to go now?" Goatee said, grabbing my arm, pulling me up off the floor.

I struggled to my feet, still doubled over. "Yeah," I whispered.

"Good," he said. "Because I ain't got all day to screw around with nutcases."

In the corner of my eye, I could see Leon wiping blood from his nose with the back of his hand. "You whack me again, little man," he said as I started hobbling past the rows of beds, "I don't stop till you're dead."

"Ain't gonna be a next time, Leon," I said.

CHAPTER FIFTY-SIX

PEARL'S OFFICE WAS SHAPED LIKE A SQUARE.

To the right of his desk was a floor-to-ceiling window-wall that looked out over a small glade. I knew the glade must serve as a sort of peaceful walking area for patients during the warm months of the year. Now the glade was dead, the trees as barren and broken-looking as the patients themselves.

The pain in my kidney had mellowed.

Enough for me to stand up a little straighter.

A brown leather couch had been pushed up against one wall decorated with custom-framed prints. One print depicted three white Adirondack chairs set on a peaceful-looking plot of over-grown grass surrounded by shrubs. Another showed wild horses in full gallop, racing around a spacious pasture. And another I recognized as a signed Jenness Cortez, with racehorses taking off from the starting gate of the Saratoga racetrack.

I sat down on the couch, still groggy, head throbbing, staring directly ahead at the numerous framed medical diplomas tacked to the wall behind Pearl's leather swivel chair. Instead of sitting in the chair, Pearl set one leg up on the edge of the desk, crossed his arms.

Casual, unaffected.

Leon, now with a bloodstained handkerchief pressed up against his face, sat on one arm of the leather couch while Short Goatee sat on the other.

"Why do you insist on fighting us, Mr. Marconi?"

"I'm being kept here against my will."

"Now if I had a dime for every patient forced to stay here against their will..." He let it hang while rolling his eyes, raising his hands in the air.

"That's not what I mean," I said, looking first at Leon, then at Short Goatee.

"Are you suggesting you were somehow framed?"

"I'm suggesting that someone has manipulated a specific series of events to suit their own purposes," I said. "And I know who the son of a bitch is."

"That's a normal schizophrenic reaction to an otherwise undesirable situation, such as being placed inside a psychiatric treatment center when you'd rather not be."

"I'm not schizophrenic."

"Schizophrenia is nothing to be ashamed of, Mr. Marconi," he said, a phony smile plastered on his skull face. "Many schizophrenics lead normal, everyday lives with the help of medication. Now, on the other hand, would I give a schizophrenic permission to carry a firearm? That's a different story entirely."

He reached over onto his desk, picked up a piece of paper, and handed it to me. Written at the top of the paper was the number 813.12, Family Restraining Order and Injunction. A copy of Val's original order filed with the county clerk. I crumpled the paper up, threw it to the floor.

"You know what I think, Pearl?" I said, right index finger aimed at his face. "Someone wants to take me out of circulation, and I believe you're being paid to help them out."

"Is that what you think? Then you should know that about one in one hundred will suffer from schizophrenia at some point in their lives. And the numbers will skyrocket with the coming decades. So you have terrific company. Like yourself, there are plenty of people who suffer from disorders of thinking or delusions, such as the one you suffered not long ago in the Albany Rural Cemetery about seeing the very black Buick that smashed into your car some years back, killing your wife, Fran. Then there is the Rambo-style shooting up of a public watering hole, followed by the faking of your own murder, and finally chasing down an innocent man at an automotive sales facility. And now we have accusations floating around over the whereabouts of Renata Barnes, the novelist—accusations that could very well point to you, Mr. Marconi."

"I have no idea what you're talking about," I said.

"Of course you don't," he said. "But then, that's a part of it, isn't it? Denial."

A buzzer went off outside the office, then a muffled announcement over the house PA. A doctor by the name of Dubin being paged. Probably a crazy bastard like everybody else in this place. Doctors and orderlies included. In the meantime, I pictured Renata where I left her, in the room at the Days Inn, the phone line unplugged. Now that I hadn't come back after I left last evening, I knew it was entirely possible that she had taken off. And if she had taken off with her new manuscript, then my whole plan was shot to hell. Without her, without her story and her eventual testimony about Charlie's death, I was as good as finished.

"Lots of people suffer from the effects of hallucinations," Pearl went on, "or perceptual disorders, feelings of being controlled or simply believing that things of a universal nature, such as the weather, carry personal significance." He paused for a second or two to take a breath. "Tell me, Mr. Marconi, do you get mad at the weather?"

I almost admitted that I did.

"So you see, Keeper—and I can call you Keeper, can't I?— there's really nothing to be ashamed of. Capital District Psychiatric Center is a wonderful place for getting well again."

I sat there on the couch, feeling a slow burn.

"Are blow jobs a part of the patient's treatment?" I asked, turning to the two gorillas.

Pearl's face went white, while Goatee's face turned a distinct shade of red.

"I have no idea what you are suggesting," Pearl said. He slid off his desk, stood up straight, his lanky body as thin and grotesque as one of those dead trees outside his window. "And if you continue to make unfounded accusations, I'd be happy to have your accommodations switched to perhaps something slightly less comfortable."

"Is that how you warned Mr. Pukas? Threatened to put him in isolation?"

"Mr. Pukas is a sick man, Mr. Marconi," he said, now walking around his desk, plopping himself down in the leather swivel chair, his eyes peeled out the window onto a suddenly overcast sky.

"Pukas is a victim," I said, "just like me."

"You don't know how right you are, Mr. Marconi," he said. "In my estimation, your separate schizophrenias are the result of post-traumatic stress syndrome. You have both suffered and withstood terrible assaults on your body. An experience that, in turn, has resulted in serious psychological consequences that far outweigh the physical scarring. The only significant difference between you and Pukas is that he suffered abuse at the hands of his parents, while you were abused by rebel inmates in 1971 during the Attica riots."

"I'm over that," I said, putting a fake, ear-to-ear smile on my face. "See, I'm one happy-go-lucky son of a bitch now."

"You got the son of a bitch part right, anyway," said Leon.

For a time the four of us just sat there, once again silent, Pearl staring out the big window onto the barren trees. Until he turned back to me suddenly, his blue eyes staring into mine. "There are two types of trauma suffered by nearly all law enforcement in this country," Pearl went on, "from the lowliest prison guard to the highest police official." He tapped his chin with the index finger on his right hand and then turned back to the window like an old friend.

"Get to the point, Pearl," I said.

"Show some fucking respect," Leon said, taking the rag away from his mouth, examining the bloodstains, then reapplying it.

"The first is a kind of episodic stress," Pearl went on, "in which a traumatic incident, like a sudden fist to the teeth, occurs to a lawman or his partner. That kind of stress, Keeper, has little lasting effect, as opposed to chronic stress, which is brought about by the daily routine, by those nagging inner voices that continually ask you where you went wrong with your life." Pearl tapped his two front teeth with the back of his pen. "Now take your wife, Fran, for instance—"

I shot up.

Leon and Short Goatee each grabbed a shoulder, pressed me back down onto the couch.

"You blame yourself for her death. And the fact that she was decapitated is particularly disturbing and gruesome. All that blood, all that mess. Tell me, Mr. Marconi, did you know that victims who suffer clean and instantaneous decapitations retain consciousness for nearly twenty seconds before the oxygen and blood run out of their skulls? Witnesses at public executions in France reported cheeks that were still rosy with life and wide-open eyes, pupils moderately dilated, the mouth closed so firmly it could not be opened by manual force when the executioner tried to pry the upper and lower jaw apart. So imagine the horror your wife experienced when she realized her own head had been sliced off?"

Pearl pretended to shiver.

I wanted to kill him.

"For you the memory of Fran's death has become a chronic torture. Maybe you don't show physical evidence of the torture, such as rectal bleeding, dyslexia, and any other of the dozen or so assorted maladies normally associated with getting the living daylights beat out of you. But you do show the neurological and schizophrenic symptoms associated with psychological torture."

Stomach turning over, head buzzing.

"For instance, I bet you drink far too much. And let me guess: You greet all forms of commitment and love not with a normal dose of apprehension but with an almost violent distaste. In some cases, your reaction may be interpreted as almost psychotic. Does the death of those two women in Monterrey, Mexico, or perhaps the kidnapping and attempted murder of Renata Barnes ring a bell?"

I felt like the linoleum was being pulled out from under me, the hole opening up onto some kind of bottomless cavern, black and so very cold. I had to wonder if the session was being filmed or recorded. I knew the cameras and microphones had to be hidden.

"Keeper," Pearl said, "sources close to me have obtained a statement from the owner of a certain ranch in Monterrey where the murders took place—an owner, I might add, who himself was shot twice in the shoulder and left alone to die in the desert by you. Now I'm not accusing you of having carried out the actual murders. I'm just saying it is possible for a man in your condition to perform such a heinous act and not even realize it. But if you were to produce Ms. Barnes unharmed, that would be an entirely different story. You do know where she is, don't you, Mr. Marconi? Can you provide me with an exact, detailed location?"

That was it, then. They still hadn't located Renata. She had stayed put after all. That's what they wanted from me. A location. If not, they were going to make me out as a killer.

"I've never laid eyes on Renata in my life," I said.

"Now, now, Keeper," Pearl said. "I'm certain that once the conditions are right, you'll be willing to reach deep down into your soul of souls to try and find the strength to cooperate with us."

I folded my hands on my lap. "And just what do you use for an incentive?"

Pearl lit up like a spotlight. "Pain, of course," he said.

I lunged over his desk, grabbed him by the shirt collar. I got in two quick blows to the mouth before Leon and Short Goatee jumped me, pulled my hands around my back, dragged me off the desk and onto the floor, slapping a plastic shackling device around my wrists, cutting the skin when they yanked it tight.

From my position, lying on my chest on the carpeted floor, I saw Pearl slide himself back into his chair.

His mouth was bloody.

"OK, Mr. Marconi," he spat, his voice thick and sick, "you're going to see just what kind of wonderful work we can do at our little hospital."

He nodded to his boys.

Leon left the room, quickly closed the door behind him.

When he came back in he was carrying a wooden straight-backed chair, which he quickly set in the middle of the floor.

He wasn't alone.

The man who followed him into the office was someone I recognized right away. A man not much older than me, taller and bulkier, with the sleeves on his T-shirt cut off at the shoulders even in March, and faded Levi's jeans and worn-in combat boots. He had a hoop earring in his left ear and a thin mustache that barely covered his upper lip and round John Lennon sunglasses that completely hid his eyes. He was smoking a cigarette. As for his head? It was completely bald. Clean shaven. A total egghead. Finally I'd come face to face with the Bald Man.

CHAPTER FIFTY-SEVEN

WHAT CAN I SAY? THAT I COLLAPSED IN FRONT OF THE
Bald Man? That what should have been fiery rage turned into something completely different? Something passive? A man humbled
over meeting his maker?

Leon pushed me down into the chair while Short Goatee
applied straps to both my ankles and around my waist. As the Bald
Man took his place in the far corner of the room, Pearl rolled down
the shades and closed the blinds on his windows. He slipped on a
pair of black latex gloves.

"Boys," Pearl said, "please gag Mr. Marconi."

Leon pulled that bloody rag out of his back pocket, stuffed it
into my mouth. I wanted to gag when I felt the warm, wet blood.
But I thought of all the things I had been taught at the academy
about hostage situations. I remembered how calm I was supposed
to be. How I should breathe long steady breaths to avoid the panic,
to create an emotional barrier between me and my captors. And
I tried like hell to breathe through my nose and I tried like hell to
stay as calm as possible. But the effort was useless.

Pearl picked up his phone. "Wendy, I'll be in therapy for the
next hour," he lied. "So, please, no calls."

He hung up the phone and used the back of his right hand to
wipe the thin film of blood from his mouth. He opened the side
drawer in his desk with one of the keys on his key ring. He pulled
out a thick, black zip-up rubber bag, set it on his desk. He smiled

and ran his fingers over the bag, as if it were alive and purring. "I think it's about time you began a little soul-searching, Keeper," he said. "Tell us, where can we find Renata?"

Leon was standing to my left, in full view, arms crossed at his chest. His lip wasn't bleeding anymore. But there was dried blood caked all around the now purple fat lip. Short Goatee stood to my right. I could see his erection pressed up against his white orderly pants. A giant bulge, as clear as day. He was rubbing the mound with the fingers of his right hand, his eyes wide and psychotic. As for the Bald Man, he stood stiff and silent, smoking one Marlboro after the other.

"Shall we get started?" Pearl said.

"Yeah," Goatee said, his voice shaking with excitement. "Let's get started, Doc."

Pearl unzipped the rubber bag, pulled out a small stainless-steel surgical instrument, the kind with two needle-sharp hooks at each end that dentists use for scraping plaque off your teeth. "You know the routine, boys," he said.

Leon reached over, gently untied the ties on my hospital gown, pulled my boxers down to my ankles.

Oh, Christ, I wanted to shout. Oh, for the love of Christ. But that bloody rag was stuffed in my mouth, the Bald Man standing in the corner...

"As I started saying, Keeper," Pearl said. "Did you know that I'm a noted expert on both psychological and physical torture?" He made his way around the desk, holding the dentist's pick in his right hand, a loaded syringe in his left. "I've also done extensive research into the resulting post-traumatic stress disorder."

My eyes tracked his every movement.

"For instance, I know that to avoid physical evidence, torture is often performed with needlelike devices in order to produce maximum pain with minimal evidence." He was standing over me now. "Stretching, crushing asphyxiations are also forms of torture that produce lots of pain with minimal physical stress. But, oh my, the post-traumatic stress is extremely significant. I'd bet the farm that you'll recall just about anything I want you to recall, just to stop the pain."

He dropped to his knees, eye level with my sex.

"Here's how it all works. First we shoot you up with a little speed mixed with an amazing new drug that stimulates the NMDA receptor in your brain. Your pain should be enhanced to the extent that even the slightest touch will send your neurotransmitters and their receptors screaming. Really, very neat state-of-the-art stuff."

I felt the prick of the needle in my thigh and then the hot pressure of the medical concoction injected into my system. When it was empty, he pulled the needle out and threw the syringe onto his desk. "Now," Pearl said a few seconds later, "does this hurt?"

When he tapped my testicles with the point of the weighted dental instrument, I thought my middle would explode in fire and ripping pain. As I thrust my body up against the restraining devices, I thought my eyeballs would pop out, my ribs would snap.

I tried to scream.

But screaming was impossible.

"Oh my," Pearl said, eyes wide and intense, "do we have a live one or what?"

Leon laughed.

The Bald Man smoked.

Short Goatee rubbed his midsection, let out a groan.

Then Pearl jammed the spike into my left testicle.

CHAPTER FIFTY-EIGHT

SHE IS TYPING THE FINAL WORDS OF THE FINAL PAGE
when the door to the room opens. Two men step silently inside,
walking out of their own shadows and into the half light that leaks
out of her little desk lamp.

One of them in a leather blazer, a pistol in his right hand.

The other in a long, charcoal overcoat and navy-blue fedora.

"Where are you taking me?" she asks the men.

The man in the fedora takes a step forward. Without a
word.

The man in the leather blazer makes his way to the phone, picks
up the receiver, brings it to his ear. When it registers that the phone
is dead, he pulls on the thin white wire, sees that it is not connected
to the jack.

He bends down and connects it, letting out a grunt as he extends
his arm under the bed to his right.

In the meantime, the fedora man picks up the travel bag that sits
in the corner of the room by the desk. He sets it on the bed.

"Get ready to travel," he says.

She stands, pulls the last page from the manual typewriter, sets
it on the stack of pages to her right.

Charlie's story. It is finished.

"Get me Homicide," the man on the phone says. "Yeah, it's Ryan."
He turns and looks Renata in the eye. "Put out a missing persons

on *Renata Barnes. That's right, nowhere to be found…Marconi?…*
Yeah, we questioned him."

The man hangs up the phone, lets out a breath.

"How've you been, Renata?" he says.

"Not too good, Mike," she says.

CHAPTER FIFTY-NINE

I WOKE UP ON MY BACK IN A ROOM SO BLACK I COULD not see the shape of my hand when I held it up in front of my face.

How do I explain the pain?

How it came to me not immediately but in a sudden wave that started at my feet, worked its way up my legs, shot up my spine, into my head.

There was the taste of blood in my mouth.

My teeth felt loose.

I would have given my life—what was left of it—for a drink of water.

Just one beautiful, replenishing sip.

My right eye was swollen shut.

I touched it with my fingertips and felt the tender sting.

The floor was cold and hard. Concrete. Not rubber. I was naked.

I curled my knees into my chest, wrapped my arms around my shins. I wanted to shout, but no words would come.

Just the shivers.

❖

After a time, a small opening appeared at the base of the metal door. A little mail-slot-sized opening through which a bright light poured in, followed by a plastic tray. In the light I could see that a bowl had been set on the tray along with a plastic spoon. I crawled over to the bowl on all fours, dipped my fingers into it.

I felt warm, wet fur and flesh.

I pulled my hand back.

In the little bit of light I could see blood on my fingers. I could smell the blood, feel the warm stickiness.

In the bowl, a dead rat.

I kicked the bowl away with my bare feet, pressed my back up hard against the wall.

Laughing coming from outside the door.

Then the mail slot slammed closed.

I curled up on my side.

After a while, I went to sleep.

❖

Startled awake, again.

This time the silhouette of a man standing over me, syringe in hand. Me using all my strength to crawl back into a far corner, trying to hold out my hands, trying to scream at him to get the hell away. But so weak, the effort was useless.

Pathetic.

First I felt the plunge of the needle.

Then the warmth of the fluid.

As it shot up my veins.

❖

When I woke up a third time, I was shivering.

But here's the strange thing: All the pain had subsided.

In the darkness, I rolled over onto all fours, felt the floor with my hands, and carefully ran them over as much of the concrete as I could until I came to the perimeter walls. The bowl with the dead rat inside it had disappeared.

From what I could gather, the square-shaped room was maybe seven by seven, with a wire drain in the center of the concrete floor. The concrete walls were covered, in places, with rubber padding. I knew the ceiling was likely constructed out of concrete planks with two holes bored out of them. The first for ventilation, the second for a video monitor fitted with a night-vision lens.

How did I know this?

I was a former maximum security warden. I knew what to expect from solitary confinement because I myself had sent men to solitary. Which meant I also knew the effects even a minute amount of solitary could have on the brain.

The brain is a funny thing.

It loses its efficiency when it's deprived of stimulation. And as for those five famous senses? They just go all to hell.

Take away the environment and suddenly you can't remember your name anymore, suddenly you begin to hallucinate like a crazy man.

You withdraw into yourself.

Your IQ melts away.

You become a babbling moron.

All within days.

I had no way of telling how long I'd been in the hole.

A day, two days. A week, maybe. Five minutes. I didn't know. I had no way of telling time, no way of knowing day from night.

I felt my face with my hands.

A day's worth of beard growth. But not much more.

Maybe whoever injected me had shaved me too. Cleaned me up a little. It was possible.

Anything was possible in the dark.

I curled up on the concrete floor, a dull, throbbing pain beginning to develop in my midsection and in my head. When the little sliding door opened, I expected to see another tray appear. But then the entire metal door opened up.

The light outside in the hall burned my eyes. I held out my hand to shield it. I squinted, but that didn't help. I didn't need eyesight to know that Pearl and his boys had arrived for round two. The three of them stood over me in the cell.

"How are we feeling?" Pearl asked.

"Who sent in the clowns?" I said, my voice dry, cracking.

Pearl let out a laugh. "That's the spirit," Pearl said, bending at the knees while Leon and Short Goatee stood poised behind him. "Does this still give you pain?" When he thrust his hand between my legs, flicked my balls with his fingertips, I thought I would go through the concrete roof. My eyes rolled up into the back of my head. There were the telltale signs of passing out—the blurred vision, the slurring of the voice, the feeling of falling into a bottomless well.

"Still very tender," he said, pulling out that dental pick from his pocket along with another syringe.

I shot back against the wall.

Pearl came close, ran his open palm down the side of my face. "There, there, baby," he said, slowly standing up. He informed me that in one hand he held an instrument that required no explanation. And he was right. In the other, he said, he held a syringe filled with a painkiller so potent it would eliminate my troubles in less than thirty seconds.

My troubles. Meaning my pain.

I was breathing hard, through my mouth.

"You must understand, Keeper," he said, "we've been very patient with you. All we need is an address. Give it to us and you get the painkiller. If you resist, well…"

He held up the dental pick.

"Die," I said, through my tears.

Pearl shook his head. "You should know that every man has his limit," he said. "And I thought we were making progress." He dropped the syringe to the floor, crushing it with the heel of his shoe. "Boys," he said.

The two goons came at me, grabbed my arms, held on tight, while Pearl went down on his knees.

"OK, OK, OK," I screamed, suddenly seeing Tony's face in my head, cursing him to hell for having abandoned me. "I know where Renata is. I swear I'll tell you the truth. I swear to God almighty I'll tell you anything."

"Of course you will," Pearl said, bringing the cold, sharp tip of the tool to my left eyeball. "I'm certain you'll tell the whole truth and nothing but the truth, so help you God."

CHAPTER SIXTY

"ARE YOU TAKING ME HOME?" SHE ASKS FROM THE BACK-seat of the cop cruiser. "Or are you taking me to jail?"

The man in the fedora turns around in the passenger-side seat to look her in the face.

"Neither," he says.

There is another woman in the cruiser, sitting beside her in the backseat. She is a thin woman, dressed in a short wool skirt and a black turtleneck sweater. Her hair is shoulder length and sandy. The woman smiles with her lips pressed together. "I'm Val," she says.

"We need your help," the man called Ryan says from the driver's seat. He is looking at Renata in the rearview mirror.

She turns away from Val and looks at the reflection of Ryan's eyes in the little rearview mirror.

"Lately, I'm a popular girl," she says, clutching the manuscript against her breasts.

"It's not you we want," the fedora man says.

"It's Richard," the driver explains, his eyes holding hers in the rearview mirror.

CHAPTER SIXTY-ONE

I WOKE UP KNOWING SHE WAS NEXT TO ME.

I didn't have to see or feel or call out for her.

All I needed was her sweet smell.

A perfume I forever associated with her, no matter where I was or no matter who else was wearing it.

When I opened my eyes, I looked directly up at a white cathedral ceiling. I panned down, grabbed an eyeful of the black bookshelves that lined the walls.

Tony's condo.

Sitting on the edge of the couch, Val was dressed in a short wool skirt with tan leggings, little brown shoes with buckles, and a black turtleneck sweater. No jewelry. Her hair was cut just above her shoulders and parted down over her forehead, above her brown, sometimes hazel eyes. When she reached out to place her hand on my leg, I noticed she was wearing the engagement ring I had given her more than a year ago.

I wondered if she had ever taken it off.

I filled my lungs with air, then let it out. I was sore all over. Propping myself up on one elbow, I looked into her eyes.

She took my hand, squeezed it. "I was wrong," she said.

Someone cleared his throat.

Tony, standing in the center of the living room. He wore gray slacks and a white button-down, the sleeves rolled up to the elbows.

"You've been in and out of consciousness for almost forty-eight hours."

I ran my hand down my leg, over my midsection. There was some padding under my sweatpants and an ice pack.

"I thought you forgot about me," I said, my voice cracking, the back of my throat parched.

Tony nodded. "The damage is nothing permanent," he said. "Albany Med discharged you almost immediately. You'll have no recollection."

"How'd you find me?"

"Barnes decided to press charges," he said. "There was nothing we could do other than buy you some time in Capital District Psychiatric. We counted our blessings. At least I did. Because the alternative was county lockup. But what Ryan and I both didn't realize was that Barnes has a friend who runs the show there."

"A freak show."

"Ryan wanted to go after them immediately when he saw the condition you were in," Tony said. "But I talked him into taking care of them later, once he had your fully executed statement in hand. The important thing now is that you're out."

"And alive," Val said.

"The Bald Man works for Barnes," I said, after a time.

"I know."

"But Barnes is *your* client."

"*Was* my client. He was using me to get to you."

"What about Renata?"

"I'm here," she said, walking out of the kitchen, a cup of coffee in her hands. "Tony found the Days Inn matches in your jacket pocket. He located me at the motel the night you left."

"And the manuscript?"

"The manuscript explains it all," Val interjected.

❖

In typical Tony fashion, he spared me the gory details:

Back in late 1994, the year I'd been appointed warden of Green Haven Prison, Reel Productions had been hired by the Republican challenger to produce a slash-and-burn campaign to destroy the Democratic incumbent in the 1996 election for governor.

"The campaign opened up some serious doors for Barnes," Tony went on. "Espccially when he was approached by the vice commissioner for Corrections with a deal he could not refuse."

"Pelton," I said.

"Washington Irving Pelton," Tony said, nodding.

The name still hit me like a brick. My old corrections officer buddy; the man I'd survived Attica with when the inmates took over D Yard and took us hostage. The same man who had set me up a couple of years ago when a cop-killer by the name of Eduard Vasquez escaped from Green Haven. When Vasquez turned up dead, Pelton conveniently tossed the blame onto me. I was well aware of his precise motive. He wanted me out of the picture so he could continue to run the drug racket he had been propagating at Green Haven for years.

But it wasn't until now, in Tony's condo, that I realized just how badly Pelton had wanted me gone. It turns out that the deal he'd offered Barnes was this: if the producer lobbied heavily for the new governor to appoint him commissioner of Corrections, Wash would see to it that Barnes was made a full one-third partner in the Green Haven drug operation.

One-third partner amounted to one hundred Gs a month.

Cash.

Guaranteed.

So naturally Barnes agreed to secretly lobby the challenger on Pelton's behalf, especially when he was convinced the campaign was sure to succeed. All that was required of Pelton was to switch party allegiance—from Democrat to Republican. Easy.

But Pelton wasn't about to let Barnes get away with all that money all that easily.

"What he wanted from Barnes," Tony said, looking down at the tops of his polished Florsheims, "was to have you killed. The Bald Man was supposed to assassinate you when you left the house that warm Monday back in May of 1996 on your way to Green Haven. But the whole thing was botched from the start. The traffic that morning was too heavy. You'd already left before he got to the house. When he spotted you going through that red light at the corner of Manning and Western, he used it as an opportunity to ram you. Only instead of killing you, he did something worse. He killed Fran."

I asked Tony what he knew about Shaw Hudson. Was he acting on Barnes's direct orders when he tried to kill us? Or was he working for himself?

"We don't know for certain," Tony said. "What we do know is that Hudson really is a hired gun for Barnes and that he went along with his order. To a degree, anyway. You see, Barnes knew that if you did not break out Renata, then the Mexican government might have extradited her to the States. That was a chance he could not take."

"But what do *you* think?" I asked.

"What do I think?" Tony said. "I think Barnes used you to break her out. Then he used Hudson to kill her. The resulting blame would be placed on your head."

I was beginning to understand everything. My motivation went something like this: I'd been going progressively nuts, seeing things in cemeteries. I skipped my wedding, shot up a bar. I even may have left a trail of murder. I thought again of those two young women at Hudson's ranch.

I ran my hands through my hair.

I wasn't sure whom I wanted dead more: Barnes or the Bald Man.

Both, I told myself. I wanted them both dead. It made me feel good to admit it. If Pelton wasn't already dead, I would have added him to the wish list too.

I got up from the couch, slow as hell. "Where're my clothes?" I said. "I need my clothes."

I started for the stairs, pushing past Tony, very unsteady, my midsection feeling like an elephant had stepped on it.

"Keeper," Val shouted. "You can't take out Barnes now."

Tony grabbed my arm just before I reached the stairs.

"Listen to her, *paisan*," he said. "You go off half-cocked now, you'll blow this thing out of the water. With the manuscript and Renata's testimony, Ryan will be able to nail Barnes on conspiracy to commit murder as well as on the first-degree murder of his son and the second-degree murder of your wife."

I pushed his hands away.

"Don't you see?" he said. "You go off on a personal vendetta, you'll blow this for everybody."

"Including Fran," Val added. "And little Charlie."

I looked at her, then at Tony, then at Renata. Looked them all in the eyes.

"When have you ever abided by the law?" I said to Tony. "You've always done what was right, regardless of the law. Look at Lenny Jones. We all know you made the hit on him. You know Barnes and the Bald Man have to die. So why the sudden change?"

"Because this one is different," he said. "Jones was already in prison. He was beyond due process. The only alternative was active vengeance. For Barnes and the Bald Man, it's different. Law and order will take them down for good."

Tears ran down Renata's cheeks. "You have to do this for my son," she said. Val wrapped her arms around the writer's shoulders, led her back into the kitchen.

I turned and took another step up the stairs. "Whatever you say, Counselor."

I felt a sharp jolt of pain in my groin with every step I took up the stairs. But I didn't care about the pain. All I cared about was revenge. Maybe I'd assured Tony that I would play by his rules. Maybe I'd made the same assurance to Renata. But it was my wife we were dealing with. My wife, her death, my life. What was left of it. So the physical pain didn't really have that much effect.

What I felt inside was anger. No, that's not even close. What I felt was anger, but what I wanted was blood. Screw it, I told myself as I made the final stair to the landing. For now I'd do what everyone expected of me. But in the end, I'd do what I had to do, no matter who got hurt, no matter who got killed.

CHAPTER SIXTY-TWO

FOR TWO MORE DAYS, I SAT AROUND TONY'S PLACE, not going outside, not talking on the phone, speaking only to Detective Ryan, who came and went two separate times on two separate days. Maybe he was hoping for two separate versions of my testimony—too bad. First of all, the story wasn't that complicated (man attempts to assassinate wife while using me as the patsy). Second of all, I had no reason to cover anything up (other than my desire to kill both Barnes and the Bald Man).

In the meantime, Renata's manuscript sat on the desk, unread.

I knew I should have been going through it, scanning each and every paragraph for the details behind Barnes's plan for killing me. But something inside prevented me from looking at it. I had to be honest with myself: Fran had died in my place. The ultimate responsibility rested with me, and that's exactly what I could not get over. So I didn't need to make things worse by reading all about it.

Not when I had already lived it.

❖

I rolled out of bed, picked up the phone.

I called information for the number for Reel Productions.

I dialed the number.

When the receptionist came on the line, I asked for Barnes. She said he wasn't in but was expected back in an hour or so. Could she take a message or transfer me to his voice mail?

I told her that I'd call back.

"Whom should I say is calling?" she insisted.

"Santa Claus," I said. "Ho, ho, ho."

She hung up before I had the chance to do it first.

CHAPTER SIXTY-THREE

IT WAS GETTING DARK WHEN VAL CAME UPSTAIRS with a tray of food.

I pretended to be asleep.

She set the tray down on the little wooden secretary pushed up against the far wall.

I sat up when Val sat down beside me. I wasn't wearing a shirt, just a pair of Tony's flannel pajama bottoms. She ran her hand along my chest, gently.

I kissed her, gently. Then I kissed her some more.

❖

After a while we lay together on the bed, Val's head in the space between my shoulder and left arm. True, I wasn't up to the task of making love. I was still in too much pain for that. But there were other things we could do, and we did them very well.

We said nothing while the lights from the cars that sped by on Eagle Street, along with the halogen lamps that lit up the governor's compound, reflected against the white ceiling. Val rolled over onto her stomach, looked up at me with big brown eyes.

"What are you going to do about Barnes?" she asked.

"I'm going after him," I said.

I listened to her breathing, heavy, from deep inside her lungs.

"And the Bald Man?"

"Yes."

"Does Tony know?"

"I think he knows."

"Why doesn't he stop you?"

"He knows there's only one thing I can do."

Val propped herself up on her elbow.

"What was all that two days ago?" she asked. "Tony trying to convince you that it has to be done his way. The legal way, with Ryan?"

"A genuine appeal to do the legal thing. Regardless of emotion."

"How could it be genuine when he knew all along what you were going to do anyway?"

"People like Barnes and Wash Pelton," I said, "they're in directly with the governor. And in this town, that's a lot like saying you're above the law."

"Pelton's dead."

"If the cancer never got to him he would have been back on the street in a couple more years. Maybe less. Probably holding some political office."

"You don't know that for sure."

"These men live a code of silence no different from the Mob. Why do you think Barnes was never implicated in any of this until now? Because Pelton kept quiet about him, even while rotting away in prison. That's the kind of brotherhood—or resolve, or whatever you want to call it—that they have."

Val laid her head back down on the pillow for a while. Then she said, "Is Tony going to help you?"

"It's something I have to do alone."

I slipped out of bed and out of the room, into the bathroom across the hall, shutting the door behind me. I ran the cold water and splashed it on my face until I felt more awake or more clean, I'm not sure which.

But the water didn't help.

I couldn't stop myself from falling to my knees in the corner of the room, between the door and the edge of the bathtub. I could feel the tears building up against the backs of my eyeballs. The tears blurred my vision. But when I tried to let them go—when I tried to let it all out—the tears wouldn't come.

After a time I wiped my face with a wet towel.

I took a deep breath, tried to compose myself. For Val.

But the effort had been for nothing. When I came back out of the bathroom, she was gone.

CHAPTER SIXTY-FOUR

TONY'S BEDROOM.

Palatial. Four-poster bed. Antique dressers and chests. Gold-framed mirrors.

Inside the walk-in closet, my Colt .45, wrapped up in the leather holster, set on the top shelf beside the three extra ammo clips.

I knew Tony.

I knew the piece would be there. Waiting for me.

Keeper, back in business.

Back in the guest bedroom, a second call placed to Barnes's office.

"Whom should I say is calling?" The same receptionist as before.

"Wash Pelton," I said.

"J-J-Just a minute, p-p-please."

The stuttering voice was replaced by smooth Muzak.

"Who the hell is this?"

Barnes, pissed as hell.

"Hell of a way to treat an employee," I said. "Especially one you haven't paid yet."

"Marconi," he said, suddenly bright, suddenly cheerful. A break in the clouds on an early spring day. "Why didn't you say so in the first place? I thought it was a prank."

"No prank," I said.

"I trust you have my wife," he said.

"You know I do," I said.

"And you want to be paid," he said. "Is that it? You want your money."

"You put me in that psycho ward," I said.

"I have no idea what you're talking about." Fake laughing, as if the charges he'd pressed against me weren't legal record. "I've assumed you were in Mexico on the job."

"How did I know you'd deny that?"

Heavy breathing.

"My turn to play *Let's Make A Deal*."

"I'm listening." His voice suddenly soft and low.

"You know that manuscript Renata was going to write and publish? The one you never told anybody about? The real one describing how you drowned your own child? The one you tried to have Renata killed for?"

More breathing.

"I have it," I said.

"Completed." A question.

"Fast writer, your wife. A real talent."

"You broke into my house."

"Give the dog a bone," I said. "But you haven't asked me what I want yet."

"Maybe I don't care what you want."

"I think you do," I said. "From where I'm sitting right this very second, I can hear Tony Angelino and Detective Michael Ryan going over their plan to nail you on the strength of this document alone. Face it, Barnes, you can either be screwed the legal way or you can be screwed my way."

Dead air.

Then, "What is it you want?"

"The Bald Man."

"How and where?" No hesitation.

❖

On the nightstand beside the bed, the Capital District section of the Albany *Times-Union,* the headline reading, COHOES FALLS OVERLOOK: AN ACCIDENT WAITING TO HAPPEN!

"You know Cohoes?"

"Of course."

"Meet me at the overlook by the falls. Midnight. I give you the manuscript. You give me the man and the rest of the two hundred Gs you owe me and Tony."

"What about Renata?"

"We'll talk about her then."

"How will I know the manuscript is the real thing?"

"The manual Royal typewriter is Renata's signature, dropped Ns and all."

"What about carbons?"

"No carbons," I said. "As far as copies go, you'll have to trust me."

"Doesn't look like I have much of a choice."

"Take it or leave it," I said.

"Twelve midnight," he confirmed. "The overlook. Don't be late."

"Don't be late? That's my line, motherfucker."

CHAPTER SIXTY-FIVE

THE CITY OF COHOES.

Located only about five miles north of Albany.

Set inside a natural ninety-degree cul-de-sac formed at the very spot where the Hudson and Mohawk Rivers merge. Home to the Cohoes Falls, the most powerful natural waterfall in the state of New York next to Niagara. Where Hiawatha, the godchild of the Iroquois nation, died.

As the story was told to me (and there are many different versions of the story), Hiawatha, having fallen asleep inside his canoe one summer afternoon, never noticed the movement of the bark craft when it broke away from the bank and drifted out into the center of the Mohawk. Startled awake, and quickly realizing that he was caught in the intense current, Hiawatha resigned his fate to the falls and his newly found Christian God.

Neither his body nor the canoe was ever recovered. But then, that's where the name Cohoes originated—from Hiawatha and his canoe. Because a literal translation of the name is "broken canoe."

A century or so ago, a massive hotel was built on the edge of the falls, constructed right into a rock declivity that measured about one hundred feet from bottom to top.

The Cataract Hotel.

A five-story Victorian monstrosity that served as a tourist destination for some of the rich and famous living along the East Coast. And just to add some high-flying adventure to the hotel, a trolley car called the Belt Line was rigged up via a cable system that started in the sublevel of the hotel and spanned the entire length of the falls, directly over the one-hundred-foot drop.

But as the years and decades passed and the city of Cohoes became the victim of economic chaos, the breathtaking falls were ignored. After all, why go to Cohoes when you could take a Greyhound to Niagara? The hotel was shut down and boarded up and the trolley car ceased to run, the cables still hanging over the river like some useless clothesline behind an abandoned tenement house.

How was I privy to all this local color?

My father and mother had both been born in Cohoes back in the city's better days, their parents having settled there years after stepping off the boat at Ellis Island. Now what was left of the city was rubble and crime, the theater closed and turned into a warehouse for plumbing fixtures, the textile mills burned to the ground, the merchants boarded up, a city curfew not enough to discourage the kids who made the trek down the hill from the projects beside Saint Agnes Church and ran crack on the street corners at all hours of the night. Even the life insurance salesmen had shut down their shops, locked their doors, and snuck out in the middle of the night, briefcases tucked under their overcoats.

The falls are still there, although no one really cares anymore.

Except for me and little Richie Barnes.

❖

I was sitting in the front seat of the rented Ford Explorer, Renata's manuscript beside me on the passenger seat. It had been no problem smuggling it or myself out of the condo. Quite simply, I'd waited until the entire place had gone to sleep. Then I dressed myself in jeans, black turtleneck, and black leather bomber. I strapped on my .45 and placed the manuscript in a plastic shopping bag lifted from Tony's kitchen. I found my keys resting in a candy dish on a coffee table in the middle of the living room, and I walked out.

Just like that.

Like that had been the plan all along.

Three minutes to midnight, the full April moon high over the Mohawk, lighting up the water that ran deep and heavy over the massive falls. A perpetual mist rose up the hundred-foot walls of the cliff and into the night sky. I turned the Explorer around so that it faced the overlook entrance.

Then I killed the engine and got out.

The overlook was nothing more than a parking lot surrounded by a dilapidated wood-slat safety fence. On the left hand side, facing the river, sat the boarded-up remnants of the Cataract Hotel—the abandoned five-story stone structure looking as desolate as the city of Cohoes itself. Emerging from a man made cave at the base of the hotel was a series of cables that I knew extended all the way to the other side of the falls, although it was impossible to see them at night.

Two headlights shone from out of the distance. Belonging to a car that made a quick right turn into the lot. I reached inside the open window of the Explorer, hit the headlights. High beams. Then I planted a bead on the windshield of Barnes's black Mercedes with my .45.

Two doors opened, driver and passenger side.

Two men.

VINCENT ZANDRI

Barnes, dressed in a long wool overcoat, and the Bald Man, in jeans and a leather jacket, still wearing the round sunglasses even in the dark.

"Did you come here to kill me?" Barnes shouted over the roar of the falls, right hand up against his brow, like a man saluting, only shielding his eyes from the Explorer's high beams.

"I'll take my money," I said.

"You have a little something for me, I believe."

"First the money," I said.

Barnes, reaching into the car, pulling out a briefcase. He set the briefcase on the blacktop and kicked it toward me.

"Now step away from the car," I said.

Barnes, staring at the Bald Man.

Me, thumbing back the hammer on the piece. "Do it," I said.

"The manuscript," Barnes said. "Where is it?"

"In a safe place," I said.

I knew he must have told the Bald Man they were making an exchange of cash for the manuscript. He certainly wouldn't have told him the truth: that he was actually making the exchange in return for his life. Unless a double cross was in the works. Which was the more likely scenario.

The mist from the falls made a slippery, wet film that coated everything and quickly turned to ice in the freezing night air. My hands felt detached from my arms, my brain having nothing to do with the actions and reactions of my trigger finger. Just a nice, slow squeeze and the show would be over. Lights out.

I knew I could just shoot them both in the face, put them back in the car, push the car over the cliff edge into the falls, and be done with it. As a former lawman, I knew I could get away with it too. So long as the physical evidence was completely whitewashed.

Heart beating inside my throat, breathing hard and heavy, body sweating even in the cold and the mist from the falls. I listened to the constant roar, and I stared at the Bald Man and I ran through the hit-and-run a thousand times. The quick slam of the black Buick, the flying forward of Fran, the decapitation, the settling of the headless body back into the passenger seat, the vision of the Bald Man giving me a quick glance. Then the tearing away from the scene.

Hit and run.

The hit intended for me, not for Fran.

And then the years that followed. The printed posters, the interviews with the cops, the composite sketches, the coming up with no leads whatsoever, the shaking of heads, the rolling of eyes, the "Don't call us, Keeper, we'll call you."

The living alone with the guilt.

I felt like crying, but I felt more like laughing, because I was God now.

Imagine me playing God?

But I should have known better than to allow my emotions to get in the way. I should have played it straight like a reasonable person. A man who has all his marbles in order. Because I waited too long. In the waiting, I gave Barnes the upper hand. Rather, I gave the Bald Man the upper hand. He had to be a trained killer. As much as I assumed I had him where I wanted him, I hadn't scared him in the least. In the end, he had been waiting for the right moment to pull the pistol out from under his jacket, aim it at my chest, fire the cap that plugged my right shoulder.

CHAPTER SIXTY-SIX

I HIT THE MACADAM HARD, THE .45 BOUNCING OUT OF my hand and sliding across the entire lower lot.

No pain. Not yet.

I rolled under the Explorer, dodged the shots that blew little chunks of frozen blacktop out of the lot. From down there I could see Barnes and the Bald Man using the soles of their shoes like ice skates, skidding down the length of the overlook parking lot.

When I knew the Bald Man's clip was empty, I slipped out from under the Explorer and jumped up. I opened the passenger-side door, grabbed the manuscript, ran for the fence, the blood running down the interior of my arm onto my hand.

Flat on my stomach, I slithered under the fence.

Nothing there but three feet of cliff edge. Beyond that, a one-hundred-foot drop down into the river and then another one-hundred-foot ride down the falls.

Two more rounds blasted through the wooden fence, one at my feet, one at my head. Not an easy thing, skating and shooting blind through a wooden fence. Not even for a pro like the Bald Man.

I got my balance and crawled along the twenty or so feet of rock ledge, using the fence as cover, the roaring water shooting up into my face. Nowhere to go other than straight ahead through the dark, the plastic shopping bag in my left hand. I inched my way toward the hotel and the now visible ladder made from iron rungs embedded in the portion of cliff face that served as the old hotel's foundation.

It took only a few seconds to make it on my belly to the cliff-side ladder.

Looking down on the ladder, I reached out with my right hand, grabbed onto the first rung as tightly as I could. Then I set my right leg onto another rung farther down. From there I climbed down into the cave where, with a little luck, I could stop the bleeding in my shoulder and maybe wait it out until morning.

But who the hell was I kidding?

I knew Barnes wasn't going anywhere, not until I was dead.

I knew the only reason they weren't coming after me from up above was that they'd already started forcing their way into the hotel. I knew they were peeling away the boards and going in through the front door. I knew as certain as the remains of that gigantic old cable car staring me in the face that Barnes and the Bald Man would be coming after me via the Cataract Hotel basement.

It's exactly what I would have done, had I been in their shoes.

CHAPTER SIXTY-SEVEN

TWO CHOICES.

Make a dive into the falls or fight them off without a gun and with a slug buried in my shoulder.

No choice, either way.

But then, I did have one more choice.

The old cable extended to the other side of the river. The cable was still strong. If it wasn't still strong, it would have collapsed under its own weight. If I used my legs and my good arm, I could snake my way to the other side.

There was a stack of old tires and chains jammed into a corner of the cave behind the old cable car. I pulled back the first three tires, stuffed the manuscript inside, and then covered them back up. You'd never know the book was there unless you were looking in it. I zipped my leather jacket up tight. Then I climbed up onto the roof of the cable car by way of a narrow ladder soldered to the side panel. I grabbed on to the cold, tightly wound cable and wrapped my legs around it. I took a deep breath and started inching my way forward, just as they came out the basement door and started blasting their way through the tunnel.

Hand over hand, foot over foot, over the cliff edge, making the mistake of looking down, the mist blowing up into my face so hard and so cold it took my breath away—and all my strength along with it.

I froze right there.

What the hell was I thinking?

I felt the spray and the razor cold cutting right through me.

I raised my head, tried to spot the cave lit up in the moonlight and now the flashing lights of the cop cruisers and ambulances.

The Bald Man was on his way, no more than twenty feet behind me, crawling with all the strength of a man who had two good arms, two good legs, and a whole lot of hate; closing the gap between us, fast.

I tried to get a full breath.

Impossible with all the mist and all the cold, the falls sucking the oxygen right out of the night.

I raised my head again, looked past my feet.

I saw the Bald Man's face.

His face, with this wild glow in the moonlight, coming for me so fast you'd swear he was a spider maneuvering upside down along his web.

A second or two later, he caught up to me, grabbed on to my right foot, tried to pry it off the cable by twisting it at the ankle.

I pulled my leg away, kicked him in the face, in his mouth and nose.

He smiled at me.

Three separate, well-placed blows with the heel of my boot against his face and he could still smile. He clung to the cable with his right hand, reached up toward his right ankle, pulled out a bowie knife, the stainless steel glistening in the moonlight. When he stuck the knife into my left calf, I felt the fire shoot up my leg into my head.

But I held on.

I kicked at him again, landed one square between the eyes, jarring his head back, sending his sunglasses down into the mist.

He was bleeding from the mouth.

Me, just holding on, knowing I couldn't possibly move. With every movement, I felt myself slipping.

And then it happened.

It was like the pain had seeped out of my body and the falls had shut off. It was as if the night had become day, all things suddenly crystal clear. I looked at the bastard, bowie knife poised high in the air, ready to slash at me again.

I took a deep breath and held it.

Just as he came down with the knife, I dropped my legs, held myself to the cable with both my arms.

The knife missed me. It swung completely around and landed in his right thigh.

He never made a noise. He just tried to pull the knife out. But he'd driven the blade too deep.

I swung my legs back up onto the cable, kicked him in the head. He lost his foothold. Now he clung to the cable with only his arms.

But then it was just his hands.

And then only one hand, which was exactly when he looked up at me with wide eyes streaked with blood.

I looked down at him, hovering far above the falls, his fingers straining to hold his weight, his round, slick head reflecting the moonlight, thin little mustache glistening in the mist, hoop earring still hooked to his left lobe.

He wasn't smiling or frowning.

He just looked curious. So this is what it's like to die, I imagined him thinking.

I stared back at him, hanging there for what seemed forever, feeling no pain, no fear, nothing. Just a nice, peaceful climax.

A second later, he was gone.

PART FIVE

NOVELIST BARNES REPORTED MISSING

ALBANY (AP) - The search began today for best-selling novelist Renata Barnes, who was officially reported missing while on
assignment in Mexico. Barnes, the wife of prominent public relations mogul Richard Barnes, had been researching the dangerous
drug wars taking place in and around the desert border lands. It
is feared she was abducted by any one of more than a half-dozen
crime families currently believed to be vying for the illicit business
being conducted in the area. While some have speculated that the
famous "method writer" was arrested after having posed as a drug
runner, her husband, Richard Barnes, denies all such allegations.
Sources close to Barnes report that he is doing everything in his
power to see to his wife's safe return.

CHAPTER SIXTY-EIGHT

SO THIS IS WHAT IT'S LIKE TO DIE, SHE THINKS. THIS IS all it takes, just a nice, peaceful drive in the dark of night to the river's edge, park Tony Angelino's Porsche at the cliff-side overlook, and get the hell out. Don't even pocket the car keys. Leave them in the ignition, keep the engine running, let the radio play, don't bother to close the door behind you. Like the song says, Just slip out the back, Jack…Set yourself free.

Here's what she does to be free: She takes a deep breath, begins the long, slow march across the parking area. With sharp blue eyes, she focuses on the abandoned overlook and the fog that rises up from the waterfalls beyond the hastily constructed wooden safety fence, beyond the old Cohoes Cataract Hotel built smack-dab into the one-hundred-foot cliff face, now boarded up with plywood, the windows shattered ages ago, the wood shingles rotted away by the constant mist, long before her birth; before her parents' births, for that matter. Other than the roar of the falls in the darkness, there is no sound. Not the sound of the car engine, not the sound of her soles on the ice-covered blacktop, not her quick but steady breaths, not the beating of her heart. There is only the permanent roar of the waterfall and the persistent voice in her head that tells her, It's time to go, baby. It's time to shake the dust of this one-horse world off your boots…

Oh man, if she could only write about dying the same way she had written so believably about so many things in her thirty-five years of living. She was the method writer, after all. At least that's the way people would remember her.

Now if only she could experience death and come back to record all the mind-blowing details. What a story it'd make. What a scoop. *Death is a process*, she'd write, *not a sudden, alarming event. Death has nothing to do with initial decay, putrefaction, butyric fermentation, and so on.* All that was physical; the result of research. It wasn't feeling or emotion. Her report would go beyond the physical to the emotional. It would grab the readers by their heartstrings, yank them right out of their chests—blood, guts, and all. *From the moment we're born,* she'd attest—*from the precise moment we're forced down that long tunnel toward the warm, bright light—we've already begun to die. That's why death is so much like being horny,* she'd write. *There's the long, dark tunnel with the light at the end. There are the faces and voices of your loved ones. There's the peace and harmony of the womb and the canal.* She'd write about it all if it were possible, because she would have placed herself in the death experience. Death would have happened to her. *Not* near *death,* but death. She'd be the only person qualified enough to write about it. So you want to know how it feels to die? she'd pen as an opener. This is what it's like.

Death has always been her shadow.

Now as she approaches the cliff's edge, she feels no fear. In fact, she feels loose, focused, free. She feels the resignation in her soul. Like the Indians used to say, it's a good day to die. A good frosty night in the city of Cohoes, anyway. As she crawls under the fence with the metal sign nailed to it that reads, DANGER: KEEP OUT, she knows she's doing the right thing, that danger no longer has any meaning for her. Back on her feet, heading for the cliff's edge, the *roar of the rushing water drowning her sighs, the mist coating her face and freezing to her skin, she knows she's beating death and her husband at their own game.*

But God almighty, if only she could live to write about it…

CHAPTER SIXTY-NINE

I DIDN'T FEEL EVEN AN OUNCE OF PAIN WHEN I DIED.

Darkness surrounded me. But then there was the sensation of moving slowly upward through a thick cloud of mist toward a brilliant overhead light.

Some people might attribute the experience to my rescue by a helicopter rigged with spotlighting and to the way the safety harness lifted me through the heavy mist of the Cohoes Falls to the safety of the chopper deck.

But it still felt like dying, as though my soul had left my body and was heading upward to heaven.

There's other evidence.

Nothing hurt.

Nothing at all. And there was an amazing warmth that wrapped itself around my body like a security blanket.

But then, here's the truth of the matter: From what they tell me now, I'd lost so much blood that I actually died, in clinical terms. As soon as I let go of the cable and hit the river, I died. And I believe it, because I'm a changed man now. Not because of the death, but because of who I *saw* in that death. As soon as I crossed over into the light, I saw Fran. Just waiting for me as if I was coming through the door of the home we shared in Albany only on weekends, a drink in her hand and a smile on her face. She came to me smiling and laughing, her black hair as smooth as her soft voice and as deep as her dark eyes. I asked her why she was laughing, and she said that I'd made a mistake. Another "whopper of a blunder." That it was so typical of me to just go ahead and "get dead" before my time. That missing her was one sorry excuse to cut my life short. She'd always be there waiting for me. Get on with living my life. Stop living in the past. She loved me, she said. Then she reached out her hand to me. And just as I reached out to her, at the very moment I was about to touch the tips of her fingers, I felt myself floating back fast and abruptly. Like going in reverse on a roller coaster. I stood outside my body, and I saw myself as a man and then as a teenager and then as a little boy with a bright smile on my face. I breathed and I was back.

The doctors had a name for it.

NDE.

Near Death Experience.

Also referred to in some circles as the Lazarus Syndrome, for obvious reasons. The symptoms are the same for everybody: the black tunnel, the bright light at the end of it, the warmth, the peace and quiet, the friends and family who await you on the other side, telling you to get back.

"I wouldn't say this to most people," the young doctor with horn-rimmed glasses suggested as he stood over me in my second-floor room of the Albany Medical Center. "But in my opinion, NDE is simply the effects of decreased oxygen supply to the brain. Hypoxia. While some fanatics believe they are actually entering the realm of the unknown, what is simply occurring is suffocation of the temporal lobe."

I tried propping myself up a little on the two pillows the nurse had stuffed behind my head earlier, careful not to disturb the plastic drain that had been inserted into the wound in my left shoulder, the pain now reduced to a constant dull throb.

"There is, of course, another explanation," the doctor said, turning back to me just as he was about to leave the room. "Some might say that NDE is simply the latent memories of the birth experience come back to us in our final moments in full Technicolor glory. Because being born is an experience we all share. Hands down. No one is exempt. Think about it: the long, dark tunnel, the bright light at the end of it, the elation and warmth of your mother's face."

"And all this time, Doc, I thought I had something to look forward to," I said.

"What difference does it make what happens to us when it's all over, Mr. Marconi, so long as it's unconscious?"

He turned to leave.

I called out to him one last time.

"What is it?" he asked.

"So you don't believe in the black and whiteness of death, do you?" I said. "Heaven for the good, hell for the bad."

He shook his head, smiled. "No," he said, "I don't."

"But you brought me back to life," I said.

"I have that gift," he said.

"I guess that makes *you* God," I said.

"Correction, Mr. Marconi," he said. "Science is God."

I was glad that he left the room before a thunderbolt exploded and fried us both.

CHAPTER SEVENTY

TWO DAYS LATER THEY DRAGGED RENATA'S BODY FROM the Mohawk River, not far from the spot where the Bald Man was supposedly killed when he fell from the cable into the falls. Unlike me, his body took the ride over the falls and was never recovered. Having given her testimony to Detective Ryan, Renata simply drove to the Cohoes Falls overlook, slipped under the fence, and leapt off the side of the cliff.

No explanation, no warning.

Just a nice, peaceful water landing.

But she had left something behind.

A letter sealed in a number-ten business envelope with my name written on it in ballpoint pen.

While I lay on my back in the hospital bed, Tony stood against the far wall of the room, beside the small vanity and sink. Val sat on the bed beside me. At my request, she opened the letter and began reading.

"Dear Keeper Marconi," she read aloud, clearing her throat once or twice before continuing. "By the time you read this, I will be dead. I don't know if you are capable of understanding the way I feel about Charlie or about the love I have for him still or about what I am willing to do in order to make amends for what I have done. I know you don't have any children, so maybe you've never experienced the love for a child as I have. Let me tell you, it is a bond you cannot imagine unless you've experienced it. At the risk of sounding sentimental, I feel I must express how happy Charlie's birth made me. I was simply happy to hold him, play with him, feed him, sleep beside him, be a mom to him in every sense of the word. He was everything to me. So much so that I did not have to write anymore to feel fulfilled. And I must say (even now) it was the same for Richard. We both loved Charlie, which makes it all the more difficult to explain what I'm about to tell you now.

"I'm not exactly sure when it happened or how it happened or what forces were at work, but after a time, the love Richard had for our son began to turn into a kind of fear. It was as if Richard had been possessed one night by something in his sleep. He began to obsess over the baby's fate. What if something terrible happened to Charlie? Something he had no way of preventing? What if one of us dropped him or left him out in the cold? What if—God forbid—he contracted cancer? There was no end to the possibilities. And because there was no end it began to seem logical, to Richard, that losing Charlie somehow, some way, was inevitable.

"Can you possibly conceive of what I'm trying to tell you, Keeper? For Richard, Charlie's death had become a self-fulfilling prophecy. And in the end, Richard felt that the only way fate could be fooled was to take control. If he was powerless to keep Charlie, then he had no choice but to take matters into his own hands.

"Of course, I begged him to get help. If not for himself, then certainly for Charlie. So he had a series of appointments with (it makes me shudder to even type his name) Dr. Pearl at Capital District Psychiatric. To my surprise, Richard seemed to come around after a while. Whatever treatment Pearl had been prescribing worked. For a full year, all talk of 'taking care of Charlie' in order to beat fate was dropped. I began to feel that Richard was cured.

"Or so I thought at the time.

"But then, I have to be perfectly honest: the manuscript is not entirely truthful. I guess after all this time, and after all that had happened, I just couldn't bring myself to tell the whole truth. Until now.

"One warm afternoon in May, I ran the bath for little Charlie. I got out all his toys, his favorite boats and rubber animals, and I set him inside the bath with them. Then I waited for Richard to come home. When he did, I told him I had to go out. Just a quick ten-minute trip out to the grocery store. But it was while I was driving that it suddenly came to me in this horrific wave that began at the tip of my toes, shot up into my spine, and traveled all the way up into my head: I had left Charlie alone with Richard.

"I remember pulling off to the side of the road, paralyzed with fear, just sitting there behind the wheel knowing I had to get home immediately. That to waste any more time meant certain death for Charlie. So I got myself together and made it home as fast as I could. Even now I can still recall the horrible weighted feeling of running up those stairs to our apartment. The too heavy, heart-broken feeling; the panic and the nausea.

"When I made it to the top of the landing I found that the door had been locked. Locked *after* I left. I had to fumble around for my keys, my eyes so out of focus with anxiety that I had to try five or six different keys until I could get the right one, all the time screaming for Richard but getting no answer.

"When I finally got the door open, I ran into the kitchen and grabbed the hammer under the sink. I can still see myself sprinting down the center hall of the apartment, with only the white light from the bathroom leaking out onto the polished wood floor. When I got to the open door, I found Richard bent over the tub, a video camera in his hands. I hit him over the head with the hammer. He dropped like a stone beside the tub.

"But it was then, when my husband fell to the floor unconscious, that I saw little Charlie laid out in the tub, his eyes closed, his lips sealed tight, his face blue and white. I fell to my knees and threw my arms around him and lifted him out of the tub. I screamed, 'Breathe, baby, breathe!' And when I got nothing I held him tighter and slapped him on the back again and again. 'Breathe, Charlie!' I screamed, with one more solid slap to the back. Then suddenly his eyes opened and the bathwater drained out of his lungs through his mouth, and he coughed and sputtered. Finally he began to cry.

"That's when I knew I had him back.

"I never took the time to dress him. I just wrapped him in a blanket. I was so panicked I hardly noticed the camera Richard had been holding—the camera he had been using to film the murder of his own son. I was so frightened at the thought of this that I just ran away with Charlie. I knew what Richard was capable of, knew how many connections he had. That for me, there would never be any hiding from him. But as for Charlie? I knew then that I could use his *near* death as his saving grace, as a rebirth, if you will. I knew that if I got him out of the apartment and away from Richard forever, I could save his life.

"So I did something no mother should ever have to do. I called Detective Ryan, told him I wanted Charlie put up for immediate adoption, that I would explain later and that for now the arrangement had to be strictly between him and me. You see, Ryan had worked closely with Richard and Wash Pelton and the governor on the campaign, strictly as a private consultant and strictly unbeknownst to his superiors in the state. He had been hired to address issues of safety and security, to deal with the constant telephone and letter threats that had been coming in since the campaign's inception. And with a drug deal going down in the prisons, he stayed on for something completely different. I could not immediately explain my motives to Ryan other than to suggest that if he attempted to speak to Richard about it, I would immediately blow the lid off his little agreement with my husband, that I didn't care what happened to me so long as Charlie was safe and hidden from his father for the rest of his life. As far as Richard went, he would never know what happened to his son. As far as he knew, he had completed whatever psychotic task he had set out to accomplish. I told him I simply panicked, hit him over the head with the hammer, and then called someone to take Charlie's body away. I never told him who took the child, only that the person could be trusted and no matter how much he threatened or beat me he could never get it out of me. From this day forward, I told him, we have no marriage. Maybe he could keep my body because he had that kind of power. But in the end he would have no real power over me."

Val took time out for a steady breath. I could tell she was holding back tears. That it would be only a matter of time until she could not hold them back anymore.

"But the story is not necessarily a sad one," she went on, slow, steady, controlled. "Because in the end, Charlie lived, despite his father. I'm quite certain that to this day he has no idea that Detective Ryan and his wife are not his natural parents. Because how much will a child recall from his first two years? Not even Richard knows it's the same child. To this day, he just assumes that I had the body disposed of quickly because deep down I feared being implicated too, which is partly the truth. The irony is that at Richard's request, Ryan arranged the funeral and burial for our child, and as you might have already guessed, there is no body in Charlie Barnes's grave. At the same time—and this is what causes me the most grief—there is, in a sense, no more Charlie.

"So I wrote *Godchild* thinking that perhaps by writing about the sadness and grief I could make it all go away. I thought it would be OK because I implicated only myself in that novel. What I didn't realize was that people would consider the fiction to be so real.

"It was only a few months after publishing the book that I learned of Richard's plot to harm you in exchange for 'a piece of the action' at Green Haven Prison. Wash Pelton and the governor, along with Richard's public-relations help, had big plans for expanding and for building more prisons under the guise of increased arrests and a dismantled parole system. They were in the process of expanding their operations south of the border, in Mexico, having already begun on a deal with the Contreras Brothers for the drug trade existent inside and around some of Mexico's prisons. It was their plan to open up a whole new lane of drug traffic between Mexico and New York. The projected profits would have been huge.

"The whole bunch of them were infected with greed to the point of murder. The point is that Richard's attempt to kill Charlie had nothing to do with fear or anxiety—or even an insurance settlement, for that matter (although we did receive a substantial settlement, of which I never touched a single dollar). Quite simply, it had everything to do with murder, and never was this knowledge more apparent than when I discovered my husband, in his office, on more than one occasion, watching the video of the drowning. It was at that time I threatened to expose the whole thing to the world. To just write the real story. But Richard threatened to lay blame for Charlie's death on me, alone. He could do it too. He had the resources. And there was always *Godchild*. So I went to Mexico to write about the drug trade and maybe, in the process, expose my husband's operation. But what I never considered was how vulnerable I'd be; how I'd be handing Richard an opportunity to do away with me once and for all. As for you, Keeper—please don't take this the wrong way—you would have made the perfect patsy.

"Now I sit here heavy hearted and I hear a voice calling for me and I know my death is only a matter of time. So I've decided to fool fate, take matters into my own hands, accept the inevitable on my own terms.

"I'd like to be able tell you how much I appreciate all you've done for me, from saving my life to giving me the courage to finish the true version of Charlie's story, even if it is not entirely the truth. (After all, in the end, Charlie *lived!)* I feel I can trust you to keep our secret safe, because in Richard's case, it really is the *thought* that counted—the *intent* to kill.

"So I won't thank you at all. But rest assured, it was worth the effort. Somewhere along the way, a soul was saved. And for that, someone will surely thank you.

"Sincerely yours, Renata Barnes."

❖

The room was consumed in a blistering silence, each of us just waiting for the other to be the first to speak. And when Val folded up the pages of the letter, stuffed them neatly back inside the envelope, and said, "Well, I guess that's that," I could have wrapped my arms around her and kissed her. I might have done it too, if it hadn't been for the drain in my shoulder.

VINCENT ZANDRI

But the feeling of relief was as short-lived as it was deceptive.

Because those were the only words that any of us spoke.

After a while, Tony released a breath.

"So Ryan's the real winner in this thing," he said. "I still don't know how he did it, but he managed to play three separate sides. Little Charlie's side, Barnes's side, and the side of law and order. He knew full well he could be implicated once he was let in on Richard's plan to kill Renata. On the other hand, he knew he could profit big time from sticking with his old boss too. But in the end he decided to protect the kid."

"In the name of the law," I said from the bed.

"In the name of all that's right and decent," Tony said. "If you can imagine such a thing."

He set his blue fedora gently on his head and walked out.

That left Val and me. But we had very little to say to each other. In the end she simply slid off the bed, made her way to the picture window that looked out over the medical center parking lot, and proceeded to have a good, long cry.

For the both of us.

CHAPTER SEVENTY-ONE

THREE MORE DAYS PASSED BEFORE I GOT MEDICAL permission for Val to drive me home.

Not downstate to Stormville, but back to Tony's place.

The guest room. The same room that overlooked Eagle Street and the telephone poles stapled with the faded image of the Bald Man. The same room that looked out onto the top floor of the governor's mansion and the white-marbled Governor Rockefeller Plaza beyond it where state workers flocked day in and day out like lemmings to the sea. I was to be Tony's guest for "as long as it took," because, after all, he felt responsible for the entire affair. He'd been duped by Barnes just as I had been. What's more, he was out quite a few bucks and had been made a fool of in certain circles that must go unmentioned here.

The room was a spacious one, with twin beds, its own bath, and a picture window that also looked out onto Saint Mary's Cathedral, the oldest Roman Catholic church in Albany. The church where Val and I were to have been married two Saturdays ago. A nurse had instructed Val how to change the dressings on my wound, and by the second day on our own, she had become an expert, silently peeling back the gauze and the tape, bringing her nose to the oily dressing, giving it a slight sniff to make sure infection hadn't set in.

She slept on the second of the twin beds, having sent her son, Ben, off to his grandmother's. We shared our morning and evening meals in the bedroom, eating off hand-painted wooden trays that

Tony had brought back from a vacation in Spain the previous year. We didn't talk much about the case. Only about the fact that Barnes was facing a grand jury in a week, the charges against him ranging from murder one (for the *supposed* death of his toddler son) to two counts of conspiracy to commit murder (the plots to have me *and* his wife assassinated) to murder in the second degree (Fran's murder) to at least a half-dozen or so assorted charges that would place the man behind bars for many more years than he had left to live. All this, and the feds had yet to examine his personal video collection for what it might reveal.

I might have made it a point to see the man, tell him exactly what I thought of him for what he did to Fran and me. I never did—not that it would have been physically possible with my sore shoulder and two sore legs (one knife wound, one bullet). But I lay back on the bed at night and I dreamed about how a meeting like that might go down:

In my mind, I see myself walking the length of the basement corridor of the Albany County lockup. I am alone, no guard sergeant to escort me. From out of the depths of the prison, I hear the voices of the caged and the corrupt shouting out for me.

When I make it to the end of the corridor, the inmates press their bodies up against the bars, stick their arms through the spaces between them, wave their fists in the air. They chant, "Kill the motherfucker," over and over again, banging the heels of their work boots against the concrete to the rhythm of their chant.

"Kill the motherfucker!"

I walk the very center of the block, on top of the yellow stripe that marks the center of the floor, three tiers of cells on either side.

Streamers made from toilet paper fly down, shooting stars from the topmost cells. Some of the streamers are on fire.

"Kill the motherfucker!'

The chant is endless.

When I finally make it to Barnes's cell, I see him curled up on his cot, back pressed up against the wall, knees pressed into his chest. He is dressed in his county blaze-orange jumpsuit, his rimless glasses crooked on his nose. He is crying like a baby. "Don't kill me," he says, his voice barely audible above the voices of the inmates. I say nothing. I just look at him, into his cold blue eyes.

I pull a set of keys from my pocket.

The keys will open the cell door.

I slip the key inside the lock.

Barnes screams, "No! No, don't!"

I close the cell door behind me and slowly make my way to him, pulling my .45 out of its holster, pressing the barrel up against his forehead, thumbing back the hammer...

But it was only a dream. And a sad one at that. So I said nothing about it to Val or Tony. I simply allowed the fantasy to play over again and again in my head like a videotape. After a time, I actually looked forward to lights out, pulling the covers over my chest, setting my head carefully back on the pillow, bringing the dream into focus.

Had the fantasy become an obsession?

Yes and no.

Yes, in that I found I could not sleep restfully until I played the scene out completely in my mind.

No, in that I knew it would always stay just a dream; that I no longer could possibly carry out the act; that although I'd had my chance for revenge, I now had no choice but to let the law take its course. I had to relegate Barnes's fate to due process, or to whatever the gods of law and order had in store for him.

When Tony came home on the third day of my at-home convalescence and told me as nonchalantly as possible that they'd found Barnes dead with a foot-long shiv stuffed down his throat inside his cell at the county lockup just an hour earlier, I was not the least bit surprised. Thinking like a former warden, I was simply curious about how the COs could have allowed anyone to get that close to him.

But Tony just waved his hands in the air as if to say, "Oh, you know, probably just one of those careless mistakes we all make from time to time."

It seemed that somebody had somehow left the cell door open during lockdown just after evening chow. No one knew how it could have happened or who might have been responsible. But several inmates were able to get inside his cell, and as you already know, Barnes was about to become infamous. His was to be the trial of the century for Albany County. "So it was only a matter of time until somebody knocked him out," Tony said. "Better for him that it happened now, rather than later."

He started walking out of the bedroom. But he stopped once he got to the door. He turned. "Oh, and did I mention that just this morning the good Dr. Pearl and his cronies were involved in a terrible auto accident on their way to pick up a patient in Poughkeepsie? Of course, they can all breathe OK as long as they don't turn off the machines." He came back in and set his briefcase on the end of the bed, opened it, pulled out a large manila envelope. He tossed it onto the bed. "One hundred eleven grand," he said. "Your share of the take minus the cost to repair the damages to Bill's Grill along with the APD you had to grease in order to stay out of lockup."

He told me to count it if I wanted.

"Why would I want to do that?" I said.

He went to leave once more but then stopped himself yet another time.

"Jesus, Mary, and Joseph, I almost forgot something else," he said, reaching into the interior pocket of his blue blazer, pulling out a small card, tossing it onto my lap.

Val came over to me as soon as he was gone. She picked up the card, flipped it over to examine it, front and back.

It was larger than a business card but smaller than a playing card, and it had a picture of the Virgin Mary on the front, her hands clasped in prayer, a set of blue rosary beads threaded between her fingers.

On the back was a prayer. "The Hail Mary," Val said.

On the bottom of the card, just under the last stanza of the prayer, was printed the name Richard R. Barnes. Beneath that, the dates September 14, 1952–April 6, 2003.

Val and I stared into each other's eyes.

"Two questions," she said. "How in the world could anyone have had these printed in just an hour's time? And second, why would Tony, of all people, have these printed at all?"

I started to laugh then, hard, my eyes tearing.

"Well, I'm glad you find this so amusing," Val said. "Here was your chance to see Barnes face a court of law, and some renegade inmates kill him before the trial even begins."

I kept laughing. I couldn't help myself. Maybe it was the pain medication.

"I mean, Jesus," Val said, wiping tears from her crying eyes with the backs of her hands. "That man tried to kill his own child, his baby. I know what it is to have a baby inside here." She patted her stomach. "I know what it is to love a child."

Suddenly there was nothing to laugh about.

And I suppose in the end, I could have told Val that it was Tony who'd had Barnes killed and arranged Pearl's accident—that he must have ordered his Guinea Pigs to make the hits. Not necessarily because of what Barnes had done to Fran and me, but because of what Barnes had done to Tony. He had double-crossed him, asked him to go along with his little charade, made him look like a fool. And if word ever got beyond intimate circles and hit the streets that somebody could make a fool out of Tony and get away with it, then the Tony Angelino Experience would be finished, effectively, his career in Albany or anywhere else in New York washed up.

So in the end Tony had no choice, and frankly, I was a little surprised that Val hadn't put two and two together herself. But then, perhaps she didn't want to think that Tony could be capable of making that kind of hit on someone, good or bad. Like I said, I could have explained the logic behind it all to Val—the logic of doing what's right, regardless of the law—but I let it go. Because what difference would it have made in the end?

Barnes was dead; Renata was dead; the Bald Man was finally dead (or so we had to assume). Even Pelton was dead. That was that. This story, which began nearly six years ago with my appointment to Green Haven Prison, was effectively concluded. I'd found Fran's killer and disposed of him. In that sense, it was a dream come true. But why didn't I feel the satisfaction that was supposed to go with it? Why wasn't I laughing, crying, or jumping up and down? Why didn't I feel it in my heart?

Val pulled off my covers. "Come on," she said. "We're taking a walk."

"My legs hurt," I said.

"We won't go far," she said. "You need some air, and so do I. We've been cooped up in bedrooms and hospital rooms for days on end. Besides, you can walk."

Val grabbed her coat and slipped it on.

"Where did you have in mind?" I asked, swinging my legs slowly around.

"Let's go visit the cathedral," she said.

"Seems like the last place you'd like to visit," I said.

"Don't flatter yourself," she said. "I'm no longer thinking about the marriage."

"What are you thinking?" I said, grabbing my jeans from the chair beside the bed, carefully slipping them on.

"I'm thinking about God," she said. "We could both use a good dose of God right now."

"Praise Jesus," I said.

"Keep it up," she said.

CHAPTER SEVENTY-TWO

VAL AND I WALKED ARM IN ARM UP THE WORN MARBLE stairs of Saint Mary's Cathedral. The night was mild but breezy, the sky clear and black, with the white lights of the city drowning out nearly all the starlight.

Val went ahead and opened the heavy wooden door for me.

Together we walked in.

The cathedral was immense.

With a marble floor and a sea of wooden pews.

A giant altar was lit up in flickering candlelight, which came from the racks of white candles positioned along the tall stone exterior walls with the angel faces carved into the polished marble pilasters. Dozens of wildflower arrangements had been laid out for Easter Sunday, the celebration for which was only hours away.

The church was empty.

Val walked ahead of me down the length of the aisle, the sound of her heels clicking against the marble floor. When she reached the front of the church, she slipped into the first pew on the right. She was already kneeling by the time I slipped in beside her.

She made the sign of the cross, prayed for maybe a minute, then repeated the sign once more, pushing herself away from the kneeler and sitting back on the bench.

For a while, the two of us just sat there staring up at the dimly lit altar, as though waiting for something to happen.

"When I was a kid," I whispered after a time, looking not at Val but at the statue of the crucified Christ suspended high above the altar, "I would turn to my mother during Sunday Mass and ask her why I had to be quiet in church."

"What did she tell you?" Val asked, her voice low, monotone, but still echoing in the wide-open cathedral.

"'Because this is God's house,' she'd say."

"And what would you say?"

"I'd say, 'So what if it's God's house? We don't whisper in our house. So why should we whisper in God's house?' And she'd bend over with her black prayer book in one hand and a rosary in the other and she'd give me this stern-as-all-hell look and tell me, 'This is Sunday morning. And God likes to sleep late on Sunday morning because he's been up all night with Saint Peter and all the saints playing cards, just like Dad. Now if you want to be the one to wake him up, be my guest. It's your soul.'"

"Cute," Val said. "But what's the point?"

"I'm not sure," I said. "It's just that every time I go into a church I think about it."

"You don't go to church, Keeper," Val reminded me.

"Maybe I'm still afraid I'm going to wake up God."

She laughed a little while I felt the soreness in my legs and the dull throb in my shoulder where the drain had been inserted. I went on staring at the altar.

"How are we, Val?" I asked.

"If that's your way of re-proposing, forget it."

"I mean it."

All around us there was the flickering of candles and soft yellow light that shone against the tall stone walls and stained glass and the black cathedral ceiling. There was the perpetual crucified

Christ and the silence of it all. I turned and stared at Val's profile. Her full lips, little nose, the triangular corner of her brown eye.

"Let's just say for now that I love you, but I cannot be with you."

I turned back to the altar.

I don't know what the hell it was, but after a time my eyes filled up and I began to feel a little dizzy. I kept my eyes focused on the altar. But instead I saw myself as a little boy. I could see myself as clear as day, like I was watching an old Super 8 my grandfather had filmed of me with his handheld camera. I was this scrappy kid again, all dressed up in some red hand-me-down jacket with torn sleeves and a matching baseball hat. I don't know what had come over me, but I saw myself running awkwardly in a field behind the split-level house my father built himself. An empty field covered for as far as the eye could see with tall, golden grass. There was the warm sun at my back and a set of heavy black clouds that filled up most of the sky in front of me. I was just this silly little kid with no clue in the world, and I saw myself waving to my mother while a distinct rumbling came from the black clouds. She was standing outside the back door of our home, calling for me to come in, not able to see me because I was hidden in the grass. But I could see her, as small as she was. I actually felt myself smiling at her, knowing there was this storm brewing but also having the good feeling of knowing she was there. I saw it all happening again inside that church with Val at my side, inside the span of a few seconds.

But then I heard the telltale squeak that told me the massive wood door to the cathedral was opening up. I heard the sound of footsteps on the marble floor. Two different pairs of footsteps, actually. The first quick and light, the second weighted and slow. Before long I saw a little boy all bundled up in a navy-blue peacoat and matching wool hat. I saw him run past me, past the farthest pews, past the altar to the rows of offertory candles that were stacked up against the walls on their ornate, black metal racks. He reached inside the cup that contained the waxy wick-starters, placing the tip of the starter into the flame of a candle that was already burning strong in its colorful red glass. But not before the man in the shiny waist-length leather blazer was standing over him, his hand on the boy's hand, helping him light not one but two separate candles. When the candles were lit, the man reached into his pocket and pulled out a dollar bill. He gave the money to the boy to deposit into the metal collection box, which he did.

When it was over, the two turned and faced me as if on cue, as if I'd been the reason for their visit in the first place. And maybe I was. Of course, had they not turned to face me, I might have altogether missed Detective Ryan and his secretly adopted son. I may never have known who the boy was had he not come to me where I was seated in the pew beside Val. The *godchild* himself, with his round face, rosy cheeks, and striking blue eyes just like his mother's. Ryan stood silent in the near distance. No longer the same Ryan who was partners with Barnes on one hand and law and order on the other. But the new Ryan, who had a little boy to watch over and raise. He came up behind the boy, took hold of his hand, and led him back down the aisle toward the wooden doors.

Maybe a second or two passed before Val took hold of my hand.

She held it hard while I cried.

ABOUT THE AUTHOR

VINCENT ZANDRI IS THE INTER-national best-selling author of *The Innocent, The Remains, Moonlight Falls, Concrete Pearl, Scream Catcher,* and the forthcoming *Murder by Moonlight.* With an MFA in writing from Vermont College, Zandri is also the author of the digital shorts *Pathological* and *Moonlight Mafia.* An adventurer, foreign correspondent, and freelance photojournalist for *RT, GlobalSpec,* and *International Business Times* among others, Zandri lives in New York State and Florence, Italy.